A HEALTHY BODY

A HEALTHY BODY

Gillian Linscott

St. Martin's Press
New York

Library of Congress Cataloging in Publication Data

Linscott, Gillian.
  A healthy body.

  I. Title.
PR6062.I54H4   1984   823'. 914   84-2136
ISBN 0-312-36534-9

First Published in Great Britain by Macmillan London Limited

First U.S. Edition

10 9 8 7 6 5 4 3 2 1

CHAPTER ONE

There were better cafés, but this one had the advantage of being alongside the bare, hot stretch of road where cars queued for the ferry across the bay. Birdie had reconnoitred it carefully the night before, wobbling along the seafront like a competitor in a slow cycle race. There were two tables on the pavement outside, inches from the wheels of trailers, caravans and small shambolic lorries loaded with crates of fizzy drinks, all waiting more or less patiently for the barrier to go up on the jetty and let them through. But nobody seemed to think it odd that Birdie preferred to sit inside the café, chair at an angle to the window. He watched the traffic and ate his tomato salad carefully, slice by slice, to make it last, mopping up the mustardy dressing with torn hunks of *baguette*. He'd ordered it because it was the cheapest thing on the menu and, in spite of his worries, was pleased when it turned out to be a single, bulging, Mediterranean tomato, elegantly sliced, a world away from the disciplined globes he'd been learning to buy in packs of four from Marks and Spencer's salad counter. Shopping, oddly enough, had been one of the worst things about it all. The single chop, the search among the family sizes for a small pack of frozen beans, had been a daily humiliation and a grief, with every fibre of him protesting that he wasn't a single chop man, had never wanted to be a single chop man, had single chopness thrust on him against his will.

But all that was a channel crossing and four days' hard cycling on French roads away. Whatever there might be to say against the situation he was putting himself into, there were small compensations: like the warmth that increased with every day south, the old, almost forgotten satisfaction of a hundred miles covered in a day, the red wine that—like the tomato—came to him without first having stood on a supermarket shelf. (The idea that the proprietor of the café might buy it in two-litre bottles from the local

5

supermarché would have hurt him.) He caught the waiter's eye and, in careful French, called for another *pichet*. Those little pottery jugs held a quarter litre, so that would mean a half litre at lunchtime, and a light lunch at that. Too much – but there wasn't much hard cycling to go now. Over the ferry, then a few miles of main road, then one of those smaller roads that, on the map, cut narrow swathes through miles and miles of woodland. Thirty miles, perhaps, but over flat land.

Just as the waiter was putting the second *pichet* of wine on the table, he saw them. And he must have tensed, or moved in some way, because the waiter was looking at him and making a questioning face. Monsieur's *pichet* of wine, he explained in condescending English, and Birdie must have said thank you or something because the waiter went away, leaving his customer holding an empty glass and staring through the window at a car with British registration plates. While he'd been catching the waiter's eye, somebody must have opened the barrier on the jetty because the queue of vehicles had moved forward. Now outside the café, where a lorry loaded with the Fanta bottles had been, was a dark green Jaguar with three people inside it. It had an uncluttered air about it, compared with most of the British cars in the queue. No sign of carry cots, Kleenex or plastic surf boards. Whatever luggage they were carrying must be neatly stowed in the boot. And the woman in the driving seat looked cool and relaxed, a pale green shirt open at the neck down to the third button. When she raised a hand and turned to say something to the man beside her he saw a watch he didn't recognize flashing on a suntanned wrist. Her long dark hair was tucked up in a sort of pleat at the back, making the slim neck look longer, more elegant, than he remembered it. Birdie filled his wine glass clumsily, too near the brim, the wine splashing on the white table top. The man beside her was tanned too, and had lost some weight. He seemed impatient at the queue and kept glancing ahead and then at the woman beside him. He said something to her and she shook her head. If he was offering to take over the driving, Birdie could have told him to save his breath. He should have learned by now that Olivia always preferred to drive. Or didn't he even understand that much about her? Then, as Birdie watched, the woman twisted round to say something to the passenger in the back seat and, a second later, the back door on the seaward side of the car opened and a teenage girl scrambled out, inelegantly. In a year or so's time she'd learn to use that length of leg to her advantage. Some of her friends at school, with shorter legs but more know-how, could give her points there. But on this child the blue athletic shorts and white track shoes still belonged with the world of long jump and school sports days. And she was sunburnt, poor love. The backs of her slim thighs were lobster red as she stood staring out to sea and Birdie knew from past experience you'd be able to feel the heat from them inches away. She was like him, she burned easily. The red skin on his shoulders, under his shirt, incandesced in sympathy and he felt his flesh prickling with heat and anger. Olivia knew she burned easily. What were they playing at, those two, letting the child bake her poor skin? It was all right for Olivia, she tanned as easily as she did everything else. And the slob with her had probably found a way to make his sessions at the solarium tax deductible. But the child – why worry? She could lie on the beach and bake while the adults swilled gins in the hotel bar or spent a long afternoon in bed. He realized that he'd gulped down an over-full glass of wine without even noticing it, and the waiter was staring at him. He made himself breathe deeply and look away from the car, telling himself that he'd known when he started it would be difficult, and if he was going to react like this every time he saw them he'd better give up the whole thing and go home. But his neck and calf muscles were knotted with the effort of not getting up and dashing across the road to the child and he could feel sweat trickling down inside his last clean shirt. He counted ten slowly before looking at the car again, and then the back passenger door was closing and she'd got her legs tucked back inside. The queue of vehicles was moving again. This time it moved steadily, and within a few minutes he saw the green Jaguar turn on to the jetty and down the ramp towards the pay booth.

Birdie asked the waiter, '*A quelle heure le prochain bateau part . . . um . . . partira-t-il?*'

The waiter replied, in English, that Birdie would have plenty of time to catch this one. It wouldn't depart for another ten minutes. His eyes strayed to the half-full *pichet*. But Birdie, abandoning efforts at French, replied that it was the next ferry he wanted, not this one. Forty-five minutes then, said the waiter, and watched Birdie drink another glass. He waited till the ferry with the green Jaguar on board was half way across the bay before collecting his bike from the café wall and freewheeling on to the jetty.

It was late afternoon at the Zoe holiday village. The flags of twelve nations round the reception building flapped in a light breeze off the sea, and scents that sank into the lungs like gas came from the geraniums and rosemary bushes alongside the neat gravel paths. For the people already in residence in the cabins, tents and caravans among pine woods that made up the village, it was the time of waking up from the afternoon siesta. The plunk of ball against racquet had started again at the tennis courts, the calm of the swimming pool was shattered as sunbathers flopped into it like seals, the evening yoga group, rush mats rolled up under arms, was following its instructor through the sand dunes to where the retreating tide had left a strip of unmarked sand, brown and succulent as fudge. The yoga class had the sand to itself for once, because it was a change-round day at the Zoe holiday village. From breakfast to lunchtime departing cars and caravans had clogged the drive and the roadway outside. Now the incoming cars and vans were clogging them all over again. And because most of the Club Zoe for this last fortnight in June had been block-booked by an English operator specializing in the off-beat, nearly all the vehicles had British number plates and travel-worn drivers. None more so than Peter Pollins, Birmingham solicitor, husband and father of three, who'd only just lacked the nerve to say he'd rather play golf in Scotland.

'Peter, what's French for goat's milk?'

The voice of his wife, Vinny, from a window of the reception building. He sighed and walked in to join her at the counter.

'Goat's milk? *Lait de* something or other.'

'I know it's *lait de* something or other. The question is, what's French for goat?'

'*Chevre*,' said Philip, Peter's fat son.

Peter rather admired the boy for managing to stay fat, in the face of Vinny's campaigns for fitness, body-awareness and fibre in diet. The twins, under the same regime, were thin as hares and had Vinny's alarming brightness of eye. Philip gave him hope.

'Do we really need goat's milk?' Peter asked, feebly.

'Of course we do. Are you sure it's *chevre*, Philip?'

The woman in the tracksuit behind the counter said, in perfect English, 'There is a goat farm near the main road. They deliver milk to the camp on Mondays, Wednesdays and Fridays. The goats are very well treated.' It was clearly a question she'd answered many times before, which increased Peter's gloom at the

8

idea of having to spend a fortnight in a camp full of Vinny's soul mates.

Vinny said, 'We'll need some before then. You'll have to ask her for directions and drive there when we've got the tent up.' And she, Philip and the twins went scrunching off on the gravel between banks of rosemary.

Peter, meanwhile, was taking a closer look at the woman in the tracksuit and rather liking what he saw. She was slim and athletic, which was a pity. All the same, he thought he detected a look in those big, black eyes which might show a plumper, more languorous type of woman trying to get out. She looked to be in her late twenties. Her tan was golden, her brown-black hair swung in a pigtail over one shoulder, and the top of her tracksuit was unzipped nearly to the waist.

'You go back up this road for about three miles . . .' She had a map out on the counter and was carefully explaining the way to the blasted goat farm. Bending over the map he saw the golden tan extended to the midriff. Her breasts, shadowed but not concealed by the tracksuit, were small but nicely rounded.

'And there you are.'

He realized that her pencil point had reached the goat farm and she was well aware that his eyes hadn't. He fell into a confusion of thanks and assurances that he'd understood, knowing perfectly well that he hadn't and would have to get directions all over again from rural toilers along the way. And he added, realizing that it was not the most original of lines, 'Where did you learn your English?'

She raised her eyebrows. 'A comprehensive in Yorkshire. Where did you learn yours?'

More confusion. 'Oh, I didn't mean, I . . . You don't look English.'

Luckily she understood that he'd meant it as a compliment. 'My mother was French-Moroccan. I grew up bi-lingual.'

'Useful in this job.'

Another lot of people had arrived to check in and she clearly expected him to go, but he had one more question.

'Can you get a drink on the site?'

'Goat's milk?'

He couldn't tell if she was joking.

'Damn goat's milk. Wine. Lots of lovely red wine.'

9

The green Jaguar, with Olivia still at the wheel, came to a halt in the car park. She switched the engine off and looked at the flags.

'You wouldn't think they'd get many Norwegians or Japanese here.'

'Dozens of them,' he said. 'Can't wait to tear their clothes off and start living.'

'Don't believe you.'

'You'll see.'

She stretched her legs in their white linen slacks, in no hurry to get out.

'It all looks terribly hearty.'

A banner between the gate posts said, in red and orange letters: 'Village ZOE'. And after the big capitals in the word ZOE it added 'Zestful, Outgoing, Energized'.

'You know, Ralph, I'd never have thought it was your sort of place.'

'You see, you're still discovering my hidden depths.' He kissed her.

From the back seat the child said, 'Mum, are we getting out?'

She broke away from him. 'Yes, of course we are. We'll just check in, then we can go and put the tent up.'

He turned round in his seat and smiled at the child.

'I'll tell you what, why don't you check in, and Debbie and I can go and be getting on with the tent? Good idea, Debbie?'

'Yes,' she said, not looking at him.

'I'll need your passport.'

'Oh God, I put it back in my case in the boot. I'll tell you what, check in on your passport and tell them I'll bring mine along later.' He got out to open the door for her and didn't start the car engine until he'd seen her go into reception.

Inside, Olivia had to wait because the woman behind the counter was dealing with a minor crisis. At the centre of it was a girl of almost alarming prettiness, her small face surrounded by such an explosion of bouncing golden hair that it seemed surprising it could all grow from one head. White shorts moulded themselves to her tight little buttocks and a simple white T-shirt made no effort at all to conceal remarkable breasts and erect nipples. From all this, came a voice that was disconcertingly Kensington, and it was a voice used to giving orders.

'We'd booked two chalets next to each other. Look, it should be there on the form.'

10

Unmoved, the woman behind the counter replied that it was not on the form. Two chalets, for a woman and two men, had been booked, and two chalets were available, but not next door to each other.

'Don, you tell her. You did the bookings.'

Don, in T-shirt and denims, advanced to the counter, looking ill at ease.

'Well . . . um . . . well, I sort of assumed they'd be together. I mean if you book together you sort of expect . . . I mean . . .'

The girl heard this impatiently, white sandal tapping the floor.

'Oh for heaven's sake. Let me tell her.' She advanced again to the counter, glaring at the woman behind it. 'Look, you silly bitch, there's going to be a hell of a row . . .'

The second man in her party, who'd been leaning against a wall looking at notices about concerts, suddenly moved forward, took her by the elbow and all but dragged her away. Olivia wasn't particularly trying to listen but she heard something about 'papers' and 'bad publicity'. Then more loudly: 'Don, why don't you take Melanie outside and get her a nice cool drink? I'll see to this.'

He gave them very little choice in the matter, propelling the girl none too gently into Don's unready arms and holding the door open for them. Then he, in his turn, advanced on the counter.

'Look, there's been a bit of a muddle.'

His voice, by contrast to the girl's, was apologetic and so low it was almost a whisper.

'It's probably the agent who made the mix-up, but you see we do need two chalets together.'

The woman behind the counter said nothing, just waited for him to go on and this clearly unsettled him.

'She's Melanie McBride, you see.'

No reaction whatsoever from the woman behind the counter, although Olivia had an idea she'd heard the name before.

'You know,' said the man. 'Harmony House.'

Again, no reaction from the woman behind the counter and an awkward silence from the man. Olivia, who was waiting patiently to book in, thought she might hurry things up by intervening.

'It's a soap opera,' she said, 'about an international finishing school. I think he means the girl's in it.'

The man glared at her. Obviously her intervention had been less enthusiastic than he'd have liked.

'You must have seen it,' he said to the woman behind the

11

counter. 'It's even on French television.'

'I don't watch television.' The woman said it as a simple statement, no moral judgement implied.

'Oh.' This nearly finished him altogether, but he rallied and started again.

'Harmony House is very big in Britain and the States. Miss McBride plays one of the leading characters, a millionaire's daughter. She has a very large following of fans, and she's booked in here because she needs a rest before they start filming the next series. And it has to be somewhere where her fans can't find her, so she can relax properly.'

'The chalets are not far apart,' the woman said.

'Look.'

He leaned on the counter.

'Look, I'm her agent. My name's James Jedd. I'm here to see she's not bothered by anything and I've brought Don along to help. It's not like dealing with an ordinary person. A girl like Miss McBride needs protecting. That's what we're here for.'

The woman looked unimpressed, but relented a little.

'There's a large, two bedroomed chalet vacant near the beach. Miss McBride could have one room and I can have an extra bed put into the other room for you and your friend. The bill will naturally be reduced.'

James Jedd considered for a while, then accepted, took the key and left. The woman, becoming human again, heaved a sigh of relief and smiled at Olivia.

'I'm sorry to have kept you waiting.'

Olivia produced her passport, with Deborah included on it, and explained that her husband would be bringing his along later. She said 'husband' with reluctance, because it had been a point of honour with her not to pretend to be married to Ralph. She refused to put herself into the category of women who were whispered about: 'Of course, you know she's not really . . .' This time, rather than make problems, she stretched the point. But, even so, she couldn't go as far as booking in as Mrs Ralph Shunner. So the receptionist took the name from her passport, and they went down in the register as Mr and Mrs Linnet. It seemed to her, in the circumstances, a reasonable compromise.

The last two who'd made bookings arrived about nine o'clock as the smells of barbecuing meat were drifting over the site and even

12

the least adept campers had wrestled their tents into moderately convincing shapes. They had a little category all to themselves on the list because they weren't paying for their accommodation. Norman Keys, colour supplement journalist, and Clancy Whigg, photographer, were there on a facility trip, to record a typical week at Village Zoe for use in next winter's holiday issues. They were a little drunk when they finally presented themselves at reception because they'd been zigzagging among the wine châteaux, freeloading enthusiastically in return for vague promises of pieces in the British press. Clancy Whigg took in the woman behind the counter at an appreciative glance and asked her name, in bad French.

'Nimue.'

'God. Nimue what?'

'Nimue Hawthorne.'

'God.'

He swung a metal camera case on to the counter and made a great show of hunting for his passport.

'Don't mind it there, do you, love? Got to look after my equipment, haven't I?'

He threw a battered passport beside his colleague's, which was already lying there, smug in a black leather case.

'Been around a bit, like me.'

She was filling in the register, unimpressed.

'This one, see. Vietnam. Last plane out of Saigon.'

He swung the camera case round to show her a big dent in the side.

'And that gash there was made by a 303, Lenadoon Avenue, Belfast.'

His companion said plaintively, 'Clancy, for heaven's sake let her check us in. I want to lie down.'

'Suit yourself, duckie.'

But he kept quiet long enough for her to finish the formalities and hand over a chalet key. Nimue watched them go, then stripped off her tracksuit and let herself out by a back door, switching off the lights in reception as she went. On long, bare feet she ran like an animal released from imprisonment, down a paved path, along the drive and into the forest. Peter Pollins, glancing up from his soya bean stew, saw her silhouette as she emerged on to the top of the sand dunes and told Vinny, who hadn't seen, that this might not be a bad place after all.

13

CHAPTER TWO

It turned out to be a longer ride than Birdie had expected – or perhaps the half litre of wine was having its effect. And it was hot, so hot that once he got past the traffic jam at the place where the ferry arrived, he took off his shirt and stuffed it into the top of a cycle pannier, adding creases to the sweat stains. So whatever the next two weeks brought, he'd just have to hope it was nothing demanding high standards of dress. He thought that the oaf probably had a dozen clean and ironed shirts (and who had washed and ironed them?) stashed away in a suitcase in the boot of the Jaguar, and even the thought of it drove the pedals round faster and faster so that the wheels hummed like hornets along the dry, white-surfaced road. When he realized what was happening he made himself slow down. No point in getting there before dark. No point either in wasting energy on hatred. He'd spent months doing that, and the futility of it was one of the things that made him decide on the present journey. If it was a choice between a mind going round like a hamster on a wheel or feet going round on pedals, then pedals it should be. What he hadn't realized was that the mind would still hamster on while the feet went round.

He said aloud to himself, 'Stop it.'

At early evening on a minor road there was nobody around to think it eccentric. He made himself freewheel, with just an occasional turn of the pedals to keep the bike going, on a road that was as long and flat as a noodle. As far as he could gather, this and similar roads went on like that for mile after mile parallel to the sea. In the first years of their marriage he'd planned cycling holidays on roads like this with Olivia. Then, as time went on and there was always something to prevent it – the child or his leave being cancelled – the plan had changed to introducing his daughter to cycle touring when she was old enough. Fifteen, say, and he'd buy her a really good touring bike and take her somewhere like the

14

Yorkshire Wolds for a few weekends to get the feel of it, then perhaps a week in Holland. Well, she'd be fifteen next birthday and the bike catalogues were tucked away in a drawer at his flat, but somehow he'd never got round to mentioning it to her.

There was that hornet hum from the wheels and he realized he was pedalling like fury again. Slowly. At this rate he'd get there much too soon. He freewheeled again, making himself think about the immediate things: the sun on his back, filtered by the trees to a point where it threatened no further harm to his sunburn, the hot resinous smell of the pines, an only just audible sound of the sea, away on his right. By French standards, it was still early in the holiday season and on this road there was only occasional evidence of activity. He passed a couple of municipal camp sites with scatterings of dormobiles and ridge tents, and as he went further south there were the occasional little bungalows – vaguely Spanish in style – almost dwarfed by huge aloe plants and even larger boards advertising *prix fixe* menus: *moules, crevette, lapin persillé, frites*. The smells were enticing and he was tempted several times to stop and eat. But, although he had plenty of time for it, the ferry trip and that sumptuous and expensive tomato had already put him several francs over his budget for the day. He rode on, slowing right down at each little bungalow for a good sniff at the cooking smells. Some people, eating on a balcony, waved at him and shouted something cheerful. He was pretty sure it was the French equivalent of 'Come on in, the food's lovely,' but he just waved and smiled. The bike was going beautifully, had gone beautifully all the way, which made him both regretful and guilty about what he was going to do in an hour or so's time.

The whole sky on his right was turning gold in a spectacular sunset when he saw the first of the signs he was looking for, a little blue and yellow affair on his side of the road: 'Village ZOE. 10 k'. Exactly the same colours as on the ticket folder he'd picked up on the oaf's hall table, that neat little mahogany table against the wallpaper with the beige plush stripes. The sort of wallpaper Olivia used to laugh at when she saw it in restaurants. It had been a piece of luck finding the tickets there – one of the little things that helped reassure him his plan was the right one – but he knew they'd be somewhere in the house. He'd heard about them the first time he took Debbie out, after the access was settled, over a seafood platter in the High Street Wimpy. It had been a disastrous afternoon, starting with the embarrassed hand-over in the town

15

car park that made him and Olivia seem like accomplices in a kidnap, going on to some awful film about a dog that was the only thing in town without an X certificate, and the whole occasion shot through with the embarrassment of making conversation with his only daughter like a stranger, now that the network of small, everyday talk had been ripped away from them. It was probably because she sensed this embarrassment, and wanted to help him, that she brought up the subject while tucking uneaten fish away under unwanted chips.

'He's taking us on holiday.'

He knew that already. It had come up in the solicitor's office.

'France,' she said. 'Some sort of camp.'

'Camp?'

That didn't sound like Ralph Shunner at all. A four-star hotel merchant if ever there was one.

'Mum says there are tennis courts and things, and a swimming pool.'

Like her parents, she was good at most sports, but tennis was a more serious passion. He couldn't stop himself asking, 'Do you want to go?'

And she couldn't stop herself saying, 'Not much.'

Then she looked down at her plate, aware that they'd just broken some sort of rule although she didn't understand what the rule could be. At that point the physical need to hug her, to let her cry on his shoulder and take her home with him became so nearly overpowering that every muscle in his body hurt from resisting it. And after he'd handed her back to Olivia in the car park he went out and got drunker than at any time in the past twenty years.

Next week he said on the phone to Olivia, 'I'm not having that car park business again.'

And probably because she'd learned to recognize that rare tone of voice that meant he was unbudgeable, she agreed that he could call at the house to collect Debbie at two-thirty, when Ralph would be out. If the tickets hadn't been on the table, he'd have made some sort of excuse to go into the living room to look for them. But it couldn't have been easier. Olivia, having opened the door and informed him that Debbie was upstairs changing and would be down in five minutes, disappeared with as much apparent calm as if he'd come to read the meters. And in the few minutes before Debbie came down he had time enough to look at every document in the folder: channel ferry ticket, overnight with berths reserved, hotel booking for the next night on the journey, voucher for a tent emplacement, thirteen days, at Zoe Village des Vacances. It was one of the few advantages of his old training that he could memorize the lot and have it stowed away in his mind before Debbie arrived in neatly pressed jeans and T-shirt.

Now, just ten kilometres away from the reality of it, he waited at the side of the road while the sky turned from gold to a pale colour like the flesh of a melon, then dusk. He turned on his lights and rode slowly, still shirtless, with the white road gleaming in front of him and an occasional pale moth looping across it. At the five-killometre point there was another Village Zoe sign, and another at one kilometre. There he stopped again, rummaged in his pannier and transferred the Swiss army knife to the pocket of his shorts. Another five hundred yards or so, he calculated, would do it. To look convincing, he'd have to do at least some walking. And at the end of five hundred yards he was already alongside a high brushwood fence that might mark the outside limit of Zoe Village territory. This was it. He dismounted and, from habit, pushed his thumb against the front tyre, finding it well inflated. He'd already decided that the smaller penknife blade of the Swiss army knife would make a more convincing job and, holding the bike by the handlebars with his left hand, he jabbed it hard at the tyre. Either the knife was blunted or Birdie's hands were reluctant to carry through the violence. In the end he had to lie the bike down flat at the roadside and grip the wheel frame with his left hand before the blade went in and air gushed out like the gasp of a weightlifter. A car swept past, doing about fifty, and luckily its driver wasn't tempted to stop and help a cyclist in distress. Birdie worked the knife downwards, making a jagged line about three inches long in inner and outer tubes. That should be enough.

He found as he walked, pushing the unwieldy bike, that the brushwood fence did belong to Zoe Village. A few yards down it there was a large sign offering, in three languages, swimming, tennis, sauna, yoga, meditation techniques and several sorts of therapies – algotherapy, aromatherapy, thalotherapy – he'd never heard of before. Discouragingly, a message at the bottom stated that this was not a public camp site. Holidaymakers by reservation only. Two weeks ago Birdie had tried, by ringing the number on Olivia's ticket folder, to make a reservation. The girl at the other end of the phone had been eager and helpful at first:

'Zoe Village, last two weeks in June. Yes, I think we can do that.

Chalet, caravan or tent? Just a couple, or family?'

Birdie replied that it was neither couple nor family, just him. The girl's voice changed.

'I'm sorry, Zoe Village won't accept singles. We could get you in at Aphrodite Village on the . . . .'

Arguing got him nowhere. Zoe Village, not the travel agent, made the rules . . . special sort of atmosphere . . . some problems in the past etcetera . . . if he fancied Mykonos instead . . .

Birdie had known that being enforcedly single made him miserable, but it had taken the travel agent's girl to make him feel guilty about it as well. The thought that the oaf – equipped with Olivia and Debbie – could walk in to the damned place without problems, had been the last piece of provocation needed to make his plan a firm one. It had also made him resentful in advance of Zoe Village, and its many therapies.

When he got to the main entrance a barrier was down across the car park and he had to push the bike round it. There were no lights on in the reception building but one powerful bulb was shining over a sort of sentry box, in the middle of a chain link fence. They'd tried to disguise the prison camp look of the thing by growing passion flowers and Morning Glories over fence and sentry box. He went up to it, still pushing his bike.

'*Pardonnez-moi, monsieur, j'ai un petit problem . . .*'

But the man in the box either couldn't, or wouldn't, understand Birdie's French, and Birdie now realized that his meticulous preparations had fallen down on one thing – he'd forgotten to look up the French words for tyre and puncture. The nearest he got was: '*Ma bicyclette est percée,*' which produced another burst of mainly incomprehensible and hostile French from the guard, in which the word 'fermé' cropped up several times in increasing volume.

'Oh hell.'

He hadn't expected this. The plan had depended on the presence of some reasonably sympathetic person who could at least understand his problem. He tried again, this time raising the bike up on its back wheel and presenting the punctured front wheel to the guard, to try to show him what had happened. But the guard – faced with a half-naked madman coming out of the darkness and waving bicycles at him – decided he was under attack. He shouted two or three words at Birdie, slammed the door of his box shut and, from somewhere inside it, pressed a buzzer.

'Oh hell.'

18

He was badly tempted to run off, but he couldn't abandon his bike and its panniers or get far if he tried to push it. A dog began barking somewhere when the buzzer sounded and kept on barking, but apart from that there was no immediate reaction. The guard stayed shut in his box, Birdie stood there holding his bike and waiting to see what would happen next.

Then, from inside the creeper covered fence, a woman's voice asking in French what was going on. A voice that sounded peremptory rather than panicked. The guard in his box was at a conversational disadvantage, so Birdie was able to get his version in first.

'*Pardonnez moi, je suis seulement un cyclist anglais. J'ai un petit problem.*'

A voice said in English: 'What kind of little problem?' And a woman appeared under the light beside the guard's box. She was zipping up a tracksuit top, her feet were bare, and a dark plaited pigtail hung over her shoulder. He was taken aback, because he'd been expecting some hulk of a security man and more French.

'My tyre's punctured.'

She took a few steps forward and bent over the tyre, and her shoulder in its tracksuit brushed against his chest. There was a smell of fresh sweat on her skin. The guard had opened the door of his box and was watching Birdie with suspicion.

'It's a bad puncture,' she said.

He took a piece of jagged glass – carefully selected back in England – from a pannier.

'That's what did it. Some wretched kid probably threw it out of the car.'

'Have you got things to repair it? We could get you a bucket of water.'

'I think it's beyond that. It needs a new inner tube and I'm not carrying one with me. I'd have to go back to the other side of the ferry.'

He'd calculated that the search for an inner tube – cunningly spun out – should ensure him two or three nights at the camp.

'I see.' She stared at the tyre, then up at Birdie. She smiled, a nice open smile.

'So what are you going to do?'

'I've got a tent. I just need somewhere to put it for the night. I wondered . . .'

'It's not a public camping site,' she said. 'There's the municipal three kilometres down the road.'

19

He'd planned, at this point, to try the weary and travel-worn line, but sensed somehow that it wouldn't impress this competent and hard-looking young woman. Instead, very slowly, he wheeled the bike round under the light, turned and thanked her, with one foot on the pedal.

'Your shoulders,' she said. 'They're burned.'

'Sunburn. I did a hundred and sixty kilometres on a hot day.'

'You should have kept your shirt on.'

But he sensed a change in attitude. This woman approved of a hundred and sixty kilometres in the heat. Possibly – although his battered sexual vanity wouldn't let him count on it – she approved of men with a presentable set of back and shoulder muscles.

'OK,' she said. 'I'll stretch a point. You can pitch your tent here tonight and I may be able to get you a lift back to the ferry tomorrow.'

That could be a problem. Still, he was in. The man in the guard box smirked as the bike was wheeled past, as if he and not Birdie had won the argument.

'Stay there,' she said. 'I'll fetch a torch.'

He waited until she came back from the direction of a little white bungalow. From where he stood he could see a children's playground and a few caravans, but nothing else of the camp.

'I'll put you at the end of Tagore. We're not using it this week.'

As they walked along the path her torchlight picked out wooden signs to the pool, the sauna, various camping areas. It seemed that each set of tent or caravan pitches was named after a poet: Brontë and Verlaine, Whitman and Mueller. It seemed that Tagore must be the part of the camp nearest to the gate, because they didn't pass any other tents or vans on the way to it.

'Anywhere you like here.'

She swept the torchbeam round an expanse of sand and pine needles. A few small trees and large heather plants were dotted round it.

'The nearest toilet block's over there. If you come to the office tomorrow I'll see what I can do about the lift.'

He leant his bike against a pine tree and tried to thank her.

'Don't worry.'

As she walked off she said to him, over her shoulder, 'If you feel like some exercise in the morning it's eight-thirty on the volleyball courts.'

What was eight thirty on the volleyball courts? She was gone before he had a chance to ask her, in long strides into the darkness. He noticed that, on her own, she didn't use the torch, confident as a fox on its own territory.

For the first hour or so Birdie behaved much as any puncture-wrecked cyclist might have done, pitched camp and made himself as comfortable as possible. The tent pegs slid easily into sandy ground and his small ridge tent was up within ten minutes. He changed into a tracksuit, and a rummage through the panniers produced a tin of steak and onions, a hunk of very dry baguette and a few inches of Courvoisier left in the bottom of the half bottle he'd bought on the Channel ferry. With brandy and water in his enamel mug, the steak and onions heating on his Camping Gas stove and a clear, star-filled sky overhead he let himself relax for a few minutes and think that this really was a pleasure trip, that he was on his own because he wanted to be on his own. A brown free-wheeling man that any independent woman might invite to pitch his tent on her patch. In this mood he found himself thinking very kindly of the competent woman with the pigtail and regretting that he'd taken advantage of her generosity. Then that brought him back to why he'd done it and the relaxed mood went, even before he'd finished spooning up the warm meat and onions. After that he hurried to finish the meal, drank the brandy and water at a gulp and rinsed the pan, plate and mug at a stand tap. Now. He knew the number of Olivia's tent emplacement, 17 Racine. The question was, where was Racine. He'd seen a large map on a board near the main gate, but going back there was out of the question, so he decided to work on the assumption that the camp would have some sort of centre and hope to find another map there.

The first step was surprisingly easy. He simply walked across the empty Tagore patch to what looked like the main drive, and down it towards some solid whitewashed buildings standing in a hollow square. It was only just eleven o'clock so there were still a few people walking around, most of them in tracksuits too, so he attracted no attention. The white buildings turned out to be a shopping centre around another children's playground: a wine shop with huge wooden barrels visible through the glass door, a small supermarket, a health food shop and a café with tables and chairs outside. The café was closed, although a light on at the back of it suggested the staff might still be washing up. And, as he'd hoped, beside a rustic wood climbing frame was another large map of the camp with a red arrow marking the shops. Racine, he

21

discovered, was about as far away from Tagore as it was possible to get. Whereas his tent was pitched quite close to the main gate and the road, the Racine emplacements were near the sea, right on the edge of the sand dunes. And number 17, as it happened, was on the very edge of the block. Was it Olivia's competence or the oaf's luck that had secured them a prime site? He started walking down the drive again, surprised at the size of the place. As far as he could gather it was about a mile square, most of it pine woods, and the main drive he was on led straight down to the sea. As he walked, the sounds of the waves on the beach sounded louder, harsh and booming even on this summer night. And it was getting cooler. Even through the soles of his track shoes he could feel the cold of the drive now the sun had left it, and he wished he'd thought to bring socks and a sweater. Most of the campers seemed to have gone early to bed. On either side of the drive, big pavilion tents glowed like grounded Christmas tree lamps. He heard an English voice from one of them:

'Phemie, where did you put the mosquito coils?'

A bit further on there were caravans, and one party of about ten people had got itself organized round a drinks table, piled with duty-frees.

'But if we're not allowed on the tennis courts till nine o'clock . . .' Apparently an indignation meeting already. He raised a hand as he passed, and they waved back at him. '. . . I mean, it says coaching included, so if we . . .'

Then an area of wooden chalets, with some lights on and murmurings of voices from inside them. Just past the chalets, if he remembered the map correctly, he had to turn off towards Racine, and there, sure enough, was a broad sandy path with tyre tracks scored deeply into it. Probably hell with a caravan in wet weather.

He went more cautiously now, glad that his footsteps on the sand made no noise. For the first few hundred yards the path kept behind the backs of the chalets, then for another hundred yards or so there was nothing but trees, then at last the tented outposts of what must be Racine. Luckily the tents, like the chalets, faced away from the path. He paced carefully, watching out for guy ropes, checking the cars that were parked alongside. On his left, between the path and the sea, the first of the sand dunes rose up, covered with little scrubby plants. The green Jaguar was parked with its bonnet facing the dunes and a large pavilion tent was pitched next to it, shining green from the light of a lamp inside.

22

This was the difficult bit. The slope of dune gave him a better observation place than he might have expected, but he had to climb it without noise. Most of the little scrubby plants proved to be thorny and tore at his tracksuit and unprotected ankles. Several times they rustled so loudly that he stopped and listened, waiting for a voice from the lighted tent. Would it be her voice, or his? But there was silence, except for the crash and drag of the sea. He climbed on, and near the top of the dune the prickling shrubs gave place to clumps of thin, wiry grass. Here, in a hollow between grass clumps, Birdie settled cross-legged, his back against the slope and the green tent perhaps fifteen feet below him. He imagined the inside of it: a nylon walled living room, two bedrooms. Debbie, on a Lilo or camp bed, divided from their room only by a membrane of nylon and a zip, hearing every sound they made, every breath. That wouldn't bother the courts or the solicitors. It was difficult to know what would bother the courts or solicitors. But there must be something, somewhere in the oaf's behaviour – in the oaf's and Olivia's behaviour – that would convince even them. And here in France, or back in England, he was going to find it.

'You must accept it,' the solicitor had told him. 'You've just got to accept it.'

Well, this was his answer.

CHAPTER THREE

Dim, undersea light filtered through the blue tent nylon and somewhere distant a bell, also undersea, was going melodiously bong bong bong. Birdie sighed, stirred and looked at his watch. Eight fifteen. Too early. But already his mind was swimming up through the undersea light into full wakefulness. Much too early. It had been four o'clock before he gave up his entirely fruitless watch on the tent. Not a sound out of it all night. Either love-making or quarrelling would have been some sort of prize to take away with him. As it was, he had made his way back through the camp, past the tents, chalets and caravans in the early light, with nothing to show for his night on the dunes except cold feet and stiff muscles. Still a bit stiff now. The bell that he'd thought was in his dreams was still bong bonging in the distance, and he unzipped the tent flap and looked out to see if he could find any reason for it.

Three children were playing on the other side of the path, on a little hillock of sand facing his tent. The sun streamed through the trees, flecked with grains of pine pollen, on to brown naked backs, legs, buttocks. There were a girl of about eight and two younger boys, all sleek and unselfconscious as salmon and entirely naked. 'Nice,' thought Birdie. 'Nice for little kids to be able to play in the sun with nothing on.' The girl noticed him, threw a quick smile and said, *'Bonjour, monsieur.'*

'Bonjour, mademoiselle,' he replied gravely.

The girl and the little boys shouted with laughter and dashed off through the trees. Somewhere from the other side of his camping patch he could hear a woman's voice calling them. He felt as pleased as if he'd seen a trio of red squirrels.

The previous night he'd found a lavatory block about fifty yards from his tent, so he strolled over to it in tracksuit trousers and bare feet, enjoying the feel of sand that still had the coolness of night about it, although the sun was warm on his shoulders. The urinals

24

were at one side of the block in the open air, and in daylight he found that mildly embarrassing. As he was standing there another man wandered up wearing a tracksuit top that swung open over a brown and pendulous chest, a gold medallion, and nothing at all below the waist. His round tanned stomach and his penis swung as he walked.

'*Bonjour, monsieur.*'

He gave Birdie a smile full of sparkling white and gold teeth and strolled away, buttocks swinging in time with his stomach. A free and easy sort of place, Birdie decided. Just how free and easy he discovered as he walked towards the source of the bell noise.

'Mathilde, what did you do with the cream?'

The cry, in German, came from a woman bending over a table outside a caravan. She was a large woman and the table was low. It's one thing on a sunny morning to see three naked children playing like squirrels in the woods: quite another in foreign country and still un-breakfasted to be confronted by the naked white buttocks of a woman who carries plenty of insulation between bones and chair seat. She looked up, saw Birdie and said in English, 'I am sorry. I thought you were my daughter.'

Spluttering words of apology in three languages and keeping his eyes firmly on her headscarf, Birdie shuffled past, then broke into a run. This brought him to the main drive of the camp and into a whole procession of people. Families mostly, husband, wife and children. Some middle-aged couples with the sort of lined faces and lean bodies that go with determined fitness and a sprinkling of younger people, including some startlingly good looking girls. They were all walking, purposefully but unhurriedly, towards the sound of the bell. But what was a lot more disconcerting for Birdie than the purposefulness was the fact that almost every one of them was stark naked. Not quite all. A few wore the tops or bottoms of tracksuits. Here and there, standing out like exotic birds among the flock, were shorts and sun dresses, and, even among the otherwise totally bare, there seemed to be a fashion for ethnic-type headbands. But, apart from that, simply skin. White skin, mostly, of the new arrivals. Glossy copper, like car bodies straight from the spray works, of those who'd presumably been around all summer. Just a few patches of red as bright as his own throbbing shoulders. Breasts pert, breasts melon-like, breasts dangling. Penises thin as sticks of bamboo or curled up in thick bushes of pubic hair. Buttocks with taut muscles under shining skin, like demonstration models of the anatomy of walking. Plumper buttocks that swayed to a private rhythm of their own. As fast as he dragged his eyes away from one awful fascination, another pressed in front of him. He realized he'd stopped dead and the gentle tide of bodies was parting to go round him. He heard somebody say, 'A bit better than that beach in Essex.'

And a woman's voice, 'Well, actually, it's a bit late for us. At home we have our exercise session at six.'

And he remembered what had been said about exercise at eight thirty on the volleyball courts. What sort of exercise for heaven's sake? And what sort of place? He started walking again, keeping his eyes on feet and rehearsing a few things to say to his solicitor. He'd come here to collect evidence, and evidence he was damned well going to collect, whatever the embarrassment.

The feet walked on down the drive, past the cluster of shops, and turned right towards the volleyball courts, met other tides of feet coming from other directions, filed through the gate in the wire netting. The bongs were coming from several loudspeakers around the courts. And there at the side of the enclosed space, about twenty yards away from Birdie, was a low platform with a microphone and on it the woman he'd met at reception the night before. To his startled eyes she looked, if anything, nuder than the rest. Her skin – the colour of expensive heather honey – seemed to glow with a light of its own, revealing muscular development of a kind he'd never seen on a woman before. It wasn't that her muscles were particularly large, just that every one of them, at shoulders, stomach, thighs, was so precisely outlined that the slightest of her movements, even when she put a hand up to adjust the microphone, brought a rippling chain reaction under the glowing skin, like the surface of water with something moving just underneath it. Just to watch her brought a reaction in Birdie too that threatened to be embarrassing. He hurriedly looked away, and found that by a lucky chance his eyes were resting on one of the few people in the assembly more or less fully clothed. The girl on his right was wearing shorts and a top in white stretch towelling, a matching white bandeau round a mass of golden-brown hair. When she saw his eyes on her she first flashed him a smile full of perfect teeth, then looked annoyed as if deciding he wasn't worth it. Her face looked vaguely familiar to him and he must have been staring, trying to place it, because he was suddenly aware that the girl had not one, but two men with her – one with denim shorts and

26

thin white chest, the other with satin boxer shorts and legs covered in a thick pelt of hair. And they were both looking at him in a vaguely threatening way. On his left, Birdie's eyes found a safer resting place: mother, father, two thin children and one fat one. The fat child was sticking doggedly to jeans, training shoes and a T-shirt with 'I'm a Self-Made Slob' in big, red letters. The rest were naked but undisturbing. The father, a plumpish dark man in his late thirties, caught Birdie's eye and grinned.

'Thought I'd come for the first morning,' he said. 'See if the scenery was worth the exercise.'

From the glare he got from his wife and the turning of heads around them, Birdie decided that such an attitude was not encouraged at the Village Zoe.

Now the girl from last night was speaking into the microphone, in English. She introduced herself as Nimue, said it was nice to see so many of them on their first morning, and announced they'd be starting with some loosening-up exercises to music. Then Jean-Paul – she indicated a six-foot-six bulk of suntan and muscle standing beside her – would organize some group exercises with light weights. Everybody should take it easy and not try to do too much, especially if they hadn't taken much exercise for a while.

'I wonder how many they cart off with coronaries,' said the dark man on Birdie's left. And got shushed by his wife.

Nimue repeated her speech in French and German, then tides of Tchaikovsky began flowing from the speakers and Birdie found himself bending, stretching and raising arms in time to the music, brain reeling all the time from a kaleidoscope of parts of anatomies in unlikely positions. After twenty minutes or so of this – with Nimue's voice giving instructions over waves of music – it was Jean-Paul's turn. Baskets full of bean bags and boxes of small dumbbells appeared from somewhere and they were instructed to find partners. Birdie got the fat child in the T-shirt.

'I wish I wasn't here,' were the child's first words.

'Where do you want to be?'

'Marbella. They've got a hotel there with a room where you can play Space Invaders all night if you want to.'

Jean-Paul threw them a bean bag and the fat child glared at it. 'What are we supposed to do with this?'

Birdie, who'd been more or less listening to the instructions, explained they were meant to sit back to back with their legs stretched out in front of them and pass it to each other.

'I don't see the point of it.'

Birdie was inclined to agree, but the child's mother said 'Philip!' in such menacing tones that both of them were scared into action. It was while Birdie was sitting with legs outstretched, trying to get the bean bag into the child's reluctant hand, that he saw Olivia and Deborah. They were there sitting back to back on the far side of the court, Olivia's long legs and flanks quite naked, Deborah in shorts. To all appearances they were intent on the exercise and hadn't noticed him. He could see no sign of Ralph Shunner, but that didn't surprise him. The oaf had never been one for unnecessary exercise.

They were relieved of the bean bags and dumbbells were handed round instead—small blue affairs of no more than two kilos, toys compared with the apparatus Birdie used in his work-outs. Jean-Paul, in heavily accented English, explained from the microphone that they should find a space for themselves, stand with legs well apart, holding the dumbbells above their heads, arms stretched. Then swing down and through legs, bending knees. Then up again . . . and swing . . . and up again and swing. He added quickly that before swinging they should make sure nobody was in range behind them: 'They are not such big weights, but they could give you a bad hit on the head.'

Some laughter, and much shuffling to find space.

Then the music started again, Jean-Paul's voice above it. Up and swing and up and swing and . . . Eighty or so dumbbells rose in the air and descended in arcs between eighty or so pairs of straddled legs. But on Birdie's right, the girl in the white shorts was making heavy weather of the exercise, and calling on her two men for help.

'But I don't see what he means. If I bend my knees I'm going to hit my hands on the ground when I go forward.'

They both stopped their swinging and started giving her contradictory advice. The one with the thin chest and denim shorts said she shouldn't try the exercise. She'd probably done enough for the morning. They'd go back to the chalet. Boxer shorts and hairy legs said it was easy. Of course she wouldn't hurt her hands. Look, like this. Jean-Paul became aware of the controversy, left the platform and came to sort it out. Birdie, continuing his conscientious swinging, was aware that Jean-Paul's ideas of sorting it out involved much laying of hands on the girl's towelling-covered hips.

'Like this, you see. Nice and easy.'

He made her lay the dumbbell aside for a while and swung her up and down between his big brown hands, her hair brushing the ground. Hairy legs looked on, scowling, but the thin chested man was swinging his dumbbell energetically, apparently taking no further interest in what was happening a few feet away. Birdie thought he was standing dangerously close and wondered whether to say anything.

'Up and down and up and down and . . .'

Jean-Paul and the girl swung together. The thin-chested man swung solo.

'. . . and down and up and down and . . . MERDE!'

The girl in the white shorts was upright, aghast. The thin-chested man was also upright, apologetic. Jean-Paul lay on the ground writhing, swearing and clutching his ankle.

For about a minute the music and the general dumbbell wielding went on, oblivious of the troubled little group in the corner. Then Nimue, from the platform, noticed what had happened, silenced the music and brought the activity to a halt with a few calm words.

'All right everybody. Just rest for a few minutes.'

She came to them through the staring crowd.

'. . . can't imagine what happened,' the thin-chested man was saying. 'I thought there was plenty of room. I didn't know he . . .'

Birdie had persuaded Jean-Paul to stop writhing and stretch out the injured leg for inspection, but he could do nothing about the swearing. That went on in a vengeful stream, directed against the thin-chested man.

Nimue said, 'Don't worry Mr Jedd. It was an accident.' She said something in French to Jean-Paul and the swearing stopped, replaced by a low intermittent groaning. There were huge drops of sweat on the man's brown forehead. Then she knelt down beside Birdie and, even in the circumstances, he was conscious of a feeling like a little electric shock when her cool bare side touched his.

'Is it bad?'

She accepted without comment Birdie's competence in first aid.

'The ankle's probably broken. He got fetched a terrific clunk with one of those dumbbells.'

She touched the ankle very lightly, took her fingers away when Jean-Paul winced and seemed to come to the same conclusion as Birdie.

29

'We'd better get him to the bungalow and call an ambulance.'

She stood up and raised her voice, 'I'm sorry everybody, but I'm afraid that's it for this morning. Same place, eight-thirty tomorrow.'

Most of the exercisers filed out quietly, rather subdued. The family next to Birdie hung around, offering help. The girl in the white shorts had broken into hysterical sobs and was being comforted, morosely, by hairy legs, while Jedd just stood there, offering apologies. Birdie noticed that although Jean-Paul was not swearing at him any more he was looking at him with hatred. The big gym instructor, by the look of it, did not forgive accidents.

Just as things were calming down a little and they were working out how best to get Jean-Paul to his feet, the girl's hysterical sobbing took a new turn.

'It's all my fault,' she wept. 'It's all my fault.'

By the third or fourth repetition she was almost yelling it.

'Shh, Melanie. Of course it isn't your fault.'

'If I hadn't tried to do that silly exercise he wouldn't have been there. It's all my . . .'

Nimue said crisply, 'I think you'd better take her away and get her to lie down.'

And the two men obeyed, supporting Melanie between them as if she too were injured. Birdie noticed that when Jedd had gone Jean-Paul relaxed a little, although he was obviously still in great pain. He let himself be raised to his feet and, hopping on one leg, supported by Birdie and the father of fat Philip, he could make it to the bungalow. They went slowly up the drive, Nimue walking in front. All round them the campers were going back to their tents and the smell of breakfast coffee rose on the warm air.

Olivia and Deborah went most of the way back to their tent without a word. They were in sight of the green Jaguar before Deborah said flatly, 'That was Dad. Helping the man with the ankle.'

And Olivia, equally flatly, 'Yes.'

There was coffee in Nimue's neat bungalow. Coffee with a good slug of cognac in it for Jean-Paul, laid out on the studio couch. Black coffee in brown pottery mugs for Birdie and Nimue. Philip's father had hurried off back to the family. The ambulance arrived surprisingly quickly and they got the invalid loaded into it without trouble. Birdie was relieved that, before the arrival of the ambulancemen, Nimue had put her tracksuit back on. Totally unable to get tracksuit trousers over Jean-Paul's injured ankle, the best they could do to make him respectable for the hospital was to get him into a black and gold caftan from her wardrobe. He looked like Mr Universe in a mini dress, and his appearance seemed to cause him at least as much pain as his injured ankle. As the ambulance turned into the road Nimue heaved a relieved sigh.

'I need another coffee. Would you like one?'

He watched while she brewed it, moving barefoot on the pine floor of her little kitchenette. The bungalow was scrupulously tidy, large blue and green cushions set square against the walls. Blue blankets by the studio couch neatly folded. On the wall was a single good print of sunlight coming through birch trees, their black shadows falling like bars.

'A nice room.'

'Yes, it's one of the best things about this job. That, and lots of exercise.'

'Been doing it long?'

'Just this summer.'

She rinsed out the cups, poured fresh coffee.

'The ambulancemen seemed quite sure it's broken.'

'I was sure from the start. Nearly a five-pound weight with a good swing behind it. Still, at least it'll be a clean break.'

She said, 'Poor Jean-Paul. He's so proud of his body.'

They sipped coffee in silence for a while. Now she'd covered up her own body, his mind was plagued with the image of those muscles sliding under honey skin. He could imagine the upward movement over her rib cage as she lifted the coffee mug. 'You're pretty fit yourself,' he said.

'Thank you.' Another silence. 'I should be out on the tennis courts,' she said. 'The first morning the instructors grade them into different classes. People can get surprisingly difficult about it.'

But she made no move to go. There was a very slight trace of Yorkshire in her voice. 'I don't know what I'm going to do about this latest.'

'Jean-Paul?'

'Yes, to be honest, he's a bit of an idle slob. But he's one of the life savers at the pool, as well as helping me in the mornings and taking the kids' exercise classes in the afternoon. I'll just have to try and

31

be in two places at once until Paris sends someone.'

He said almost without thinking about it, 'I've got my life saving certificate.'

She said nothing, just looked at him out of dark eyes.

'And I take the general fitness classes at the youth club every week. I expect I could manage your kids.'

Eyes wider.

'Well,' she said.

'So . . . if you wanted . . . I could help out here for a day or two if you liked . . . till you get somebody.'

His brain, catching up with his impulses, was saying yes, this was a very good idea. A way of staying at the Village Zoe for several more days at least, getting evidence, and the slob powerless to do anything about it. But he wondered even so why he was so eager her answer should be yes.

'Why not?' She laughed suddenly, square white teeth between rose-gold lips. 'Why not? If you're sure you wouldn't mind. Until they can send somebody from Paris.'

'I'd be glad to.'

She looked at him for a few moments, then became all efficiency.

'Right, you can start work with the kids this afternoon. I'll find some money to pay you out of the petty cash. And you can move your things into Jean-Paul's chalet if you like. They'll probably put him in traction for weeks.'

'I'll stay in my tent, thanks.'

Easier from there to keep an eye on Deborah, Olivia and the oaf.

'If you like.'

Another short silence, and he hoped she wasn't reconsidering her decision. Suddenly she asked, 'The youth club and so on – are you a teacher?'

'No, I just got involved in a lot of youth liaison work.' He decided to take the plunge. 'I was a policeman.'

He watched carefully, and wasn't sure if there'd been a slight change of the look in those dark eyes. People reacted in all sorts of ways.

'Was?'

'Until this year. Something happened.'

Now her expression had changed, and he understood why she might be having second thoughts. He said hastily, 'Not little boys or little girls, if that's what you're worried about. You can trust the kids with me.'

She just nodded, registering what he'd said, accepting it. 'Good.'

She stood up, collecting both coffee cups, and took them to the sink.

'I'll have to go and see to the tennis. The first kids' exercise class is at three, on the volleyball courts again. I'll meet you there at a quarter to and show you where everything is.'

She was unzipping her tracksuit top, changing into the nudity that seemed to be her official uniform. He agreed hastily to meet her at the volleyball courts and left.

It was about two hours after that that he met Olivia. He'd been wondering how he could manage it without Deborah or the oaf being there and had gone down to the beach to think about it. A quick swim that was more of a wrestling match with the sinewy Atlantic waves, a brisk run along the beach to get warm, and he was walking back along the path over the sand dunes when he saw her. Olivia, now wearing slacks and open-necked shirt, was standing on the top of the dunes, staring out to sea. A breeze whipped at the thin grass round her feet. She was so deep in her thoughts that Birdie was within a few feet of her, had asked her the question, before she saw him.

'Why did you bring Deborah here?'

In the instant it took her to turn and look at him she'd blanked out any surprise. And her answer was in the same tone of desperate patience as when they'd first discussed Deborah's school holidays several weeks before.

'You agreed to it. And you're not doing any of us any good by behaving like this.'

'I wouldn't have damned well agreed to it if I knew where you were bringing her. Does the solicitor know about it?'

'You realize I could get a court order to stop you trailing us like this. It's harassment.'

'I said does the solicitor know about it?'

'About what?'

'About bringing a fourteen-year-old girl to a bloody nudist camp. Sleeping in the same tent as her mother's lover.'

She said, patiently, 'Naturist is the word. They don't like nudist.'

'I don't like it either. And what do you think it's doing to her? Bending and stretching all over the place with crowds of gawping perverts.'

'For heaven's sake, Arthur . . .' (She'd never called him Birdie.) 'For heaven's sake, Arthur, do they look like perverts?'

She waved a hand at the long stretch of beach in front of them. Kids and parents flying kites, falling off surfboards, putting up striped canvas shelters against the wind. The screams of a toddler who'd probably just had it broken to him that there was no ice cream stand rose above gulls' cries and waves.

'Just like any other families on holiday. And probably a lot healthier than most.'

'So that's it. A health kick. You're trying to turn bloody Shunner into a muscle-man, are you. Well, if you think bringing him to a place like this . . .'

'As a matter of fact . . .'

'. . . is going to make him take any exercise beyond drinking himself insensible and swivelling his eyes after every female within range . . .'

'. . . it was Ralph's idea to come here.'

'. . . you must be even more besotted with him than . . . what do you mean, his idea?'

'It was Ralph who suggested it.'

'His idea to bring Deborah here? And you just agreed to it, I suppose. Just as you've agreed to every other bloody thing he's suggested. Oh yes, darling. Let's all go and romp around with no clothes on. Without a thought of what it might do to Deborah.'

He was practically shouting, and a woman with two children flying a kite from an adjoining dune was beginning to look their way with interest. Olivia dropped her voice practically to a whisper, but an angry one.

'Deborah's fine. She's over at the tennis courts.'

'She didn't look fine to me. Yesterday waiting for the ferry or at that session this morning. She looked pretty miserable to me. And you've let her get sunburned.'

'If Deborah looks miserable, it's probably the tension of being trailed around by her own father like an incompetent private detective. What do you think that's doing to her?'

'What do you. . . ?'

'You think about it. After all the insecurity, just when she's beginning to settle down and go on holiday like any other child of her age, there you are, staring, spying on her. Is that supposed to help her to adjust?'

34

'I don't want her to bloody adjust . . .'

He'd been intending to say that any life with Ralph Shunner in it could never give security to his daughter, or anyone else. But he stopped short, realizing that – as in every argument with Olivia – he'd just scored an own goal. And she knew it.

'Yes, that's just it, isn't it. You're determined that she won't get a chance to have a normal life. You're so vengeful about Ralph and me that you'd wreck Deborah's mental stability for good rather than accept what's happened.'

And useless then to try to explain that although he'd said the words, he didn't mean them the way she thought. Or did he? Among all the other things the past year and a half had taken was any certainty about what words meant. He just stood there, toes curled in the hot sand, while she went on in the same low voice.

'I won't let you do that. As soon as we get back to England I'm going to tell my solicitor exactly what's happening. Because if I have to go to court again to stop this, believe me, I'm going to. Even if it costs another thousand.'

She paused, waiting for him to say something, but he said nothing. Just stared down at the pink trumpets of flowers like Convolvulus that grew straight out of the dune without leaves or stem.

She said, 'So you'd better leave now. The longer you stay, the more harm you'll be doing yourself. And Deborah – if you care about that.'

No reaction. She stared at him for a few seconds, then turned away and slid down the inland slope of the dune, the sand following each thrust of her heels in miniature avalanches.

The sun was directly over the café verandah, casting broad shadows from the vine leaves on breasts, thighs, trays of apèritifs. A woman's hand, plump and smooth, fingers heavily ringed, stretched out for a glass of *pineau de charente*. Two male hands followed it to the neighbouring glasses.

'Here's to the Resistance,' said Peter Pollins.

They sipped, considered.

'You have to drink it really cold, like this,' the other man said. 'I went in the kitchen half an hour ago and made them put the bottle in the ice compartment. It isn't enough just to leave it in the fridge.'

The woman said, 'Can you get it in England?'

'A few places, but it's inferior stuff. I always take a bottle or two back with me.'

Peter Pollins said, 'It reminds me of that joke about the Irishman and Benedictine. You know, "What Protestant bastard made the glasses?" You don't get much in them.'

The plump woman, who obviously hadn't heard the rest of the joke, giggled obligingly. She was in her late forties with a body that was all of a piece, as rounded, smooth and white as her hands. Her limbs splayed out, relaxed, against an orange towel she'd thrown over a hard chair in an attitude full of comfort but without sexual challenge.

She explained to Ralph Shunner, 'Mr Pollins and I are being very wicked. We're the . . . what was it. . . ?'

'The Drunks, Gluttons and Layabouts' Defence Commando. Joan and I have just invented it.'

Peter Pollins had already achieved a state of mild drunkenness on two glasses of white wine and one *pineau*.

'Sounds interesting. Can I join?'

Pollins pretended to look at Ralph judicially.

'That depends. Do you promise to abstain from all forms of voluntary exercise?'

'I do.'

'Do you promise never to lay hands on a tennis racquet, volleyball, parallel bar or dumbbell?'

'I do.'

'Do you solemnly swear throughout the length of your stay never to fail to imbibe at least one alcoholic beverage before twelve noon, local time.'

'I do so swear.'

Peter clapped him on the back. 'Then I have great pleasure in welcoming Mr Ralph Shunner as a member of the Drunks, Gluttons and Layabouts' Defence Commando.' He caught the eye of the waiter, a slim brown lad in blue satin shorts. '*Trois charentes encore, s'il vous plaît. Très froid.*'

He settled back in his chair.

'The trouble is for any normal individual, this place is too healthy by half. Joan's here because her husband's the sort who actually likes going for five-mile runs before breakfast. My dear wife Vinny's never happier than when she's tucking her left toe behind her right ear. Our theory is that in every healthy family there's one like us screaming to break out. What about you?'

Ralph Shunner smiled. 'I'm only here for the wine. My wife and step-daughter get the exercise. I'll be touring round some of the châteaux deciding what to buy.'

'A bottle from each?'

Ralph Shunner looked amused, tolerant. 'Good heavens, no. I buy in bulk, don't you?'

The leader of the Drunks, Gluttons and Layabouts' Commando looked dashed. 'Well . . . I mean, I've thought about it. They've got some very decent red at the shops here, and I was thinking if I could get hold of some of those empty orange juice containers, the big ones . . .'

He stopped short, seeing Shunner's expression. 'You didn't mean that kind of buying in bulk?'

Shunner shook his head, smiling tolerantly.

'I usually buy four cases of claret a year, for drinking in about three or four years' time. Except for the occasional really special case, of course.'

'Of course.'

Peter Pollins took off an imaginary hat and held it at chest level.

'Joan, this is no ordinary member of the Drunks, Gluttons and Layabouts we've recruited. I believe we shall have to make him a Brigadier.'

The café was beginning to fill up with early lunchers and every table under the shade of the vine was taken. This was causing some displeasure to an English group, two men and a woman, who had just arrived. Melanie McBride had changed from the white towelling outfit of her morning exercise section into a bikini bottom of vaguely Wild West style, cut from an expensive scrap of fine chamois leather and much hung about with fringes and dangling beads. In a café mostly full of naked people, it drew every eye in her direction. Her two escorts were still in shorts, and James Jedd looked nervous and worried, not helped by Melanie's latest problems.

'Of course not. It's right in the sun there. Make-up will be furious if I go back with a face full of freckles.'

Joan said in a piercing whisper, 'Isn't it that girl from whatsit?' And got an angry sideways look from James Jedd.

Melanie's other escort, Don, had laid hold of the table and was dragging it into the shade, its metal legs screeching on the stone floor. This caught the attention of a waiter, who tried to drag it back again, and a tug-of-war developed with Don and the waiter shouting at each other in English and French. Melanie joined in, shouting at the waiter.

'Oh dear.'

James Jedd sighed from a bottomless weariness and moved in to mediate, but with very little success. Don and the waiter stopped pulling and let the table rest half in and half out of the shade. But the waiter was adamant that it would block the way from the kitchen unless it went back where it started.

'Excuse me.'

Ralph Shunner, who'd been watching and looking bored, left his two companions and walked over to the arguing group. In crisp white shirt and shorts there was an official air about his large, slightly plump figure, and Don and the waiter fell silent. Only Melanie went on talking, her back to him.

'. . . after all, we're paying for it. I don't see why he should . . .'

Ralph put a hand on her bare shoulder and said, in a quite unexpected East End accent, 'Give it a rest, Rosie love. You can all come and sit with us.'

She spun round, mouth open.

'What are you doing here?'

James Jedd seemed relieved at anything offering a compromise, though he'd scowled when he saw Shunner's hand on the girl's shoulder.

'Hello, Ralph. You've got a table?'

Collecting three more chairs presented no diplomatic problems and, after a little more moaning from Melanie, she and her two escorts were sharing a table with the three members of the Drunks, Gluttons and Layabouts.

'I'm right, aren't I, love?' Joan asked as soon as they sat down. 'You're that girl from whatsit.'

'Harmony House,' she said quickly.

And Jedd, almost as quickly, 'She doesn't want to be recognized. She's on holiday.'

'Of course she wouldn't. That one's a right little bitch, isn't she? The one on the television I mean.'

Simultaneous dirty looks from Jedd and Melanie were beamed at Joan's plump face, but without effect. Ralph Shunner made some introductions.

'Rosie, love, these are Peter Pollins and Joan Meek. Joan, Peter, this is little Rosie who once used to work for me and went on to find fame and fortune as Melanie McBride. This is James Jedd, her manager . . .'

'Agent,' said James.

'. . . and this gentleman I don't think I've had the pleasure of meeting.'

'That's Don,' said James. 'He works for me.'

Don said nothing, staring at the menu card.

'My, haven't we all come on.' He turned towards Peter and Joan. 'I used to run wine bars and Melanie was one of my waitresses. Know why we called her Rosie?'

'Gypsy Rose Lee?' asked Peter, nearly tearing his eyeballs from their sockets with the effort to smile into Melanie's eyes and look at her cool, conical breasts at the same time. She appeared to take no notice of him.

Ralph shook his head. 'No. She was a quiet little thing, just come to the big city from Crewe or Luton or somewhere . . .'

'Croydon,' said Melanie, between her teeth.

'. . . and this man came in and asked whether we had any rosé wine. She said no, but she'd mix some red and white together for him. After that we always called her Rosie.'

'She wasn't with you that long,' said Jedd coldly. Even though Shunner had rescued him from an embarrassing scene over the table, he didn't seem pleased by his company.

'No.'

Ralph Shunner, apparently not noticing his bad humour, went on talking to the table at large.

'No, she wasn't. James here whisked her away to a film career.' Somehow he managed to say the words 'film career' in a way that made it quite clear what sort of films he had in mind. Joan was either the only one at the table to miss the implication, or had grasped it perfectly well and wanted to stir up trouble. She asked Melanie, 'What films have you been in, dear? Anything I'd have seen?'

And Melanie, without saying a word, got up with a swaying of fringes and clicking of beads, and went away. They watched silently as her neat little buttocks in their covering of chamois skin and her round heels in their backless sandals bounced indignantly across the café terrace to an empty chair at another table. Arrived at the chair, she crossed her legs, accepted a glass of wine from her new companions and was immediately as deep in conversation with them as if Ralph Shunner's group had never existed.

'Well, little Rosie has come on.'

Coinciding with James Jedd's, 'Oh no. It's that fucking

photographer.'

Don came to life and put down the menu card. 'Want me to do something?'

'It's too late now. I know him. If we try and warn him off he'll be even more of a pest. Oh fuck the woman.'

'What's wrong?' Joan asked.

'She's supposed to be here incognito. Not recognized. No publicity. So what does the bloody woman do but make for the first photographer she can find.'

'Who?'

'That man she's sitting with. He's a freelance, does a lot of colour supplement work. Probably his caption writer with him. Why does she have to be so bloody stupid?'

Ralph Shunner said calmly, 'Perhaps you should have explained to her what incognito meant.'

And Jedd rounded on him. 'She's just doing it to annoy us. It's your fault for starting that bloody business about the films.'

'My dear man, how was I to know?'

'Pâté for everyone?' Peter Pollins, deprived of Melanie, had turned his attention to the menu. As a way of calming down the quarrel it worked as well as anything. By the time they'd decided between pâté and prawns and red carafe or white, Ralph Shunner had turned the conversation back to wine again.

'But seriously, Peter, if you're interested I might be able to put you in the way of a good thing or two. What would you say to a decent cru bourgeois 1978 around £40 the case?'

And Peter: 'Tempting, Ralph. Very tempting.'

A tall woman in shirt, slacks and sunglasses arrived at the top of the café steps and stood looking around. At once Ralph Shunner was on his feet.

'Olivia darling.'

Her tense face broke into a smile. She kissed him and slipped her arm round his waist. He fussed over her gently.

'You look tired, darling. It's too hot for walking far. Come on, you sit here.'

He gave her Melanie's chair, conjured up more prawns, another glass, introduced the group to her by their first names.

'My wife Olivia.'

'Not legally. We're living in sin.' But she smiled at him as she said it, and he smiled back.

As she peeled prawns efficiently and sipped wine they went on talking round her, but with Olivia's arrival Ralph Shunner's behaviour was noticeably different, with none of the innuendoes at Jedd's expense, or wine snobbery at Peter's. He drew her into the conversation. Had she enjoyed her walk along the dunes? Was Deborah still at the tennis courts? And she, under the influence of food, wine and his care, relaxed visibly. Even the disclosure that Peter Pollins was a solicitor brought only a momentary tightening of the muscles round her mouth.

Ralph Shunner explained, 'We've been going through some rather difficult divorce proceedings, haven't we, love? I'm afraid solicitors are a bit of a no-no at the moment.'

And Peter Pollins said hastily that he did mostly conveyancing, no good at the matrimonial side, left that to his partner. To cover the slight confusion, she turned the conversation to James Jedd, who was sitting opposite her and drinking red wine at about twice the rate of everybody else.

'Are you feeling better? It must have been a nasty shock this morning.'

It seemed Ralph and Joan had heard nothing about it and, although obviously sorry she'd opened the subject, Olivia had to explain.

'He had some bad luck at the exercise session. We were all swinging dumbbells but there wasn't really enough room, and one of the instructors got in the way.'

'For heaven's sake, what did he do to him?'

Shunner sounded quite alarmed. She reassured him.

'It was only his ankle.'

'Even so . . .'

Shunner was staring at James Jedd as if he expected him to produce another dumbbell and start laying about him.

'Well, obviously the instructor shouldn't have been standing there,' she said.

Joan's eyes were alight with pleasure at another embarrassment.

'You mean you actually got an instructor in the ankle with a dumbbell? 'Broken?'

James nodded.

'Well, that's first blood to the Drunks, Gluttons and Layabouts Commando. I mean, if Ralph here gets made a Brigadier for knowing about wine, putting a keep-fit instructor out of action should make you Major General.'

41

Peter Pollins ordered another carafe of wine on the strength of it, but Olivia made an excuse to draw Ralph away from the table and over to the bar. As he settled up the bill for all of them she said to him quietly, 'Arthur's here. In the camp.'

'Are you sure?'

'I've spoken to him.'

He pushed a little pile of francs back towards the waiter, took her arm and led her down the steps to the shopping square, where a big eucalyptus tree gave shade.

'The man's mad,' he said.

She nodded. 'We'll have to go away. Spain perhaps.'

'No,' he said.

She looked up at his face, near to tears, but just keeping herself in control. His arm went round her waist.

'No, Livvy. You can't deal with things by running away. He'd follow us from here to Cadiz on that bloody bicycle. What sort of holiday would that be?'

'What sort of holiday is it going to be anyway? And if you go off to Paris for those two days and we're here on our own . . .'

'I'll see him and settle it before I go to Paris, I promise.'

'What can you do? I've already threatened him with getting a court order.'

His arm round her waist went tight. 'I'll threaten him with more than a bloody court order.'

'Ralph, please don't . . . don't do anything to him.'

'Like what?'

His face softened. He sat her down gently on the edge of a concrete tub of geraniums and settled himself beside her. 'I'm not going to fight him, if that's what you're worried about. But I'm damned if I'm going to see you and Debbie scared.'

She leant against him and closed her eyes. It touched him still that her lean, firm body that usually found it so hard to relax would nestle up against his like a child's. For a few minutes they stayed like that, oblivious of the few people that passed them on the way to the café, or the whirring of insects in the eucalyptus.

At last she said, 'I should be at the tennis courts to collect Debbie.'

'I'll come with you.'

They walked hand in hand along a succession of sandy paths. When they got within sight of the courts Deborah came running to meet them, looking happier than for months past.

42

'Mum, Nimue says I should be in the adults' class. She's coming to ask you if I can. I can, can't I?'

'Of course you can. Who's Nimue?'

'You know. She's the one who was taking the class this morning. I think she runs the camp.'

'Is she still at the courts? We'll go back and see her now, if you like?'

Ralph Shunner hung back, letting mother and daughter go ahead. Both the woman and the girl shared this quality of tension, of making the smallest decision – like this one about the tennis lessons – hum with importance. In Olivia, it still puzzled and attracted him.

Nimue was standing talking to a man by the umpire's chair.

'He's the chief coach. Better wait till they've finished, Mum.'

But Olivia, less diffident, walked straight up to them. 'I'm Deborah's mother. She tells me you think she should go in the adults' class.'

Nimue, at least four inches shorter than Olivia, turned and smiled at her. 'Yes, your daughter's very good for her age. She wouldn't get stretched in the children's class, so we thought it would be useful experience to play with the club class women. But that's in the afternoons.'

'That's all right. We shan't be going anywhere.' Olivia turned to go, but Deborah was reluctant to leave a place where she had shone for a while.

'Can I help Nimue collect the balls up, Mum?'

And Olivia realized, as Deborah bounded around the courts and brought back balls to Nimue with the enthusiasm of a young gun dog, that the child was already deep in one of her spells of hero worship. It would be 'Nimue this . . .' and 'Nimue that . . .' for most of the holiday and she'd deeply resent being torn away to Spain or elsewhere. Olivia sighed and a hand fell on her shoulder.

'Everything all right, love?'

Ralph was standing beside her.

'Everything's fine. I think Deborah's getting one of her crushes on Nimue.'

Nimue and the child came back together, carrying between them a large bucket full of tennis balls. They were talking to each other, and didn't notice Ralph's arrival until they were a few yards away from him. Then there was a little gasp from Deborah.

'Oh!'

43

And tennis balls were careering in all directions over the red rubberized surface of the court.

Nimue chased a clutch of them into a far corner, followed by Deborah. Ralph and Olivia gathered up the nearer ones and dropped them into the bucket at their feet without exchanging a word. Olivia had been clinging to the hope that Deborah was becoming more relaxed with Ralph, but this clumsiness at an unexpected sight of him seemed to show there was still a long way to go. She was grateful that he'd made no comment on it.

'They've got the rest. We'll wait on the bench outside.'

She was grateful to him for that, too. Not crowding the child, giving her a few minutes to recover.

When Deborah had rejoined them, without Nimue, and they were walking back in the direction of their tent, Olivia said gently, 'You were a butterfingers, weren't you? Letting go of the bucket like that.'

And Deborah, pride hurt, 'It wasn't me, Mum. Nimue let go of it.'

And Olivia worried more, that Deborah was learning to lie and hide her feelings.

CHAPTER FOUR

Birdie held a child's ankles in his hands, warm from the sun and thin as sticks.

'Right, I'm letting go now.'

For a split second the child stayed balanced, then the legs started thrashing and the handstand collapsed.

'Oh, fuck,' said the child.

It was one of the twins, Leonora.

'You were nearly there. You just need to arch your back a bit.'

'Here, Mister, are you going to teach us kung fu?'

'No.'

'But she said we . . .'

'No. We're doing pyramids.'

'I'd rather do . . .'

'I said no.'

For Birdie the last few hours had been bad, from the moment that Olivia had managed, for a third time, to turn his entire view of his place in the world upside down. And, God knows, it hadn't been much of a view she'd left to him anyway: a father with just a few rights left in his daughter's life and a natural concern about what might be happening to her. Then Olivia, on her sand dune, had started talking about solicitors and harassment and suddenly he'd seen himself in court again, eyes focusing on the coat of arms above the judge's chair and the words refusing to come. Refusing to let him explain to the judge that this wasn't harassment. It was what any father would do, wasn't it? Where did the courts come into that? But then how did a court come into it in the first place?

'Sir, what's pyramids?'

'. . . like in that film, where there's two of them coming at him with a knife and . . .'

'Polly's hurt her knee. It's all bloody.'

At first he'd panicked, had been half way back to his tent with the idea of taking his wounded bicycle and trudging for a repair shop and home. But before he got there he realized that this would be the worst of both worlds. His boats were burned anyway, and if Olivia really did want to make trouble, he'd given her the material for it already by following them to the camp. So why should he abandon this hope, this certainty, of finding something in Shunner's behaviour that would make any court change its mind about custody. And in that direction things were on his side, for once. The providential crippling of the instructor that morning and Nimue's acceptance of him as a stand-in meant that he now had an excellent excuse for staying at the Village Zoe.

'Right, we need three big strong ones to start with. Pete, Steve and . . . er . . . you, Jenny. Then two little ones and two who can do handstands.'

Another thing, if he went now he'd be letting Nimue down, after her touching and immediate acceptance of him as an answer to her particular problem. All the more so because he sensed she wasn't a woman who accepted help easily for herself. Her efficiency, the quickness of her decisions, matched the hard muscularity of her body. And yet she'd almost taken his assistance for granted, from the time of the accident, when they helped the injured Jean-Paul to her bungalow.

'We'll try it kneeling down first. The idea is that the twins put a foot on your outside knees and you swing them up on your shoulders.'

At least, that had been his thinking two hours ago. But Birdie was more than a little annoyed to find that he was apparently expected to get the children's exercise classes arranged without any help from Nimue. She'd promised to meet him at a quarter to three to explain what he was supposed to do and show him where the apparatus was kept. Having made his decision, he was there five minutes before time, but there was no sign of her. Instead, a succession of parents, bound for after-lunch siestas, deposited about twenty kids, varying in age from about six to thirteen and in temperament from respectful to bolshie, and left him to get on with it. At five past three, with the customers getting restive and still no sign of Nimue, he had to patch things together as best he could.

'That's right. Pete and Jenny, if you put a hand round their legs to steady them . . . Philip, either eat that pancake or put it down somewhere . . . now where are the handstanders?'

Eventually he got them organized into two quite respectable

pyramids, even if the foundations of one of them included fat Philip still gorging crêpe.

'That's not bad. Hold it a second.'

A cool voice from behind him said, 'When are you going to bring on the walruses?'

He turned, and there was Nimue, screwing up her face in disbelief.

'Isn't it what I'm supposed to be doing?'

She hesitated. 'Well, they tend to go for the more contemplative sort of thing here.'

'Like what?'

'Concentrating on your solar plexus and thinking of deep sea waves. This sort of formation work probably strikes some of them as a bit . . . authoritarian.'

She was, as usual about the camp, completely naked but looked less cool than usual. There were drops of sweat between her breasts.

'You have to be a bit authoritarian with kids. Anyway, if you wanted . . .'

She was instantly apologetic and it struck him that she seemed more keyed up than in the morning. The day was probably taking its toll.

'I know. I'm sorry I wasn't here. Something cropped up. In fact . . .'

Squeals from the kids as one of the pyramids collapsed.

'Oh God, not more knees.'

But there was no damage and it became simply a case of sorting out a giggling recriminating heap into its component parts and finding them something else to do. Nimue did this deftly, although abstractedly, and took up where she'd left off.

'In fact, I was coming to ask if you'd help me out some more. I've got to go off for a few hours. If you could finish the exercise class and then do my two hours at the pool from six to eight . . .'

She hesitated.

'All right.'

'It's a lot to ask on your first day, and I wouldn't land it on you, except it really is a crisis.'

Her eyes were on his, full of an appeal that seemed out of proportion to such a small request.

'Of course I will. Anything else I can help with?'

She shook her head. 'No, thanks. Just don't let any of the kids kill

47

themselves. You wouldn't believe the insurance problems.'

She turned to go, then, 'Oh God, I'm going mad. You'll need the balls and so on. Big blue box by the table tennis place.'

Then she was gone at a run, too fast for a hot afternoon. He watched her go, puzzled at what this latest crisis could be. He hoped this wasn't going to be a regular pattern of events for an instructor at the Village Zoe. If so, there wouldn't be any time for watching Shunner.

'Hey, Mister, can we. . . ?'

'Five-a-side football. Run to that box over there and get a couple of balls.' It would probably give them heatstroke, but he'd stake nothing on his chances of getting this lot to concentrate on its collective solar plexus.

The green tent nylon filtered the light and cooled it so that the inside was like an aquarium in which two pale and languorous fish moved. Olivia was stretched out at full length on the groundsheet, its plastic cool against her thighs and buttocks. He was sitting back on his heels, pumping up their double Lilo. At some point in their love making a valve had malfunctioned and, as a background to its climax, there'd been a hiss of escaping air. By the time he'd withdrawn from her they were just a few inches from ground level. Now she watched intently as his arm muscles, under their coat of black hair, relaxed and tightened at the pump.

He said, 'It's having the same effect on me.'

'Um?'

'Seeing you stretched out like that. It's pumping me up again a damned sight quicker than this air bed.'

It was the thing that had shocked her most about him, at first: his cheerful bawdiness. She and Birdie had enjoyed sex, but never talked about it. Ralph talked about it almost all the time, or at least let her know he was thinking about it. He loved to grab a few seconds alone with her when they were dressed up and on party manners at some formal dinner dance and tell her in detail what he suggested doing in bed when they got home. Then a quick spin round and – 'Ah, Mr Mayor, we were just saying the Parks Department has done miracles with the geraniums . . .' – as she tried to will the blush from her cheeks.

She said, 'I've never made love in a tent before. Another first.'

'There'll be more, love.'

'Was this why you wanted to stay here, so that we could make

48

love in a tent?'

He disconnected the pump and climbed back on to the Lilo, patting the place beside him.

'All safe again.'

But she stayed stretched out on the groundsheet beside it. He made a child's face of disappointment.

'Not recovered yet?' He stretched out a hand towards her and she took it.

'I just want to lie here for a while.'

Silence for a few minutes, except for the sound of their breathing and the sea from the other side of the sand dunes.

'Well?'

But she stayed where she was.

'Tonight,' she said.

She was aware of a sudden tension in the aquarium of light, as if a smaller fish had darted through it. He said, in a different tone of voice, 'Look, love, I was going to tell you, I shan't be here tonight.'

'Why?'

He said awkwardly, 'That telephone call. This Paris thing's moving faster than I expected and they need me there early tomorrow morning. I think I should travel down tonight.'

'But we've only just got here. France is full of wine. You don't have to go rushing off to Paris to buy a few dozen cases.'

He sighed and also sat up. 'Look, love, we have a good life, don't we? I mean, I don't have to get up at seven and go rushing into some damned office every morning, do I? Well, the price of that is just now and again I have to do something in a hurry, when I'd rather be doing something else.'

Silence.

'After all, you didn't want a nine-to-five man or you wouldn't have taken up with me.'

She said, as if he'd made an accusation, 'Arthur wasn't a nine-to-five man. He was a nine-to-midnight man, that was part of the trouble.'

'So? I'm not pulling on my boots and going down to the police station, am I? We do all right, love.'

But she just sat there, arms round her knees, in an almost childlike pose.

He tried to console her. 'It won't take long. If I can get the deal tied up tomorrow I might be back by tomorrow night. At the worst it won't take more than two days, then we can get on with enjoying

49

our holiday.'

'I don't want to stay here.'

He put a hand on her shoulder, but she was unresponsive.

'You'll be all right. Lots to do here, and Deborah's happy as a tick with all the tennis.'

'And what about Arthur?'

'Judging by the slagging off you gave him, he's probably on his little bicycle and going hell for leather for Calais. You can cope, that's one of the things about you I fell for, isn't it?'

She stretched out her legs again, staring at her slim, green-shadowed feet. Yes, Olivia could cope. But what scared her, what was the other side of the confidence and happiness in being with Ralph, was this need for his company all the time. She'd loved Birdie thoroughly for quite a few years, and more or less for quite a few years more, but never at any point had there been this need to be with him all the time. But with Ralph, even an absence of twenty-four hours made her as panicky as a sixteen-year-old. She said slowly, 'You see, when I'm with you, things are right.'

'And when I'm with you. You know that.'

He meant it, but she could tell he was puzzled. And she couldn't go on to tell him the other half of what was in her mind: that when she was separated from the excitement of his physical presence, the buoyancy of his personality, the doubts crept in. Doubts about her ex-husband, doubts about Deborah. With him, she was certain she'd made the right decision, that things were always going to be all right. Without him, the plaintiffs for the other side had a field day. She believed they'd give up and go away in time, but they hadn't yet.

She said, 'You will try and get back as soon as you can?'

'Of course. You know I don't want to be away from you.' He patted the airbed again, and this time she climbed on to it, but just to lie beside him, sides and feet touching, listening to his breathing and the sound of the sea.

Footsteps padding on sandy soil, coming closer. A voice from outside the tent calling 'Mum.'

She was off the airbed as if it had erupted under her.

'Debbie.'

Before the child came in, she slipped on a long towelling jacket and went into the living room part of the tent to meet her. There'd been urgency in the child's first call, but once she knew her mother was there it ebbed away.

50

'I've been swimming, Mum.'

'I can see that. Pool or sea?'

'Pool. I did twenty lengths, but I had to put my feet down a few times because people kept getting in the way.'

'Hungry?'

'A bit.'

Olivia rummaged in the ice box and put cheese, tomato and crispbreads on a plastic plate. It was only after Deborah had eaten the food and was drinking a second glass of orange that she came to what was really troubling her.

'Mum, did you know Dad's *working* here?'

Ralph, also wearing a towelling jacket, had just come out of the bed compartment when she said it. Olivia gave him a quick, worried look.

'What do you mean, Debbie?'

'He's an instructor. I saw him when I went to the swimming pool, and I met Thea and Leonora later and they'd been to class and they said he was running it.'

She added uncertainly, 'I didn't tell them he was my father.'

Ralph said, 'You're not to speak to him, Debbie.'

Both mother and daughter gave him amazed looks. He stood there, staring at the child intently, head slightly bent under the tent roof.

Olivia said, 'Ralph!' Then, to Deborah, 'I expect he was just helping out for the day. He won't be staying.'

'Why not?'

'Well, he's got work to do at home.'

Deborah stared into the orange juice glass. 'I see.' Then, with a sudden change of tone, 'Is it five o'clock yet? I'm going to practise backhands with Thea.' She picked up her racquet and ran off, and Olivia rounded on Ralph.

'You can't do that. Telling the child not to speak to her father. What do you think that's going to do to her?'

He seemed genuinely surprised at her reaction. 'I'm sorry. It just seemed to me that the less we had to do with him . . .'

'Of course. But don't you see she's confused enough already? If we start making a bogey-man out of him there'll be such a conflict of loyalties she'll just break down.'

'I'm sorry.'

She said, 'Do you think it's true?'

'It might be. You said one of the instructors had an accident this

51

morning. If he offered to deputize . . .'

'Oh God. And he was fussing round that woman who runs the place.'

Ralph said slowly, 'You know, if he'd shown half this determination before, he might have kept you.'

She flared up, 'Don't talk about keeping me. I'm not a bloody dog.'

'Love.' He put a hand on her shoulder, but she pushed it away.

'Anyway, it's not me he's determined about, it's Deborah. He's obsessed about the whole custody thing.'

A silence, hot and prickly. Then she said, 'Are you still going to Paris tonight?'

'I've got to.'

'Well, we'll come with you. I don't want to stay here.'

'Love, it'll be hot and noisy and boring. And Debbie would hate being dragged away from her tennis.'

'So I'll just sit here by the tennis courts all day?'

'I'll leave you the car. You said you wanted to see inland?'

'And what about Arthur?'

'We can't go on regulating our lives by what he might or might not do. And the effect on Debbie's going to be worse in the long run if we up sticks and rush off the minute he puts in an appearance. This is as good a place to stay and sort it out as any.'

'But you won't be here.'

He sighed. 'I promise faithfully I'll have a talk with him this evening, before I go.'

'What will you do?' There was apprehension in her voice and eyes.

'Do? Nothing. I'm going to have one last go at talking to him as a reasonable man. And in spite of all this, I think basically he is a reasonable man.'

'Be careful.'

'I'll be careful.' He kissed her, but her lips were tight and unresponsive.

On his way to lifeguard duty at the pool Birdie passed the tennis courts and saw Deborah. She was playing with one of the scrawny twins from the exercise class – or rather, he saw with amusement, the twin was getting a comprehensive lesson in backhand from a determined teacher.

'. . . no good watching the net, watch the ball.'

The words came cutting through the early evening sounds of the camp with the incisiveness of one of Deborah's own serves, and he thought of how the child was a different person on the tennis courts. Her father's diffidence fell away from her and she became, in voice and movement, the image of her quick, decisive mother. But he didn't resent the tennis. It touched and surprised him that a child of his should be so very good at something. But it was not the time to go over and speak to her, even if he'd decided what to say. He plodded on to the pool.

This part of his duties was mercifully less complicated than the children's exercise class. He took over a whistle on a white rope toggle and a blue cloth cap from a beautiful but bored French boy, these apparently being the lifeguard's badges of office. The beautiful French boy had worn nothing else, but Birdie patrolled in his khaki cycling shorts. After a few circuits he gave up patrolling and sat on a high stool by the railings, taking in the scene. The sun was past its peak, slipping down towards the pine woods, and the temperature was perhaps in the low seventies. There were only a few bathers left in the water, and these mostly determined exercise swimmers doing their daily ten lengths or so, but the flagged pool surround was still quite crowded with people taking in a last dose of the sun before dinner. Birdie had never seen such a spread of relaxed nudity. It reminded him of an exhibit of champion potatoes he had guarded, along with its silver cups, as a very young constable at an agricultural show. There were scrubbed and translucent King Edwards with their rounded contours tinged pink, red Desirees whose bright skins seemed too tight for the flesh inside them, tender little Channel Islands, big brown Pentlands, ready to be oiled and baked and served with rock salt. Some of them were as glossy as if they'd come fresh from the deep-fryer. He watched, fascinated, as a King Edward sat up to rub lotion on its pink bits or a tender young Channel Islands rolled from its back to its front. As with the potato stand, surprise struck him at what were usually commonplace things. So there were that many kinds of potato, he'd thought. Odd to have lived so long and not known it. So there are really so many different sorts of bodies, he thought now.

For an hour or so, Birdie and his flock of potatoes took in the evening sun. The customers in the pool dwindled to two cheerful German women who showed absolutely no sign of drowning. Then they too, having completed a staggering total of lengths, heaved themselves out of the water, leaving little waves that caught the sun and glinted on an unbroken blue surface. The sunbathers began to roll up straw mats, collect their bottles of Ambre Solaire and drift away.

'Great, we've got it all to ourselves.'

Enter Clancy Whigg, photographer, in denims and bare chest, carrying his much dented metal camera box. And, clutching his arm, walking unsteadily in high-heeled white leather mules, Melanie McBride, actress. She was wearing long ear-rings of little looped gold chains and another chain round her waist, above a vestigial bikini bottom in a metallic gold fabric. The photographer put down the camera case almost on Birdie's feet, then condescended to notice him.

'Going to take a few pictures here. OK?'

His tone suggested that it would just have to be OK. He arranged Melanie on the end of the springboard, with a few giggles and squeals from her.

'Clancy, I'll fall in. I can't swim.'

'It's all right, darling. The lifeguard will fish you out. Won't you?'

Birdie moved up closer to the springboard, discarding hat and whistle. This might be where he started working again for his share of the Village Zoe petty cash.

'Right, cross your legs and arch your foot. That's it, toes up. Just get the ball of your foot touching the water if you can. That's right.'

He fired off shot after shot, with the girl moving fractionally between each one, then freezing. Birdie was surprised by the precision of it all. The photographer kept up a constant stream of instructions, some of them minutely anatomical. 'Shoulders back a bit, stretch your boobs. Fine, hold it. Straighten that knee, no, the right knee. Don't forget those toes.'

And the girl responded instantly and exactly, as if they were surgeon and theatre sister working on some complicated operation.

'Right, round the other side. We'll get some silhouettes.'

Once the camera had stopped clicking, Melanie made a great performance of changing her position on the springboard and Birdie put out a steadying hand. She stumbled, and her weight came against his chest so that he had to tense his muscles to stop them both falling.

'Here, that's not bad.'

Clancy had his camera up again.

'You sit on the edge there, and if he kneels beside you I'll do some shots with his chest as a background.'

He inspected Birdie's chest critically. 'Pity it's not browner, but it's quite nice and muscular. Here.' He unlouped a gold St Christopher medallion from his own neck and hung it round Birdie's. 'Keep it to one side, so that it just touches her earring.'

Her hair, unbelievably soft, unbelievably thick, settled against his chest, and his stomach muscles stirred and tightened. But her attention was firmly on the camera.

'That's it. Face sideways a bit. Half close your eyes. Great. Hold it. Here, lifeguard, get your chin out of the way. Head down a bit, darling. Eyes closed now. Not asleep-closed, dreamy-closed. That's right.'

They finished using his chest as a prop and went back to the springboard. This time Clancy arranged her so that she was lying prone along the board, her breasts pressed against the end of it and her face over the water.

'My neck's stiff.'

'Grin and bear it, darling. These are going to be great ones.'

He took his camera from his neck and handed it to Birdie. 'Hold this.' Then, still wearing his denims, he walked down a side ladder until he was up to his waist in the water and leaned out towards the girl on the diving board.

'Forward a few inches, darling. Just a touch of nipple. Now.' He clicked his fingers and Birdie tried to put the camera into the hand he wasn't using to hold on.

'No, round my bloody neck, halfwit.'

Then, with the camera strap round his neck, one hand operating the shutter and the other clinging to the pool ladder, Clancy went through another long sequence of instructions and clicks, with the girl inching infinitesimally forward over the water. Birdie would willingly have pushed him in if it hadn't been for the professional constraints on a lifeguard, but he couldn't help being impressed by the dedication. After a long ten minutes Clancy had had enough.

'That's it, darling.' And to Birdie, 'Take the camera and put it in the box. I might as well have a swim.'

He set off down the pool at a splashy crawl, leaving the girl spread out along the diving board.

'Clancy, I'll fall in. Clancy!'

There was real panic in her voice. Birdie dashed to put the

camera in its case then came back to help her.

'You won't fall. Just kneel up, if you can. That's it. Now, get hold of my hand.'

He calmed her down, and they ended up sitting beside each other on the landward end of the springboard. All the sunbathers had gone, and it was time for him to lock the pool gate for the evening. Although it was still quite warm, the girl was shivering and he wished he had a jacket to put round her.

'You're getting cold.'

'I'm scared.'

And she really looked it. Now she wasn't posing any more, there was a sharpness about her features, a jerkiness in the way she moved her arms and legs, that showed she was full of tension. He tried to comfort her.

'You were quite safe. We wouldn't have let you drown.'

She shook her head and some of her long, soft hair flicked against his shoulder. 'Not that. Scared of him.'

He looked at where the photographer was threshing his way back up the pool.

'Of him, you mean?'

'Of course not.' She was contemptuous, and it seemed as if Birdie's ignorance was giving her back some of her confidence. When she spoke again her voice was steadier.

'Clancy's nothing to be scared about. It's the other one.' Was she beginning to enjoy herself a little, beginning to act the role of scared beauty? Certainly she was angling for Birdie's attention, and although he didn't particularly want to know, she'd manoeuvred him into giving her the cue line.

'Which other one?'

She looked at him sideways. Clancy had flipped round and was swimming away from them on another length.

'You saw him this morning.'

'At the exercise session. There were two of them with you this morning.'

'Only one that counts. The thin one, Jedd. He's my agent. The other one's just a tame gorilla.'

'Why are you scared of your agent?'

'You don't know him,' she said.

Birdie was beginning to find the game a bit tedious. 'Of course I don't know him. I don't know any of them.'

'He's a killer,' she said.

56

Definitely enjoying it now. The lowered voice, the straight, direct look into his eyes, could have come from any of a hundred films.

'Literally or metaphorically?'

It threw her and she had to think a bit. 'I mean, if people don't do what he wants, things happen to them. That's why I'm scared.'

'Haven't you been doing what he wants?'

She glanced around, as if expecting half a dozen eavesdroppers to appear from nowhere. 'He's furious because I've gone off with Clancy. And he'll be more furious if he finds Clancy's taken these photographs.'

'Will he? Why?'

Birdie remembered uneasily that his bare chest figured as a background in some of them.

'Contracts and things, that's what he says. But it's really that he wants to own people, to control people. We had this sort of . . . sort of game when I first knew him, and I had to stand or sit in the same position, for hours sometimes, and not move until he said I could. To show he was in control. That's the sort of man James Jedd is.'

He said, not knowing much about these things, 'Couldn't you go to another agent?'

'It's not as simple as that.'

Again, the same technique. Distancing him, but leading him on to ask questions. He decided not to respond this time. When she realized he wasn't going to speak she said: 'He's not even a very good agent.' There was a little girl wail in her voice, the child with the second biggest ice cream. 'I mean, I'm not going to spend the rest of my career in a soap opera, not even Harmony House.'

'I'm sure you're not.' He was sure of nothing of the kind, but anybody tries to comfort a wailing child.

'Clancy wants to do a poster of me,' she said.

'Great.'

'It will be good exposure.'

'I'm sure it will,' he said, thinking of the breasts brimming over the end of the springboard.

'I mean, it could tip the balance for film parts.'

'Like Marilyn Monroe and the calendar, you mean?'

But her interest in other blondes seemed to be zero.

'Jedd will be furious when he knows. Really furious.' She said it as if Jedd's fury were a sort of ornament to her, like an outsize diamond pendant. 'But I've got to break away from him

57

sometime.'

Back straight, eyes staring into the forest. A girl's gotta do what a girl's gotta do. Again, he didn't know how he was supposed to respond and his silence seemed to needle her. She looked at him full on.

'Don't you think I've got to break away from Jedd sometime?'

Since they'd only met properly about half an hour ago, he didn't see how he could have an opinion in the matter. But perhaps all that professional cuddling up to his chest had ripened the friendship.

'You know best.'

But she was dissatisfied. Obviously as a co-star in the scene he was not coming up to expectation. She hesitated a moment, and appeared to change the subject.

'You know what happened at that silly exercise class this morning?'

'You mean the man getting his ankle broken?'

'Yes.'

'Nasty accident.'

She said, 'It wasn't an accident.'

'What?'

This time his question was right on cue. It rang out as a yelp over the pool and even Clancy looked up, startled, from his crawl.

She repeated, lowering her voice, 'It wasn't an accident.'

'But . . .'

'I thought it was, at first.' She was talking fast and low now, seeming more intent on getting her story over than creating an effect. Clancy was swimming back towards them.

'Then I heard him and Don talking . . .'

'Don the gorilla.'

'Yes. They were arguing, and Don said something like Jedd should leave that sort of thing to him. And Jedd laughed and said Don wouldn't have done it as well.'

'Did they know you were listening?'

She nodded, lower lip between her teeth. 'I think Jedd may have meant me to hear. As a sort of warning.'

'But . . . but why should he want to break an instructor's ankle?'

'I don't know. He must have annoyed Jedd in some way and that was Jedd's way of getting back at him.'

'Bloody hell.'

'So you can see why I'm scared. When Jedd finds out about

58

Clancy and the photographs . . .'

'Will he find out?'

'Jedd finds out everything. It's one of his things.'

Clancy had reached the edge and was pulling himself out of the pool.

'Why don't you just go away?' Birdie asked her.

'Away? Where?'

Clancy walked towards them, denims dripping water. 'Jeez! That was good.'

She said, softly and hastily, 'Don't tell Clancy. It will worry him.'

He suspected it was not so much the photographer's peace of mind she was concerned about, as the possibility of her poster promoter disappearing over the horizon in a cloud of dust.

Then, even more softly, 'But would you, sort of, keep an eye on me?'

Before he could even think of a reply, Clancy was with them. He placed a cold, wet hand on Birdie's shoulder and the other on Melanie's. 'Have to leave your big hunk of lifeguard, darling. Time for drinkies.' He straightened up, deftly twitching his medallion from round Birdie's neck.

'Ciao.'

Melanie gave Birdie a long, expressive look over her shoulder as Clancy led her off, one hand hooked round her waist, the other clutching his camera box. Bloody hell. He'd come to Zoe Village less than a day ago with plenty of his own problems. He was now lumbered with some of Nimue's, including twenty awful kids needing exercise, and a blonde-haired damsel in distress. Well, Melanie would just have to cope with her own problems, if there really were any problems outside her dramatic little mind. But this story about the broken ankle – could she really have made that one up? And what should he do about it? Nothing, he thought. Nothing, nothing, nothing. Not even mentioning it to Nimue. He'd got enough to worry about, and so had she, probably. And it was most likely just a spoiled little girl making reasons for taking on a new agent or lover. It was well past eight and the sun was touching the tops of the pine trees on the seaward side of the camp. He walked once round the pool to check there were no bodies lying at the bottom of it, then locked the gate in the low railings with a key that hung alongside the official lifeguard's whistle. He assumed that key, whistle and hat would have to be returned to the office for whoever came on duty in the morning, and walked with them up to the reception building. He gave them to a dark-haired girl beside the counter, who told him she hadn't seen Nimue since lunchtime and didn't know when she'd be back.

As soon as he was out of the office he broke into a run. Running had always been his safety valve when pressure was on him, and the day had produced a build-up of pressures that pushed and pumped at the inside of his skull like machinery. He sprinted down the drive, past the caravans – keeping well clear of Ralph and Olivia's tent this time – along the path between the sand dunes, and did not settle to his normal long loping pace until sea was breaking round his feet and the beach stretched in front of him, clear and empty, mile after mile.

Ralph Shunner got to the reception building about ten minutes after Birdie had left it, and managed to hire a car by phone from a local garage. Then he asked, 'Do you know where I can find the new instructor – the English one?'

The girl regretted that she didn't. If there was anything she could help with.

'Not to worry.' But he lingered at the counter. 'What about the boss lady? Is she around?'

The girl explained for a second time that Mademoiselle Hawthorne was not there and no, she didn't know when she would be back.

'Tell her I've been asking for her, would you. No other message.'

He walked slowly along to the café where Olivia was waiting for him. She was sitting with a group of other English visitors, some of them from the Drunks, Gluttons and Layabouts Defence Commando. There was the solicitor Peter Pollins, already flushed and loud of voice, and his wife Vinny with a full glass of wine standing untouched in front of her. With the evening growing cool, most of them were in track suits, except for plump Joan Meek, splendid in a red, black and gold caftan. Beside her, eyes following every move she made, sat a man in a red track suit, as slim and agile as a marmoset with a brown, creased face, who turned out to be her husband, Alexander. There was a welcoming chorus as Ralph arrived. They found him a seat, filled his glass from the carafe.

In the bustle Olivia whispered to him, 'Have you seen him?' But he shook his head slightly.

Olivia was still surprised at Ralph's capacity to make friends. All the people round the table had, like them, arrived only the day before, but they were already forming themselves into a social planetary system, with him as the sun. The cries of welcome seemed genuine, the talk was wittier and more confident when he was there. The wine went faster. Even disapproving Vinny smiled when he said something to her, picked up her glass and took an experimental sip. He talked vintages with Peter Pollins, complimented Joan on her caftan, and she stretched out her succulent white arms to show off its pattern, nearly flattening a man at the next table. Apologies and more laughter. Then he turned his attention to Joan's husband and within seconds the little man was trying to convert him to the joys of yoga. A little persuasion from Ralph, and Alexander was demonstrating a headstand beside their table and maintaining it for minutes on end, to the pride of his wife and the annoyance of the waiters.

This inevitable sociability of Ralph was something Olivia had resented at first, while being fascinated by it. If she and Birdie went out for an evening together, it was just that. They might by chance meet friends or colleagues, wave to them, exchange a few words and go their separate ways. By contrast, an evening out with Ralph was like a South Sea voyage, with ports of call uncertain and eventfulness guaranteed. What began as a quiet, almost clandestine evening at the pictures was quite likely to end as the sun was coming up, at a club just opened by one of his long lost friends. A quiet table for two would become a crowded table for four, then six, or twelve, with waiters who were always helpful when Ralph was around, bringing more chairs, more glasses, more bottles. It was like that now at the café of the Village Zoe, with new arrivals turning up by the minute, the scraping of tables being pushed together, the slightly resentful looks from customers on the periphery as more noise and laughter rose from the central group. Olivia would have liked to spend the evening alone with him, and worried more and more as time went on about his promise to speak to her ex-husband. But he gave no sign of having anything on his mind. At one point, he turned to Peter Pollins, 'Peter, you still interested in that case of wine?'

And Peter, disregarding his wife's censorious glance, said at once, 'You bet I am.'

'I'm seeing a friend tomorrow, and I think . . .'

He lowered his voice, and the two men put their heads together conspiratorially, while Joan was trying to recruit the rest of the table for a card party.

'. . . a poker school. I mean, poker's so marvellously unhealthy, don't you think? We could play till daylight.'

When Ralph had stopped whispering to him there was a glint in Peter Pollins' eyes, like a schoolboy who thinks he's beaten the system. He gave Ralph what was probably meant to be a quick, decisive nod, but because of the amount of wine he'd already got through it became a series of jerky head bobbings which he had some difficulty in controlling. Ralph, aware that most eyes were on them, put a finger alongside his nose, a joke appeal for discretion.

'Between you and me, then, Peter?'

'Between you and me, Ralph.'

Vinny, who hadn't missed a gesture, asked, 'What's going on?'

'Just a little transaction, my love. Just a little transaction.'

Judging from her expression she'd have dragged him away there and then if Joan hadn't distracted her. 'What about you, dear? Will you join our poker school?'

'I don't play cards,' said Vinny, frostily.

'Really, dear? Not even Happy Families?'

Vinny gave her a withering look and sat tight.

Olivia realized that Ralph had left his seat and was crouching beside her.

'Love, I'm going now.' It was his way. Never any protracted goodbyes. He said they didn't need that.

'You said you'd . . .'

'I'll see him, don't worry. Then I'll have to go. You stay here and enjoy yourself.' A quick kiss on the back of her hand and he'd gone. He was down the café steps and half way across the square before the others realized he was no longer with them and began an outcry at being deprived of him.

'Where are you off to, Ralph?'

'He's got to see somebody in Paris,' she explained dully. 'He's driving there tonight.'

They stared at her, surprised at her apparent acceptance of it. She wondered if he knew when he said 'Enjoy yourself' how bleak she felt, how marooned among these alien people without him to warm them for her. How cold it was when he left. Probably he didn't know. That was one of the things she had to accept. Joan patted her on the knee, 'Cheer up, dear. He'll be back. Have a Calvados.'

Slightly warmed by the kindness and the drink she stayed there for half an hour or so, until the voices and the laughter at the edge of her consciousness became intolerable. She whispered to Joan, 'I've got a bit of a headache. Enjoy the poker.'

The light was going. While she was still in sight of the café she walked quite slowly, but once she was off the main drive and heading for their tent she was almost running. Ralph moved quickly. By now he'd probably seen Birdie, picked up his things and gone. But there was a chance she'd still find him at the tent and, whether he wanted it or not, she'd see him before he went. Just that, to see him, like a love-struck teenager. But as a teenager she'd been much more in control of herself.

'Birdie is that you?'

Birdie froze to the spot, his ribcage still heaving up and down. He'd run much further than he meant to, miles along the sand. By the time he'd made it back to the beachguard's hut and the start of the path between the dunes the light had almost entirely gone and the sea had receded by several yards from a deserted beach. His body was tired, but the pounding in his head hadn't stopped. Now a voice he recognized from the other side of the beachguard's hut.

'Birdie.'

'Who's there?' But he knew.

'Ralph Shunner. Can I have a word with you?'

A gulp came from his throat. He tried to walk past but Ralph Shunner had left the wall of the hut and was standing across the narrow path, giving Birdie the alternative of pushing him aside or making an undignified scramble up a dune.

'I don't want to talk to you.'

'It's about your daughter.'

The big man stood irresolute, swaying a little on his feet from tiredness. Ralph Shunner was above average height but Birdie overtopped him by several inches. He looked as clumsy, as powerless as a bear with the hunter's bullet in him, the second before falling.

Ralph said quickly, as if to prevent the fall, 'There's a bench here. Why don't we sit down.'

A narrow wooden bench sticking out from the wall of the beachguard's hut, probably meant for people to sit on while taking shoes off. Birdie settled on it, seeming almost unconscious of what he was doing.

'What about Deborah?'

And Shunner, settling more cautiously on the narrow ledge, 'This isn't doing her any good, you know.'

'What's that to do with you?' Birdie's voice came thickly, his chest still heaving.

'Because I care about her too.' Shunner's voice was quiet and even. 'I love Olivia, so of course I care about her daughter.'

Silence, then stubbornly, 'She's nothing to do with you.'

'You want to think that, but it's just not true. Olivia got custody, I live with her and, as you know, I'm going to marry her. So whether you like it or not, Deborah is something to do with me.'

A growl from Birdie in which only two words were audible . . . 'bloody courts.'

Shunner sighed. 'I don't think it's the time to go into that again.'

For the first time in the conversation Birdie looked straight into Shunner's eyes. His breathing steadied suddenly and there was no labouring in his speech.

'You don't think it's time to go into that again. You tear my whole life apart and you don't think it's time to go into that again. All in a day's work to you. Get it finished and on to the next thing, on to the next woman. All over. There hasn't been a day in the past eighteen months when I haven't woken up thinking about what happened. And there won't be a day.'

Shunner said, 'You seem to think I did it to you.'

'If you didn't, who did?'

'The position I was in, I couldn't do anything else. And you'd put me there.'

'The law of the country put you there.'

'And the law of the country found me not guilty.'

'That? Law!'

'It was your law.'

'It wouldn't have been my way of fighting.'

There was silence again. Shunner sighed and leaned back against the wooden wall of the hut, trying to get comfortable. He said at last, quietly 'You don't know what you'd do if you were facing fifteen years inside.'

'I wouldn't have done that.' Total certainty, answered by another kind of certainty in Shunner's voice, 'Nobody knows what he'll do till it's happening to him.' A pause, then he went on. 'I suppose it's no use telling you this, but it wasn't my idea. It was the lawyer's.'

'Oh yes.'

'All right, you don't believe it, but it's true.'

'You must have discussed it with him.'

'No. I was as surprised as you were when he used it in court. I mean, he knew about me and Olivia, but it hadn't occurred to me . . .'

'It wouldn't, of course.' Heavily sarcastic.

Shunner, in spite of his efforts, was beginning to get annoyed. 'And it wouldn't have happened if you hadn't been so pig-headed. If any of your superiors had known what the situation was, there was no way they'd have let you give the evidence.'

'I was the only . . .'

'If you'd sunk your pride and gone to them and said . . .'

'And let you get away with it? Let you take my wife then let you get off scot-free from the other thing as well?'

'It would have been less damaging all round in the long run.'

Silence from Birdie.

'Wouldn't it?' Shunner probed. But Birdie's head was down on his chest again and he seemed not to hear. Shunner went on in a quieter voice, 'But whether you like it or not, all that's history. The point is, the other court knew all the facts and they still gave Olivia custody of Deborah . . .'

'Goodness knows why.' Another half audible growl from Birdie and an instant response from Shunner.

'You know damned well why. Because Olivia's a good and caring mother. And even a court knows that a teenage girl's place is with her mother.'

'And with any pervert or petty crook her mother happens to have taken up with?'

Shunner refused to rise to it. 'Look, I'm trying to tell you it doesn't matter what you think of me. The point is, following us around like this is going to do you nothing but harm, and that child's going to crack up if it goes on.'

'That's not true.' Was there a hint of doubt in Birdie's voice? Shunner pressed on.

'If you leave now, we'll forget about all this. We'll be back in England in a couple of weeks, and you'll have the usual access to Deborah.'

Pause.

'Perhaps we could even arrange a bit more frequent access.'

Silence again, and Shunner imagined Birdie might be thinking seriously about the offer.

'She could even go away on holiday with you next time.'

The moon was rising now and the tide so far out that it was visible just as a thin line of white water. The sound of disco music came from a long way off, in the centre of the camp. The two men sat side by side on the narrow bench, wordlessly, for a minute or two more. Then Shunner spoke again, in a voice that was still quiet, but more hurried.

'Look, while you're thinking it over, there's something I've got to say. You talked about me going on to the next woman. It's not like that.'

A sound of protest from Birdie, but Shunner went on. 'I just want you to know that I really love Olivia. There's something about her that . . . something that tells me that I'm . . . all right, that . . .' He was struggling, looking down on the sand, unaware that Birdie's head was lifting again, and Birdie's eyes were staring at him unblinkingly.

'. . . an honesty about her . . . knowing what things are worth in the right way . . .' Then he looked up and became aware of Birdie's expression, seemed to interpret it as scepticism. Shunner's tone changed, became more confident. 'And she loves me. God knows why, but she really loves me.'

Birdie stood up, his whole body obviously straining to be away, but his face still turned towards Shunner.

'Look, I'm sorry, but there's no point in not saying it.' Shunner was on his feet too, had taken a step towards Birdie, not trying to hold him there physically but appealing to him to go on listening.

'I know it was a good marriage you two had, but there comes a point for a woman when she feels all the dice have been thrown, all the exciting things that are going to happen to her have already happened. Then she starts . . .'

He stopped there. The look on Birdie's face was now unmistakably one of fury. Instead of straining to get away, his body, his whole attention were turned on Shunner.

'Look, I didn't mean to . . .'

'She talked to you,' said Birdie. 'She talked to you.'

It was a meaningless howl of pain, and Shunner felt the hairs rising on the back of his neck as if he'd heard a wolf calling in the sand dunes.

'There's no point in . . .'

But Birdie was on him, covering the few feet between them at a

66

bound. Shunner had his arm up to try to ward off the blow, had a split second to turn his head sideways, but that was all. Birdie's fist, propelled with all the force of a well muscled shoulder, struck him explosively just in front of the left ear. He slumped like a sack on the wooden bench, and Birdie, after one terrified glance, ran back into the camp along the path between the sand dunes.

CHAPTER FIVE

His left foot had gone numb from being in the same position so long. He moved it slowly and looked at the luminous numbers on his watch. Eleven forty-five. Nearly three hours perhaps, since he'd hit Shunner. Three hours and a world away. All that time he'd sat there on his sleeping bag, only dimly conscious of things going on round him, of the dusk turning to darkness, of the disco music in the distance, of the occasional voices of people passing outside his tent. Just sat there with a sense of having done something irreparable and waiting for the world to crash in on him. He imagined what Shunner would be doing: returning to consciousness, going back to Olivia and telling her about it, perhaps even telling Deborah. No, surely not telling the child too. But in a tent she'd hear anyway, wouldn't she? 'Hit him . . . your father hit him . . . violent man.' But surely she wouldn't believe them if they did tell her. She knew her father wasn't a violent man, didn't she? She was wrong then, wasn't she? Because her father had hit him, could still feel the tension of the blow in his shoulders and the ache of it in his knuckles. So what would they do now? Go to the French police in the morning or wait and see the solicitor when they got back to England? '. . . hit him . . . a violent man . . .' And change the access agreement. Can't let a violent man have access to a fourteen-year-old girl.

And again, sitting hunched in the darkness, he protested that he wasn't a violent man, that this was just a terrible mistake like everything else that had been done to him. And he hated Shunner all the more because it was Shunner who had done this to him as well, and he imagined him lying sore-headed but smug in that other tent less than half a mile away, in the certainty that he now had all he needed to crush Birdie entirely. He must have been crazy to follow them to the Village Zoe. The excitement, the sense of righteous crusade that had kept him going in that long, mad ride through France had gone entirely and he looked at his actions with cold horror. Olivia's voice came back to him, '. . . trailed around by her own father like some incompetent private detective', and he saw himself through Olivia's eyes.

'Show me the way to Amarillo . . .' came the music from the disco. He straightened himself into the kneeling position which was all the tent allowed, found his enamel mug and poured the last of the Courvoisier into it, rooted around in one of the pannier bags until he found a torch, a pad of paper and a ballpoint pen. Then he crouched on the tent floor and, by torchlight, managed to write:

Dear Debbie,
    I'm going back to England today. I hope you have a nice holiday. See you when you get back. Love, Dad.

He wanted to make it much longer, to ask her not to believe the things they told her about him, to tell her about his fear that they'd stop him seeing her ever again. But he couldn't burden the child with that. He took a long swig of brandy before writing the second note:

Dear Miss Hawthorne,
    I'm sorry, but I have to go back to England urgently. I don't like having to let you down like this, and I hope you'll find a proper replacement soon. The swimming pool key is at reception. Best wishes, Birdie Linnet.

He planned to put both notes through the door of the reception building as he left. Then he carefully packed all his possessions into the cycle panniers. It was past one o'clock by then and the disco music had stopped. He'd intended to strike his tent and go as soon as he'd got the notes written. Then he remembered two things: his slashed cycle tyre and the bad-tempered night guard on the gate. The thought of what he'd done to the tyre now filled him with almost as much horror as the blow against Shunner. How had he turned into the man who did these things? And, when it came to it, he couldn't face the idea of slinking out with his wounded bicycle, under the eye of the guard he'd bested only one night ago. With any luck, they'd open the main gates about six and the guard would go off duty. He'd go then – hoping not to meet Nimue – and with any luck he'd get through the trudge to the ferry and find a shop that sold inner tubes before evening. Meanwhile there was nothing to do but wait.

By four o'clock it was beginning to get light and he couldn't bear sitting around any more. He decided to go and walk along the beach for an hour to try to calm down. Then it would be almost time to pack his tent and go. He stuck to the smaller sandy paths, rather than risk waking anybody by the sound of his footsteps, and when he saw the dunes rising in front of him he decided to climb straight up the nearest one. He couldn't face the main path past the beachguard's hut. The morning air was cool, almost cold. Inland, to the east, there was a tight-stretched paleness about the sky, with the sun not yet visible. When he'd scrambled to the top of the dune, the sea was still the colour of pewter, with long cloud bars just visible above it. The tide was coming in, and the beach was completely deserted. To get on to it he'd have to slide down into a wide valley, a favourite place for sunbathers during the day, then over another dune on the further side. Any sort of activity was better than thinking. Once down on the valley floor he chose a grassy crease between two dunes as his best route and brushed between bushes like stunted willows to get to it.

His eyes were on the small bushes and on his own feet, picking a way through them, so he first saw the obstacles as a shoe and registered vaguely that some sunbather must have left it. Then, at an angle to it, another shoe. Then . . .

'Oh God.'

The crazy part of his mind was telling him a dozen things – it was a tramp, it was a joke, it was some other man. But he recognized the pale expensive trousers and, when he glanced towards the head end and immediately away again, he caught a blur of reddish brown hair. So then this other part of his mind started clamouring that the man was unconscious, had been out there all night, must be got to a doctor. He should be feeling for heart beats, looking into the eyes. But the last time he'd seen that face it had been slewing itself away from his own fist, eyes screwed up. That memory kept him at Shunner's feet, holding on to one of the ankles as if only that could prevent both of them from sliding away under the sand. But that ankle – bare above a canvas yachting shoe and colder than the sand – was enough to tell him nothing could be done. Birdie was aware of a sobbing, gasping sound as he forced himself to edge forwards, knees pressing the sand. He knew the sound must be coming from him, but there was

70

nothing he could do about it. It stopped briefly when he took hold of a wrist but began again as soon as he'd confirmed there was no pulse. The arm too was quite cold and flopped back heavily when he let it go. He still couldn't look at the face.

'Oh God.'

Once he'd put the wrist down, he just knelt there beside it. One of the little bushes was bent sideways by the weight, its upper leaves pressed against the sand. Birdie kept looking at the leaves, listening to the sound of his own breath gasping, trying to stop himself from thinking.

'Didn't hit him that hard . . . must have got up and walked away . . . couldn't have killed him . . . got up and walked away from the beach hut . . . or how did he get here?'

There were sea birds swooping and crying on the beach. Down in the valley he couldn't see them, but they sounded as close as his own breathing.

'Thin skull. Some people have thin skulls. Remember that case of the yob at the youth club . . . reduced to manslaughter . . . medical evidence that some people have thin skulls and you can't know . . . got up and walked away . . . internal bleeding, haemorrhage . . . cerebral haemorrhage . . . got up and walked away then collapsed and . . .'

'Oh God.'

Stop that noise. Stop it . . . that's better.

But although the sobbing-gasping sound stopped he couldn't move, couldn't as much as move his eyes from the thin, dark green leaves or their silver undersides.

He didn't know how long the other sound had been going on before he was aware of it, whether he'd been crouching there for hours and the other sound had been going on all the time or whether it had just started when he heard it. But the instant he was aware of it he was on his feet and his heart was pounding. The sound was coming from the direction of the wire fence, invisible beyond the further dune, that marked the boundary of the Village Zoe on the beach side. A pinging sound. The sound of somebody climbing over the wire.

Somebody climbing out, or somebody climbing in? If he went up on the dune, he could see. Or run. Run off back to the tent and not wait to see. But he did neither. To move at all, whether towards the beach or back inland, would connect this thing with reality. While he stood there, as long as he didn't move, didn't think, there was no connection. It didn't exist. A step in either direction, and he gave the thing beside him an existence outside this crease in the dunes and the small bush it was crushing. And it would be an existence he couldn't cope with. The pinging sounds from the wire had stopped. Whoever had climbed it was either coming towards him or going away. Then he heard a slithering sound, a sound of moving sand, far quieter than the seagulls' cries, but nearer than he'd thought possible, near enough to threaten the shell of silence around him and Shunner's body. He heard breathing that wasn't his own, lighter than his own, but labouring a little with the effort of climbing the dune. He still couldn't move, stood there with his head twisted towards the sound. Whoever it was stopped for a moment or two at the top of the dune. Then the sand began slithering again, this time towards him. The person doing the breathing had chosen this same route between the dunes. He looked up, could see the sand sliding in little regular spurts as feet pressed it, then . . .

'What are you doing?'

The shell of silence was broken. Nimue Hawthorne stood on the slope above him. Nimue Hawthorne, hair falling loose around her shoulders, wearing jeans and an anorak. When she spoke she was looking straight down at Birdie, either not seeing or not yet registering, the body in between them. Involuntarily he glanced down and immediately away again. She said nothing, not even a gasp. The head was nearest to her, and she stopped beside it, looked at the face, crouched down and took it between her hands. Then she put it back down on the sand, straightened up and came towards Birdie, who was staring at her to save himself from looking at Shunner.

'There's no pulse,' he said.

She shook her head slightly. Her eyes had dark, tired circles round them. She said, 'Well, what are we going to do with it?'

Then, slightly impatient, as he looked at her dumbly, 'Had you thought of that?'

He shook his head. She was frowning, much as she'd frowned at the problem of how to find a new gym instructor. A competent woman facing a problem. She said after a few seconds: 'We'll have to carry him quite a way. Can you manage it?'

He nodded. As long as nobody expected him to think, he could manage anything. He thought, when he saw her, that this was reality breaking in. Now the reverse had happened. She was part of the unreality and as long as he went along with whatever she told him to do, the thing still had no existence apart from them. He listened meekly to her instructions.

'You'd better take the feet.'

She glanced at her watch. 'Half past four. We're all right for time . . . just.'

They got themselves arranged, Nimue with her arms hooked under its armpits, Birdie with the ankles tucked under his arms and the heels of the yachting shoes in his hands, facing outwards like a horse in the shafts of a cart. That way he didn't have to look at it. It occurred to him, mistily, that this arrangement meant Nimue, being shorter, was carrying much more of the weight, but he didn't have the will to protest. Perhaps she'd sensed that he couldn't stand a journey looking down at the face.

The sea birds were still crying on the beach and the sky was changing from white to blue. She directed him further along the sunbathers' valley between the two ranges of dunes, parallel to the sea, speaking a word or two in a flat voice. He walked slowly, heavily, eyes on the ground, with the rough canvas of Shunner's yachting shoes chafing his wrists. Sometimes his grasp shifted a little and it was one of the cold ankles that came in contact with his own skin. When that happened, as it did three or four times, he stopped to readjust his grip and Nimue said nothing. In a policeman's life there'd been bodies from time to time, some of them burnt or battered or decomposing. This should be nothing to him – and that was just the trouble, it was nothing, non-existent, until the touch of those ankles threatened to make it real to him. More real than any of those bodies in the course of duty had been. He tried to concentrate on the ground in front of his feet. The everyday bits of litter left by the sunbathers – the occasional peach stone, the empty sun tan oil bottles – looked sharp and surprising to him, like museum exhibits from a remote way of life. She had to tell him twice to put it down for a while. He lowered the legs down to the valley floor and turned to watch her put down head and shoulders. She was breathing hard and looked tired to the point of unconsciousness, but her voice was normal.

'You see that little path? We turn left there, into the trees, and about four hundred yards along till you see a square concrete building. All right?'

He nodded. The body seemed heavier when he picked it up again, and the small part of his mind that was recovering from

73

numbness began to worry about how it felt to her. But they plodded on, turned on to the smaller path and into the pine trees, where a chorus of inland birds replaced the gulls' cries. It was a very narrow path, hemmed in by broom and heather bushes, and looked as if it was not used often. His hands, clasped round the feet, brushed against dew-covered branches. The square concrete building, when they came to it, was almost covered in a tangle of bushes.

'Right.'

They put the body down in a clearing of dry grass, scattered with rabbit droppings. Birdie's mind was doing odd things to him again, trying to convince him he should, after all, look at the face – look at the dent his fist must have made in that thin skull. But he knew he couldn't expose himself to the reality of it, not until the thing was finished. He made himself concentrate on the objects round him. Some battered chairs, made of pine branches, stood by the wall of the building, along with a blue plastic water tank. The whole arrangement looked disused and deserted. There was a strong smell he couldn't identify.

'Hang on a moment.' Nimue pulled back a bolt on the door and went inside, reappearing in a few seconds. 'It'll do.'

She pushed the door wide open and they carried the body inside. It was a simple cube of space, about the size of an average living room. On one side of it were two large pine benches, covered in sandy dust. The other side was divided into two concrete tanks, their sides raised about two feet from the floor. They were filled with a slimy, greenish-brown substance that looked more like compost than anything and smelt bad.

'Alginotherapy,' Nimue explained. Then, taking his blank expression for a query, 'Soaking people in tanks of warm seaweed. For rheumatism and so on. They tried it last season apparently, but it didn't catch on.'

She found a rusty, long-handled shovel leaning against the wall and climbed on to a narrow gangway between the two tanks. As she prodded at the seaweed its rank, salty smell got even stronger and a few flies rose and buzzed. There were shutters over the windows, warped by the sun so that they let some light through. The body lay on the floor, a long, dark lump.

'There, that should do.' She'd made a long, deep hollow in the seaweed. 'If we can get it up on the gangway here, we can tip it in.'

They managed it, with Birdie taking the feet again.

'Right, swing it out, and let go.'

She let go a second before he did, so that the head and shoulders hit the seaweed while the feet were still in Birdie's hands. They jerked and twisted and he flung them away from him, just saving himself from falling backwards into the other tank.

'If you could help cover it over . . .' She was already busy shovelling the stuff over the face and shoulders.

'Sorry.' He knelt down and began scooping up the stuff in great sticky handfuls, covering the shoes, the ankles, the shins. It took them perhaps twenty minutes to cover it thoroughly, and when they'd finished the surface the seaweed was as smooth as it had ever been. The only suspicious thing was the dampness of the disturbed weed compared with the other tank next door.

'Won't matter,' Nimue said. 'nobody comes here. The smell keeps them away.'

She looked exhausted, the hair round her face damp and matted.

He said, 'There's seaweed in your hair.' He put out his hand and removed the greeny-brown clinging strand. It was the first voluntary movement he'd made since discovering Shunner's body.

'I could have been swimming,' she said. But she made no attempt to stop him. The movement, more than anything they'd done so far, seemed to make them accomplices. They looked at each other for a moment, then across at the tank.

'Come on.'

She led the way out of the building and bolted it behind them. 'Twenty to six,' she said. 'I've got to get back.'

'Should I . . . should we go back separately?'

She stared at him. 'Why?'

His mind was beginning to work again, but slowly. 'If somebody sees us together . . .'

'So what?'

Just as the body was becoming real to him, it seemed to turn non-existent for her. The path that she took led to the main drive and he walked along it beside her in silence. They met just one person on the way, a young man crossing the drive with a towel, on his way to a shower block. He said good morning to Nimue in English and she replied. A few yards further on she said, 'That's the way to your tent.'

He looked at her and turned away.

'Don't forget the exercise class,' she said. 'Eight-thirty.'

And before he could say anything she was walking away,

towards her bungalow by the main gate.

The tent was just as he'd left it, the floor bare, and everything packed in the panniers. And, on top of one of the panniers, the two neatly-folded pages from his notebook: one addressed to Deborah Linnet and the other to Miss Nimue Hawthorne. He tore them in half then in half again and put the pieces tidily away in his pocket. The possibility of leaving now simply didn't occur to him. She'd taken it for granted he was staying, and although his mind was beginning to come out of anaesthetic, he wasn't yet capable of independent action. But what was she doing? As his mind unfroze he began worrying away at that question, tentatively at first, then with urgency. Was she crazy? Really deeply crazy, so that tidying away a body was no more to her than picking up litter? Was she sorry for him? Even in its dazed condition his mind made short work of that one. Oh sure, so smitten with the charms of Birdie Linnet that on the strength of about thirty hours' acquaintance she helps him cover up a murder. Was she scared of him? Now, that's more likely. Look at it from her point of view. Climbs into camp by the back way and finds murderer crouching over victim, assumes he'll kill her next. Calmly saves her life by pretending to help him then . . . then runs like hell the minute she's out of sight of him and rings for the police. Ringing the police now, from her bungalow. He was pleased to have solved the mystery of her behaviour. It made everything simple again. In a little while the police would come to the main gate and she'd show them his tent and they'd come and arrest him. And she'd take them to show the body in the seaweed – talking her competent French – and they'd tell her how brave and resourceful she was. And they'd take him away, to Paris probably, since he was a foreigner, and he'd have to keep very calm and ask to see the Consul and find a lawyer so that he could tell him about some people having thin skulls and – oh God – did they have a manslaughter verdict in France? Or wasn't there something, that if you killed a British citizen abroad you could be sent home and tried in a British court . . .

And at that thought his calm was gone immediately. Instead of the idea of a hypothetical French court there was the terribly clear memory of a British coat-of-arms over the judge's chair, of a barrister's wig on slightly sideways, of questions that shouldn't be asked and words that refused to come right. Sweat broke out all over his body. Supposing they called Olivia as witness? Even

Deborah? But the plea would be guilty, wouldn't it, so they needn't call any witnesses. Guilty to manslaughter. But if they called it murder. . . ? He thought if his bike had been working he could have got on it and pedalled away before the police came. Make for Marseilles, Morocco. Then he thought there was a sort of justice that his own action in disabling the bike had cut off even this possibility. He'd insist on being tried in a French court. Could he do that?

How long would the police take to get there? He glanced at his wrist to look at the time, then glanced away again without seeing it. To arrest a murderer they'd send . . . Not murder, manslaughter.

The camp was waking up around him. There were children's voices outside, perhaps the same children he'd seen the day before. He hoped they'd be gone before the police came for him. Hoped Deborah . . . oh God, don't let Deborah be there. Adults' voices on the path now, talking German, laughing. Sounds of traffic from the road outside. A fast car, could be . . . no, going past. Not that one. He glanced for the time again, and realized now that he wasn't wearing his watch. Must have packed it with the other things in one of the panniers, but he couldn't be bothered to unpack them and look for it. Leave them all tidy for the police to take away.

A little later the bonging began, just like the day before, but he had trouble in remembering what it meant. When he did remember he could hardly believe it. The invitation to the morning exercise class at eight thirty. When they left the seaweed building Nimue had told him it was twenty to six. That meant she'd had around two and a half hours since then to get the police there. Surely if she'd telephoned as soon as she'd left him they'd be here by now. So . . .

So Nimue hadn't phoned the police. His mind adjusted to the idea slowly, almost reluctantly, because it meant things weren't settled after all. So what was she doing? Blackmail—was that it? He didn't want to think of her as a blackmailer, but that was surely the only other thing that made sense. If so, that only delayed the arrival of the police by a few days. His sort of money wouldn't buy off a blackmailer from a shop-lifting charge, let alone a killing. But did she know that? 'Don't forget the exercise class,' she'd said, as a command. And he had to do what she said.

And there she was, nude and gold-skinned, her dark hair back

77

in its pigtail, standing at the microphone on the volleyball courts.

'Good morning, everybody. I hope you've slept well. Some nice easy stretching exercises first. Slowly, with the music.'

Forests of arms rose and stretched and swayed. A slightly smaller forest than the day before. No sign of Melanie and her minders. No sign either of Olivia and Deborah.

'Now the other side. Up and stretch and down and stretch. Lift those rib cages.'

Birdie, standing next to her, could see the tiredness in her face, but she wasn't letting it into her voice. And to him, her manner was exactly the same as it had been the day before.

'Walk round a bit,' she told him. 'See they're doing it right at the back.'

He moved through the forest of swaying arms, of swinging breasts and buttocks, seeing all of them, in his mind, against a cushion of green-brown seaweed.

'. . . up as high as you can. Don't lift your heels. Now flop forward and try to touch your toes . . .'

Her voice and the music went on, and nearer at hand another voice, low but angry. He recognized it as belonging to Vinny, the thin mother of fat Philip. This morning, though, it seemed to be her husband rather than Philip who was in trouble.

'Really, Peter, you might at least try.'

The man was leaning against the railings. 'Haven't got the energy, Vinny. Not after last night.'

'That's your own fault,' she said. 'I didn't ask you to go off and play poker, did I.'

He sighed and dragged himself away from the railings and began a few half-hearted gestures in the direction of his toes, pausing as Birdie went past.

'My back wasn't designed for this,' he said.

'It gets easier with practice.'

Birdie was amazed at the normality of his own voice.

'I'll take your word for it. How long is this going on?'

'Not sure.'

Birdie automatically glanced at his wrist before he remembered he wasn't wearing a watch. But this time something began nagging at the corner of his mind. Now he thought about it, he didn't believe he'd packed the watch with the rest of his things. There'd been no reason to do that. Surely he'd been wearing it as usual at the time.

'Breathe in when your arms go up, out when they come down.'

'What happens if you don't?'

'Nothing much,' said Birdie. His mind was very much elsewhere. He'd just remembered that he was wearing the watch when he'd left his tent to go down to the beach. He remembered quite clearly looking at it to see how long it was to six o'clock. But he wasn't wearing it when he got back to the tent. Therefore . . .

'Oh God.'

'Is something wrong?' asked the reluctant exerciser.

'No . . . No, I just don't feel too well.'

'Must be all that exercise.'

Birdie sprinted down the side of the volleyball court and out on to the path. He was certain that Nimue would see him go, but she was trapped at the microphone and could hardly bring the exercise class grinding to a halt for a second day running. He'd just worked out where the watch must be – in the seaweed with Shunner. What was worse, it was neatly engraved with his name. ('You're sure to leave it in a changing room somewhere,' Olivia had said, when she gave it to him ten years before.) He remembered the dead man's feet jerking against his wrists and could, now he thought about it, remember the relief of pressure as the links of the watch bracelet parted. And with his nerves almost as over-stretched as the watch strap, the second he'd remembered that he had to go and get it. It was an action of panic, a world away from his resigned decision to wait and let the police get him. From being passive he'd become tense with activity, sprinting down the drive at a speed that made several joggers shake their heads. He had to slow down to locate the narrow path to the seaweed place, and at this point he used a little caution, glancing round to make sure nobody was watching him. When he'd gone a short way along the path he stopped and listened. Nothing. He walked on, quite slowly now. The dew had dried from the bushes, and more flies were buzzing.

More flies, too, inside the building, and the seaweed smell even stronger in the warm air. Now, in spite of his anxiety to get the watch out of the way, he hesitated at what he had to do. He made himself climb on to the gangplank and lie down on his stomach, his nose only inches from the seaweed. Then he rolled up his tracksuit sleeve and plunged his arm into the warm, decaying ooze. Almost immediately his fingers came in contact with a trouser leg. He followed it down, reluctantly, to the ankle, then felt around to one side of it. Within seconds his fingers closed on metal and the watch, sticky with seaweed, was back in his hand. Relief made him move too quickly. He got to his knees, tucking the watch away in his tracksuit pocket. Then, doing up the zip, tried to stand. His foot slipped on a piece of seaweed, he lost his balance and, arms waving wildly, plunged head-first into the tank.

His first thought was that the dead man had reached up and pulled him in. The tank was full of Shunner and every movement Birdie made to get free made the corpse, lubricated with seaweed slime, flop against him. He choked, cried out, and scrambled for a foothold, but every time he managed to get a knee or a foot against the bottom of the tank it slid away from him, tumbling him on top of Shunner, even underneath Shunner. His lungs were bursting, his eyes and mouth clotted with weed. He managed to kneel, to put a hand down on something to support himself, then realized that the something was Shunner's neck rising from a green-stained shirt. He grabbed his hand away and fell forward again, instinctively saving himself from drowning in the muck by throwing all his weight against the dead chest, using the corpse as a raft. And, exhausted, he clung there, his face inescapably, at last, against the dead face.

And with the pressure of his weight on the lower body the face was pushing upwards, shedding layers of seaweed as it came. He tried to shove it away from him, but the last slab of weed slithered from under his fingers. Like a plaster, he thought. He was half hysterical. A plaster Shunner didn't need any more. Not for . . . not for such a neat . . . And recognition stabbed his slithering brain and, in spite of himself, he was looking again at the place the seaweed plaster had covered. Looking at it and, in the shock of what he saw, managing without knowing it to find a foothold on the bottom of the tank. Managing to take a firm hold of the gangway and drag himself on to it, clear of the seaweed. Then, grabbing an arm, he pulled Shunner's body alongside and looked down full on the face. He found the place again and examined it quite calmly this time, the hysteria replaced with a numb coldness. It was there, above and just in front of the right ear, half hidden by the slime-plastered hair. A neat round hole, its edges still crusted with blood in spite of the heavier traces of seaweed. A neat, unmistakable bullet entry wound. He sat back on his heels, flies buzzing round him. He'd hit Shunner just in front of the left

80

ear. Nimue, who'd been looking down at that head all the time they were carrying the body, must have seen the hole, must have assumed that was the way that Birdie had killed him. How could he convince her now, or anyone else, of the certainty that was flooding through his own head, that Ralph Shunner had indeed been murdered but that the murderer – almost unbelievably, even to him – was not Birdie Linnet?

CHAPTER SIX

Waves crashed around him and retreated slowly, full of seaweed – ancient seaweed that had spent the past year at least seething in a concrete tank and was at last set afloat again from Birdie's hands, face, feet and tracksuit. The second burying of Shunner under the weed had been at least as messy as the first, and he'd had to do it single handed. It had been a matter of luck, not planning, that nobody had seen the tall, green-smeared figure running out of the sand dunes and into the sea to wash. His path from the alginotherapy hut had taken him to a small gate in the fence and a deserted part of the beach, about half a mile from where he'd met Shunner the night before. Birdie was fairly confident that nobody was watching him. About a hundred yards out from the shore there was a canoe with two figures in it, rising and falling on the waves – too far away to have any interest in what he was doing. Fifty yards or so along the sand a yoga class was waving legs slowly in the air, clearly in no position to watch him or anybody else. He straightened up and stripped off his wet tracksuit, still smeared in tentacles of weed, trod it up and down in the surf. In this place a naked man carrying a bundle of rolled-up clothing would be far less conspicuous than one in soaking wet clothes. The day before the idea of walking naked through a camp full of people would have been unthinkable – almost as unthinkable as illegally disposing of a body. 'Illegally disposing of a body.' He let the words run round in his head. Not murder, not even manslaughter. And yet, obstinately, he was still behaving as if he had been responsible for Shunner's death, almost convincing himself that the bullet hole in front of the right ear never existed. Already he was having to fight off the impulse to go back yet again to the seaweed place and assure himself that he really had seen it.

He picked up the tracksuit top and trousers and wrung them out. Still some weed clinging to them, but that might have come fresh that morning from the sea. If anybody challenged him about it, he could make up some story about running into the sea to cool off. A quick look round to make sure nobody had been watching him, and then . . .

'Olivia!'

He hadn't been watching the canoe for the past few minutes and now it was no more than a few steps away from him. And there she was, in the back seat, eyes fixed on him, face a little flushed from hard paddling, her blue seaman's smock soaked from the spray.

'Dad!'

A cry of protest from Debbie, in the front seat. Now that Olivia had stopped paddling, her own efforts couldn't keep the canoe from drifting out to sea again.

'Sorry.'

Automatically he grabbed the rope at the front of the canoe and pulled until he felt its bottom touch the sand. Debbie was out immediately, and if she was surprised to see her father standing there naked she gave no sign of it.

'Thanks, Dad.' A quick, tight smile at him, then she turned to her mother, still sitting in the canoe. 'Mum, can I . . . ?'

'Yes, you run along. See you lunchtime.'

Half way up the beach the child turned and gave a quick embarrassed wave – impossible to say whether to Olivia or Birdie or both of them. They both watched, without saying anything, until she was one figure among many on the more popular part of the beach. Then Birdie put out a hand to help Olivia from the canoe and, abstractedly, she accepted it.

'Debbie's been bothering me to go out in a canoe.'

'Yes.'

Amazingly, until the canoe arrived alongside, he'd forgotten Olivia. Or, he supposed, his mind had deliberately blanked out the most unthinkable fact of the whole sequence – that the body twice buried under seaweed was Olivia's lover. That she'd been waiting in the green-walled tent all night for him to come home, must have been wild with anxiety when it got light and he still wasn't there. They stared at each other, ankle deep in sea. Her eyes were tired, worried, but there wasn't the desperate anxiety in them he expected to see. And her first words to him weren't about Shunner.

'You're still here then?'

'Yes.' But it wasn't exactly anger in her voice, more like irritation at a job not done.

83

'Didn't he talk to you?'

So that was it. Shunner's approach to him at the beach hut had been discussed in advance, had it? She knew, at least, that he'd gone out looking for Birdie on the night he didn't return. His heart beat hard and heavily and it was difficult to control his breathing.

'No,' he said. 'No, he didn't.'

Again, the look of annoyance. Annoyance, he thought, at Shunner rather than him. Then, because one of them had to open the subject, he asked, 'Are you looking for him?'

'Who?' Her head went up and her eyes were on him, blank and hostile.

'Looking for who?'

'For . . . For him. Ralph Shunner.'

She looked away and shook her head. 'He's gone to Paris.'

'What?'

'Why shouldn't he? He had to go there on business. He went last night.'

'Oh.'

'He was looking for you. He was going to talk to you.'

'When will he be back?'

'Perhaps today, perhaps not for two or three days. He didn't know.'

He couldn't say anything. He supposed he should have felt relief that the hunt for Shunner hadn't started yet. But what he felt instead was an angry pity for her – anger as if her ignorance of Shunner's death were somehow her fault, and pity for the blow that would fall in two or three days. It came out clumsily.

'So he's left the two of you here?'

She flared up at once, as if he'd accused Shunner of deserting her, and perhaps it had been in his mind.

'For goodness' sake, I can manage by myself for a couple of days.'

She turned away from him, took hold of the canoe rope and jerked it several feet higher up the beach. He took the back of the canoe, intending to help her, but she rounded on him, 'I said I can manage.'

And he just had to watch as she towed it towards the high tide line, leaving a long gash in the sand. It seemed she resented even his eyes on her, because she turned after a few yards, 'Why don't you go and leave us in peace?'

And, after watching her for a few more yards, he went, the

84

soaking tracksuit rolled up under his arm. The sun was almost overhead now, and the beach was filling up fast. A few people who knew him from the exercise classes said hello and waved as he went past. He was horribly conscious both of his nudity and the seaweed smelling bundle he was carrying, but nobody seemed particularly interested in either. There was a bad moment as he passed the beachguard's hut. A toddler was sitting just where Shunner had slumped the night before, her father bending to empty sand out of her shoes, and he had to remind himself firmly it had still been Shunner then, not Shunner's corpse. Shunner had got up from there—groggy from the blow, probably, but he'd got up and wandered off into the valley between the dunes. And there, sometime between about nine in the evening when he'd left Shunner and just after four the next morning when he'd found the body, somebody had put a bullet into Shunner's brain. Or they'd done it elsewhere and dragged the body into the dunes. Had there been any signs that it had been moved? He didn't think so, but he couldn't remember. He was back at his tent before a worse thought struck him—that somebody who wanted to kill Shunner had come across him at the beachguard's hut, still unconscious from Birdie's blow, had carried him into the dunes and, before he could get his consciousnesss back, blotted it out entirely. He sat and worried about that for a while, then tried to pull himself together. He found that he was hungry and thirsty, brewed a mug of black coffee and dunked into it lumps of rock-hard baguette. As he drank and chewed he got his thoughts in some sort of order.

Firstly, for anything from twenty-four hours to several days, Shunner wasn't officially dead. 'Perhaps today, perhaps not for two or three days,' Olivia had said. Had he made any arrangement to phone her? But then, phone calls to a camp site would be difficult, so if she didn't hear from him for two days, say, she might not be desperately worried. What about the business people he was supposed to be meeting in Paris? They might be surprised when he didn't turn up, but surely not worried enough to send out search parties. So, two days perhaps before Olivia got really anxious, and longer than that—say another twenty-four hours—before she officially reported him missing. Three clear days then.

Three days to do what? That was the second problem, and far less tractable. Three days, he supposed, to prove that he hadn't killed Shunner. If he went to the police now—not that he had the slightest intention of doing it – there was more than enough against him to get him held on suspicion. Who found the body? Birdie Linnet? Who disposed of the body? Birdie Linnet and Nimue Hawthorne. Who was known to have a grudge against the deceased? From what he knew of Shunner's past, quite a few. But if the French police found out, as they inevitably would find out as soon as they checked with Britain, the size of Birdie's grudge, that would put him top of that particular category as well. And that was not even counting the probability that he was the last person beside the murderer to see Shunner alive, and the fact of that potentially lethal blow. 'Innocent men don't get charged.' That was what an older and case-hardened constable had said to Birdie, soon after he joined the force. 'Now and then, they may be innocent of what they've been charged with, but you can bet a month's pay they're guilty of something.' At the time he'd nodded, drunk his tea and kept his mental reservations to himself. Now the memory of the conversation made him furious. He wanted to shout across the years: 'Innocent men do get charged, you old fool. Look what's happening to me.' But he wasn't charged yet; if he kept his head he had three days to make sure that he never was charged.

Then there was Nimue Hawthorne. It wasn't only a matter of convincing the police, he had to convince her. And he was by now becoming certain that the name of her game must be blackmail. Otherwise, she'd have phoned the police long before. In his wild relief when he saw the bullet wound in Shunner's head he'd imagined that he could prove his innocence to her, but that thought hardly survived a few seconds. Nimue must have seen the wound from the moment she slid down the dune. She was standing at Shunner's head, then, in that walk of several hundred yards to the seaweed place, she had her hands hooked under his arms, looking down at that face with every step. And she'd naturally assumed that Birdie had fired the shot – knowing nothing of the knock-out punch at the beach hut. If he went to her now with that story she'd just assume that he was making a belated and confused attempt to cover up. Absence of gun? So what? Birdie would have had time to bury it in the sand, wouldn't he? He gulped the last of the coffee, remembering the sound of somebody climbing over the wire fence, feeling the hairs rising on his neck.

Then, with the memory of the sound, the last paralysed corner of his mind began to move again and, once started, to race and make up for lost time. Nimue Hawthorne. Stunned into passivity, he'd got the whole sequence the wrong way round. As he'd seen it Nimue was – inexplicably – helping him dispose of his victim. Put it the other way round and Birdie Linnet was – more explicably in the circumstances – helping Nimue dispose of her victim. 'What are we going to do with it? Had you thought of that?' Nimue had shot Ralph Shunner. He tried looking at it from that viewpoint and found some sense, some problems. Nimue was awake at four o'clock in the morning, and clearly had been awake all night. Nimue who, of all people, could surely have walked in by the camp's main gate, came climbing in furtively over the wire. But why did she have to climb in? Shunner, after all, had been shot inside the wire and, judging as far as he could from the entry wound, shot at close quarters. But then if she'd shot him, climbed over the fence to get rid of the gun and was on her way back in when Birdie saw her . . . But why had it taken her so long? The body was cold when he found it.

And why had she simply accepted that he'd help her hide the body? She couldn't, after all, have known that he was standing there imagining himself to be Shunner's killer. His presence should have come as a bad shock to her, and yet she'd quite calmly conscripted him and, presumably, trusted that he'd keep quiet about it afterwards. He played only briefly with the idea that this sort of thing was routine duty for instructors at the Village Zoe. Did she think she'd scared him into it? But as far as he could remember – and the whole thing was becoming blurred – she'd never even hinted at a threat. And yet she'd seemed so certain of his co-operation. This was the part of the puzzle he couldn't make fit, whichever way he turned it. But something else did fit, and that was Nimue's obvious uneasiness the previous afternoon, and her apparent absence from the camp after that. When he met her he'd been impressed and a little intimidated by her obvious efficiency in running the place. Then the efficiency had slipped quite suddenly. She'd kept him waiting at the children's exercise class, turned up just long enough to unload some of her duties on to him, and that evening the reception office had no idea where she'd gone. In the half day or so before Shunner was shot, something had jolted the efficient Miss Hawthorne right out of her routine. If he could find out what had given her the jolt, he'd probably have his hand on the motive for Shunner's killing – and, if not proof itself, that would certainly be well on the way to proof. It had become urgent for him to fill in the blank of what Nimue had been doing during those thirteen hours between her brief appearance at the children's class and her reappearance beside Shunner's body. Had she really been away from the camp all that time? Had she met Shunner, quarrelled with him? Could she have gone somewhere to pick up a gun? And here, at least, he found firmer ground among the quicksands. This sort of investigation had been part of his life for seventeen years and the technique would surely be much the same among sand, tents and bare sun tans as in rainy streets back home.

His watch, which had survived the seaweed, told him that it was just past midday. He made himself stroll as casually as possible towards the café, but when he got there found that he was still too early for the lunchtime rush. There were only two tables occupied on the balcony. At one of them a group of French teenagers were drinking Coke and listening to a beautiful black-haired girl playing a mandolin. The other table had just one man, sitting beside a half-empty litre carafe of red wine and Birdie recognized him as the solicitor, Peter Pollins, husband of the formidable Vinny. He looked up as Birdie's shadow fell across the table, and cringed.

'Oh God, I hope you're not trying to make me take exercise.' His speech was a little slurred.

'It's not compulsory.' Birdie sat down beside him.

'Mind if I join you?'

'Have a drink.'

Birdie picked up a glass from the next table and accepted. 'Enjoying it here?'

Pollins' reply was heartfelt. 'I wish I were back home on a rainy Monday morning with a desk full of conveyancing files. That's how much I'm enjoying it here.'

'Not what you'd expected?'

'I dare say it's what *she* expected. I don't get much choice in the matter.'

Birdie remembered dimly the words between Pollins and his wife on the volleyball court that morning.

'Still, you made a break for it last night, by the sound of it.' He'd intended no more than a casual remark and was surprised at the alarm and annoyance on Pollins' face.

'This bloody place. Everything you do . . .'

Hastily he tried to smooth things down. 'I wouldn't have thought anybody minded you playing poker.' And unmistakably the look on Pollins' face turned to relief.

'Poker . . . yes, Joan's idea. Great girl, Joan.'

'Was it a good game?'

'Not very. Too pissed to concentrate.'

They drank in silence for a while, then Pollins asked suddenly, 'Can you change travellers' cheques here?'

'I don't know. They might at the office.'

'Bloody place. You'd think they'd have a bank.' It seemed to wrench the conversation round to where he wanted it.

'I thought it seemed quite well organized here. Miss Hawthorne runs a very tight camp.'

Pollins thought this over for a while, frowning. 'You mean Miss Health and Beauty?'

'That's the one.' Birdie tried to sound casual. 'I was looking for her last night.'

'No accounting for tastes.' Pollins poured the last half inch of wine into his glass and Birdie took the hint and caught the waiter's eye.

'I mean, I wanted to ask her about something. I couldn't find her anywhere.'

'I suppose they get time off.' Pollins' eyes were on the waiter, decanting more wine into a carafe. He seemed so uninvolved that Birdie risked a direct question.

'Did you see her around yesterday evening?'

'No, but then I wasn't looking for her. Wasn't around anyway.'

'Out playing poker?'

'Yes.'

But for some reason the alarm was back in his eyes again. Birdie supposed the row with his wife had made the subject a sore one. As far as his investigation was concerned, Pollins seemed to be a dead loss. But since he'd had to pay for the carafe of wine he decided to stay and help drink some of it. He was about half way down the second glass – and already feeling light-headed from too much wine and too little food – when a heavy hand clamped itself on his bare shoulder. He gave a strangled gasp and rose about six inches into the air, slopping wine on the table.

'Oh dear, your nerves *are* in a bad state. Too much healthy living.'

It was the photographer, Clancy, relaxed and grinning. He was on his own for once, but still had a camera slung round his neck. He sat down without an invitation and called to a waiter to bring another glass. Pollins seemed too deeply sunk in gloom or alcohol to resent it. When Clancy's glass was full Birdie sailed straight in.

'We were talking about the girl in charge here, Nimue Hawthorne. I was trying to find her last night.'

He got much the same reaction as from Pollins, but this time as a sideways look rather than in words. He pressed on: 'I mean, you'd expect her to be around all the time, wouldn't you. In case of emergencies. She just landed me with her swimming pool stint and disappeared.'

Clancy shrugged.

'Did you see her around last night, Clancy?'

'No.' But there was at least a flicker of interest from him. He asked, 'Do you know her then? Before you came here, I mean?'

'No,' said Birdie. 'Did you?'

Clancy's reply was not instant. 'No-o-o, I don't think so. I just had this feeling I'd seen her before somewhere.'

'A model?' Birdie suggested. But Clancy shook his head.

'No, I can tell them a mile off. No, it would have been somewhere . . .' He screwed up his eyes, trying to remember, then gave up. 'No. Why are we talking about her anyway?'

Birdie didn't need to find an answer, because at that point something like a tornado came upon them. A thin man in denims, white chest and dark glasses came up the café steps at a run and immediately homed in on their table.

'Where is she? What have you been doing with her?'

It was James Jedd. He planted his hands on the edge of the table, setting the wine glasses rocking, his eyes in their dark glasses only a few inches away from the photographer's face. Don the gorilla stood impassively a few paces behind him.

'Where is she?' he repeated, so close that his saliva flecked Clancy's face. His voice wasn't loud, but his anger and intensity radiated out so that even the group round the mandolin girl had their eyes fixed on Birdie's table. Clancy half got up, sat down again, tried a nervous grin.

'What y'talking about?'

'You know what I'm talking about.' Jedd's voice was lower, if anything, but his whole body was rigid. 'If she's not here in five minutes, I'll bloody take you apart.'

Clancy's eyes went nervously to Don, then back to Jedd again. He looked worried.

'Look, mate, it's no good coming on like this. I just don't know what you're talking about.'

'You know.'

And, for a count of ten seconds or so, they just looked at each other. Birdie, sensing violence in the atmosphere like thunder, was on the edge of his chair, ready to drag them apart if necessary. Pollins was watching with his mouth open, pale as a mushroom. Clancy gave in first.

'Look, if it's Melanie you're talking about . . .' He paused. Jedd hadn't moved a muscle. 'If it's Melanie you're talking about, you've come to the wrong place. I don't know where she is.'

'You were taking photographs of her yesterday. At the swimming pool. He was there.' The dark glasses veered fractionally towards Birdie, then back to Clancy again. Clancy licked his lips. There were drops of sweat on his forehead.

'Just a few atmosphere shots. For the colour supp piece.'

'Where is she?'

'How should I know?' There was bewilderment as well as fear in the photographer's voice and Birdie thought it sounded genuine. 'So I took some shots of her. That doesn't make me her keeper.'

'She was with you last night.'

Clancy shook his head. From the look on his face, the bewilderment was growing fast. 'She wasn't. If you must know, she stormed off before we even had dinner, let alone anything else.'

'Stormed off?'

Without taking his eyes off Clancy, Jedd sat down in an empty chair between him and Birdie.

'Yeah, stormed off. You know, stamped her little foot and twitched her little arse and went. Scrammed, took a powder, vamooshed.'

Jedd took a deep breath. 'Where did she go?'

'She didn't say. Didn't get a chance to ask her. One minute there she was in the chalet, the next . . .' He paused, probably feeling he'd made a tactical mistake by admitting to being in the same chalet as Melanie McBride, but that didn't seem to be bothering Jedd.

'What time was this?' Jedd's tone was fractionally less hostile and Clancy wrinkled his forehead and thought.

'It must have been around nine o'clock, because we were going out for dinner, then we had this argument and off she went.'

'What was the argument about?'

Clancy looked at Jedd in silence for a while, then he said, in a voice that wasn't quite as casual as it tried to be, 'Melanie was having a touch of the dramas. Got the idea she needed protecting.'

91

'She . . .' Birdie couldn't quite stop himself speaking, and both turned to look at him. Reluctantly he had to continue. 'Melanie was saying the same thing to me. At the pool.'

Jedd gave him a ten-second blast from behind the sunglasses, then turned back to Clancy. 'What did you say?'

'I told her she'd been reading too many telly scripts and not to be a silly girl. Something like that.'

Birdie could believe it. His reaction had been much the same. And it seemed that Jedd believed it too. 'And that's when she lost her temper?'

Clancy nodded.

'And you don't know where she went?'

'I've told you, no I don't.'

The glasses swivelled back to Birdie. 'Do you know anything about it?'

It seemed to Birdie cosmically unfair that with so much else to worry about that he was being dragged into Melanie's affairs.

'No. She spoke to me at the pool. I saw her go off with Clancy some time after eight o'clock. I haven't seen or heard of her since.'

Jedd leaned back in the chair and took off his sunglasses. The eyes behind them were tired – but the same was true of practically all the eyes Birdie had seen at the Village Zoe that day. If Jedd had spent the night crashing around looking for Melanie, he might have seen something of the comings and goings of Nimue Hawthorne, but Birdie couldn't work out how to bring up the subject. He tried.

'Did you ask them at reception if they'd seen her?'

'No. Not yet.'

It was clear that Clancy had been Jedd's Number-One suspect and he hadn't considered any other possibilities.

'Did she take any clothes with her?' It was an automatic question from a former policeman, and he was surprised at the precision of Jedd's answer.

'Yes. Her tote bag's gone. A green dress and a blue silk boiler suit. Some underwear. Most of her make-up.'

Perhaps one man in twenty could have been as precise about a woman's possessions. Even in the days of his marriage, Birdie knew, half of Olivia's wardrobe could have disappeared without his being aware of it. Would Shunner have known? Pushing down the thought of of Shunner with Olivia as firmly as he'd pushed his body under the seaweed, he tried to concentrate. Jedd's answer reminded him of what Melanie had said by the swimming pool about his need to exert control over her. Even, it seemed, her underwear.

'When did you notice she was gone?'

'Yesterday evening. But I thought she was away having it off with somebody and she'd come back when she got tired of him – in half an hour or so.' The look he threw at Clancy showed the photographer wasn't out of the wood yet.

'If you want to know, I didn't . . .' Clancy began.

Birdie asked hastily, 'When she didn't come back. . . ?'

'About one o'clock, I went out looking for him.' A jerk of the chin towards Clancy.

'I couldn't find him. I went to his chalet and he wasn't there.'

'So what? I'm not under house arrest am I?' Clancy was becoming more truculent.

Birdie asked, 'What did you do then?' It was a lead up to asking him if he'd seen anything of Nimue, or anything else unusual, but Jedd was beginning to look at him suspiciously.

'I walked round a bit to see if I could find her, then I went back to the chalet and waited.'

Birdie had a mental picture of what Melanie would have found if she had returned: Jedd, vengeful, implacable. He was beginning to find her fear of the man more convincing.

'When she wasn't back by morning I checked the cupboard and found the clothes gone.'

Clancy said, 'So, she'd just decided to bugger off.'

'She wouldn't do that.' It wasn't an expression of trust from Jedd, rather a statement that she wouldn't dare do it.

'I mean,' said Clancy, 'it was *you* she said she wanted protecting from.'

Birdie waited for the explosion, but Jedd said, quite flatly, 'She's crazy.'

He stood up, replacing his sun glasses. Don, who had been standing throughout, moved back a step. From behind the glasses Jedd delivered a statement, mainly towards Clancy, but catching Birdie in its range as well. 'She hasn't got the wit to go off on her own. She's gone off with somebody, and I'm going to find out who it is.'

He left, more slowly than he'd arrived. Clancy looked at Birdie and drew a long breath.

'Silly little cunt.'

93

Whether he meant Jedd or Melanie wasn't clear, He stood up. 'Proper put me off my food. I'm going for a swim. Ciao.'

He raised a hand, grinned tightly and went off in the opposite direction from Jedd and Don. Which left Birdie and Pollins at the table, Birdie angry with himself for not finding out what he wanted from Jedd, Pollins apparently well on the way to alcoholic stupor. But it was Pollins who stood up first, with some difficulty.

'You can finish the wine. Got to see about damned travellers' cheques.' He made his way unsteadily down the steps. Five minutes after he'd gone, Vinny came looking for her husband, hot, angry, and in no mood to listen to round-about chat from Birdie. Nobody but himself, it seemed, was even slightly interested in the activities of Nimue Hawthorne.

Except, if he'd known it, Birdie's daughter. Deborah was back at what was the centre of Zoe Village for her, the tennis courts, and Nimue's side. The morning's coaching session (men's improvers' class) was coming to an end and Nimue was taking a few minutes' rest from her duties of giving appropriate encouragement and seeing that everybody got a fair share of the instructor's time. Now she and Deborah were standing by the umpire's chair, watching critically as two men kept a sickly rally in intensive care.

Nimue's voice was low, and Deborah nodded without taking her eyes off the play. The shorter, plumper man advanced closer and closer to the net. His opponent performed miracles of balance on the base line, wielding his racquet on the end of an outstretched arm like a wild butterfly catcher. The ball hit the racquet to collect from it just enough impetus to fly over the head of a man at the net before dying in the red dust of the court behind him.

'Game, set and match.'

'See what I mean? At this level, it's not a question of who's going to win. It's who loses first.'

Luckily the two men, shaking hands at the net and congratulating each other on a jolly good game, didn't hear her, but Deborah flashed a smile of pure devilment, the first Nimue had seen on her usually solemn face. The men strolled off the court, sheathing their racquets and looking for praise, and got it in carefully ambiguous words from Nimue. Before they parted from her, the butterfly catcher asked her if the kids' exercise class would be on again that afternoon.

'Best idea out. Get rid of the little blighters for an hour.'

Nimue assured him that it would be. 'They had a smashing time there yesterday. Good instructor you've got for them – that English chap.'

A quick glance at Nimue from Deborah. The butterfly catcher went on, 'Fit bloke too. We were having a little stroll on the beach after dinner last night and there he was tearing along like an Olympic champion. Two weeks of this and perhaps I'll be the same.' A sideways glance at Nimue clearly meant to suggest that she might join in the process of bringing out the champion in him.

She fielded it. 'I'm sure you will. We'll see the children this afternoon, then.'

When they'd gone, Nimue and her shadow Deborah made the round of the courts, slackening nets, gathering up discarded headbands and eyeshades. At the first net Deborah said, in a subdued voice, 'That's my father.'

'Who is?' From Nimue's expression, she thought Deborah meant the butterfly catcher.

'The one they were talking about. The one that's taking the children's classes.'

The expression changed to a different kind of surprise, more guarded. 'Birdie Linnet's your father? I thought the man you came with was your father.'

The child shook her head, no trace now of a smile. 'That's Mr Shunner. He's not my father. He and Mum are going to get married.'

'Oh.'

Nothing more was said while they dealt with the next two nets. Nimue was thinking hard, her hands going through the chores automatically, and the child seemed oppressed either by her silence or what they'd been talking about. After a few minutes Nimue said, 'Your mother and father got divorced?'

'Yes. Last year.'

A pause, and then Nimue asked gently, cautiously, 'Did your father mind very much?'

An uncomprehending stare from Deborah. Divorce she knew about. The concept of divorce with no hard feelings was clearly not something within her experience. That stare was Nimue's answer, rather than what Deborah said.

'He didn't want to. Mum said, when a marriage has . . . broken down it's best for everybody . . .' Her voice broke off, as if forgetting some equation in chemistry. She was twisting a white

95

towelling headband in her fingers.

Nimue said hastily, 'You don't have to talk about it.'

'No . . . I want . . .' Two wide brown eyes locked on hers, tears gathering. 'I don't mind talking about it. It's only . . .'

Nimue hooked an arm round her thin shoulders and led her to a bench. 'Don't worry, love.'

'No. I want to talk. It's the worst thing not being able to. But if I ask Mum things it only worries her, and the only time I asked Dad he got so sort of . . . angry, and . . .'

'Angry?' Nimue felt her arm tightening over Deborah's shoulders and forced herself to relax it.

'Not with me. I don't think it was with me. It was when I wanted to ask him something about what happened in court.'

'When they had to decide whether you lived with your Mum or Dad?'

'Oh that.' Deborah's voice was almost dismissive. 'Custody and access? No, that was something different. That's civil law, you see. Mum explained that to me all right.'

'So what was this other thing in court?' Nimue's voice sounded too sharp, too interested, in her own ears, but it didn't seem to alarm the child. Deborah spoke as if she were dragging things up from her memory and seeing them for the first time, almost unconscious that anybody else was there.

'The other case happened first, just after Dad went away. I knew something was wrong, but Mum wouldn't tell me about it. Then Jessamine – she's my friend at school – Jessamine said it was in the papers, so we went out at lunchtime and bought the *Daily Mail* and . . . it was in there.'

'When was this?' This time her tone was too sharp. The child glanced at her, half alarmed.

'Last year. A year ago in March.'

Nimue made herself breathe deeply, calmly. The child went on, fingers still twisting the towelling band:

'There were photographs. Of Dad and . . .'

'And Mr Shunner.'

A deep sigh from the child. 'Yes.'

Nimue asked very gently, 'What was the trial about?'

'It was something to do with drugs. You know, serious drugs that kill people. Not pot or anything.'

'How did your Dad come into it?'

Deborah stared at Nimue as if she should have known. 'Dad was a policeman. He had to go in court and give evidence about things Mr Shunner had said. Then this lawyer – the one that was working for Mr Shunner – said they shouldn't listen to Dad because he was only trying to get his own back because Mum had left him and gone to live with Mr Shunner. That made it something or other evidence.'

'Unreliable evidence?'

The child nodded. 'So they didn't send Mr Shunner to prison, and Dad had to stop being a policeman.'

'You mean they sacked him?'

A look of alarm from Deborah. 'No, that was what I asked Dad about. He said they hadn't sacked him, he'd resigned because he didn't see much point in doing it any more when people like Mr Shunner could get away with things. He was really angry, and I got sort of scared, and he said he was sorry, he hadn't meant to be like that with me and . . .' She paused for several seconds, staring at the ground, '. . . and he was crying.'

Her voice was so low that Nimue could hardly hear it.

For a few minutes they sat in silence on the wooden bench, Nimue's arm still round the child's shoulders. The sounds of the camp came from a long way off and the surface of the tennis courts was shimmery with heat haze.

After a while, Nimue said in a normal tone of voice, 'What about some backhand practice?'

'Oh, yes please.' Gratitude and relief in Deborah's voice at being helped back to dry land. She added immediately and politely, 'If you can spare the time.'

'Twenty minutes.'

She couldn't spare the time, and the temperature was in the nineties, but with so much churning round in her mind she desperately needed some physical activity.

CHAPTER SEVEN

Vinny Pollins looked after the family travellers' cheques and currency. She was good with money. Vinny looked after the bookings and the tickets and the car insurance and the personal holiday insurance and the Michelins. Peter Pollins' own preparations had been less complicated – just a hundred pounds worth of his own travellers' cheques, tucked well down in his wallet where Vinny wouldn't see them. For eventualities: that was what he'd told himself when he queued at the bank for them in his lunch hour, hoping that she wouldn't come in and find him. Eventualities? Well, supposing the gear box went, or one of the kids broke a leg or the ferries went on strike? But all those things, of course, were provided for in Vinny's big buff folder of forms and brochures. And when he pushed the idea a little further he had to admit that his eventualities took the shape of bottles and glasses, of small tables with definitely no room at them for three children and – if he pushed the idea further still to a point where he had to abandon it in panic – of a presence on the opposite side of the little tables which was clearly not Vinny. When he'd eventually come face to face with the bank cashier he'd been pink with guilt and embarrassment. Now, with the five twenty pound travellers' cheques fanned out in front of him on the reception desk at the Village Zoe, he was embarrassed all over again, fumbled while writing his signature five times and glanced at dark-haired Marie behind the counter to see if she'd noticed. If so, it didn't seem to bother her. She thanked him, gathered up the cheques and pushed over rather fewer francs than he'd hoped for. Still, it would have to do. Emerging from the reception building into the glare of the afternoon sun, he looked round carefully before walking over to the family car. Vinny should be safely occupied delivering the kids to their various activities, but he couldn't afford to take chances: at least, no further chances than he was taking already. The car was baking hot inside and cluttered with family things. He made a cursory attempt at tidying it, stuffing T-shirts into the glove compartment and plimsolls behind the passenger seat, then, after a last look round, set off southwards at a cautious speed. The empty road shimmered in the heat. Then a huge advert for brandy he remembered as a landmark and, five kilometres on, the place itself, a rectangular blot on the landscape, the motel.

It was a girl behind the check-in desk this time. He gave his name, and he thought she looked at him suspiciously while she rang the room number he'd asked for. He tried to relax, letting his eyes roam round the foyer, the modern tapestry wall hangings, the rampant rubber plant.

'She says, will you go up.'

He felt the girl's eyes following him as he mounted the beige carpeted stairs to the first floor.

'Come in.'

The shutters were closed so that the room was in dusk, but still stiflingly hot. Melanie was stretched out on the bed, wearing the outfit she'd been wearing the evening before, a sort of jumpsuit in turquoise silk with a zip down the front, heavy gold chains round her neck.

'How are you?'

He stood, ill at ease, just inside the door.

'Close the door,' she said. Then: 'Did you get some money?'

He nodded, sitting down on the edge of the one chair in the room, covered in beige velveteen to match the carpet. Even with only a small bagful of possessions she'd managed to make the room untidy – a wispy bra and a small triangle of panties over the back of the chair, make-up and perfume bottles on the small table, along with unwashed coffee cups and empty tublets of dairy cream substitute.

'How are you?' he repeated. 'Did you sleep?'

'I couldn't sleep. I've got a stinking headache.'

There was a heavy sweetness in the room he couldn't identify but assumed it must be the perfume she was wearing.

'Perhaps some fresh air.' He opened the shutters a few inches, letting a shaft of sunlight in. 'What about a drink?'

He'd bought a bottle of white Bordeaux, two tumblers and a corkscrew surreptitiously at the camp supermarket that morning, reasoning that it would work out cheaper than room service at the motel. She watched without interest as he poured two glasses of the disastrously warm drink, and just sipped at hers while he took a great gulp.

'The money,' he said. He made a space on the table and spread out the notes and a handful of coins.

'How much is that?'

'A hundred pounds. But you'll . . . we'll have to go carefully with it. I've been looking at what they charge for a night here and it's not cheap.'

There was no reaction. He crossed the shaft of sunlight, into the dusk beside her bed.

'I've been so lonely,' she said. It was like a child's voice. He sat down, very cautiously, beside her.

'Poor little thing.'

He put a hand on her shoulder, just where it curved into the white neck above the silk of her jumpsuit. The zip was open almost to the waist, showing breasts round and pale as helpings of sorbet. Her skin was cool too.

'Poor little thing.'

Unresisting, she leant against him, letting him stroke her hair. He went cautiously at first, then plunged his hand up to the wrist in its soft, yielding silkiness with no reaction from her, either of protest or pleasure. Her eyes were closed, her lips slightly parted. He let his hand slip down from her hair to the triangle of cool, pale skin between the lips of the zip, then further to the tongue of the zip, inched it down until the silk fell back from her breasts and gently rounded stomach with its neat disc of navel.

'I'm so scared,' she murmured. 'So scared.'

'No need to be scared. I'm looking after you.' And he meant it. Being there with her, touching her, he'd recaptured the excitement, the sense of danger, of their flight from the Village Zoe, of the crazy, short-tempered drive from village to village looking for somewhere to stay, of the early morning hours when the ugly rectangular motel looked like a rescue ship sailing on exotic waters. Away from her he'd remembered only the confusion and embarrassment of it all, and the doubt about whether the danger she kept talking about was anything more than hysteria. Now he was the man of action again, decisive, protective. He let his fingers wander slowly over her stomach and breasts, waiting for her to respond to them. She said, 'Has he been looking for me?'

His fingers halted an instant, remembering Jedd's anger in the café that morning. 'Yes, he thinks you've gone off with that photographer.'

This time her stomach muscles did tighten, but not in response to his fingers.

'Is he . . . angry?'

'Yes.'

'He'll find me,' she said. 'He always finds people.'

'Why should he?'

'He'll find me.' By now she was too tense to respond to him at all. He removed his hand from her stomach and put it back on her shoulder, his eyes still on the broad white triangle of skin.

'Why are you so scared of him?'

'I told you. He thinks he owns me. Like a slave. He used to have this game . . .'

'You told me.'

Silence. She asked him to hand her bag over, burrowed in it and found a thin, rather battered cigarette. A line of sweet, heavy smoke rose. After a few deep drags at it she passed it to him and, not liking to refuse, he put his lips to it, trying not to draw the smoke into his lungs.

He said, handing it back, 'You can leave him. Wait till you get back to England and see a lawyer about the contract. If you don't know one, I can find one for you.'

'That's back in England.'

Under the influence of the smoke she was relaxing a little. He let his hand begin its downward journey again.

'I'll help you get back to England. Just give me a couple of days. I could drive you to Paris, put you on a plane . . .' (How would he explain a day's absence to Vinny? Could he get a plane ticket on his Barclaycard?)

'He's got my passport.'

He was beginning to notice an air almost of smugness about her when she managed to put up yet another obstacle.

'I could get it from him.' But remembering Jedd's face at the café he didn't relish the idea.

She shook her head. 'He wouldn't let me leave here. He thinks I know too much about what's going on.'

'And what is going on?'

She looked sideways at him. 'I don't know.'

'I think you do.' His fingers traced a slow spiral up her left breast.

'Nothing . . . nothing I can talk about.'

'Why are you so sure something's going on?'

'Because . . . coming here. He was suddenly so set on coming here. We were supposed to be going to Barbados, then at the last minute he said we were coming to this place instead. I said I hated France, but he . . . I just had to do what he said.'

'Perhaps he just felt like coming to a nudist place.'

She stared at him, incredulous. 'Him? He wouldn't need to come to a place like this.'

He felt like a bumpkin and a voyeuristic bumpkin at that, hurried back to the main argument.

'So why. . . ?'

'That's just what I'm saying. Why? It's just the sort of place he can't stand. Wooden chalets and cold showers and families with kids all over the place.'

That reminded him all too vividly of Vinny, and brought a surge of guilt and anger that made his fingers dig deeply into her breasts. She gave a little gasp and his fingers slid down and opened the zip a last few inches. She leant back against the pillow, the cigarette still between her fingers.

Later, when the bar of sunlight had shifted several yards across the room, he poured what was left of the wine into their glasses. His head was muzzy from the cigarette smoke.

'It's getting late,' he said. 'I've got to go back.'

'Don't leave me.' But the urgency had gone from her. The appeal sounded almost a matter of routine.

'You'll sleep. I'll be here again tomorrow.'

'I'm scared he'll find me.'

'He won't.'

'I'm scared.' Tears came slowly, from under her closed eyelids. He stroked her hair.

'And we'll talk about getting you back to London. I'll find a way.'

On his way downstairs he wondered if a Consulate could issue a temporary passport. That would be the sort of thing Vinny would know – if only he could ask her.

Towards the end of the afternoon Birdie decided one of the things wrong with him might be lack of sleep. It scared him that he was having to fight harder and harder against what he knew would be a lunatic thing to do – to go back yet again to the seaweed place and reassure himself, by seeing and touching, that the bullet hole was really there in Shunner's head. His attempts to find out anything about Nimue had got nowhere. In a dutiful haze he'd superintended the children's exercises, but he could remember so little of that now that for all he knew he might have sent the lot of them swimming out to sea like lemmings. And all the time the image of a face tilted against a bed of seaweed like a poached egg on spinach, of a neat entry wound punched in front of the right ear, had been growing clearer and clearer. From an afternoon of haze, he could remember all too clearly the first time the thought came to him: suppose I imagined it? He'd been wandering somewhere on the fringes of the camp, where the pine woods were thickest, and his eyes focused sharply on one tree out of a thousand trees. He could remember a drop of resin on the bark, hardened in the sun, a thin fly with feelers longer than its body. His eyes locked on them while his mind tried to come to grips with this new idea. Suppose the bullet hole had never been there, that in some convoluted mental effort to clear himself of Shunner's death he'd imagined it? He argued with himself: but I touched it. I could see it. And he remembered the old woman who, back in the days when he was duty officer, would come into the station every Friday to report giant butterflies in her bedroom. Very vividly she'd describe them: their brown-orange wings big as bed sheets, the rustling noise, the smell of them, like old wet cardboard. And the form had been to tut-tut a bit and promise to get somebody from the council round to see to them. And she'd trot off happily enough and be back there next Friday, the details never varying. She'd seen giant butterflies. He'd seen a bullet hole. Then he'd found that he was walking fast, that his feet were on a narrow sandy path between bushes and seemed to know where they were going. And where they were going was towards the seaweed place.

He'd managed to stop himself that time, to tell himself that he knew the bullet hole was there, that this need to see it again was nothing more than a compulsion of overstretched nerves. He'd dragged himself back to the main part of the camp, heard his own voice, sounding surprisingly normal, answering people who spoke to him, mostly jokey remarks about exercise. He'd even thought of going for a swim in the pool, until he remembered that Nimue might be doing lifeguard duty there. And all the time, the effort of fighting down this need to go back to the seaweed place was like wading through deep water. The thought that he hadn't slept for thirty-four hours and this might be one of the results came as something of a relief.

He went to his tent and stretched out on the sleeping bag, eyes closed, but if he slept at all it was only the most superficial doze, with the sounds of the camp filtering through it and vivid mental pictures making it unrestful: the poached egg on spinach, the muscles that rose over Nimue's ribcage when she lifted her arms, the newly painted coat-of-arms over the judge's bench. After an hour or so of this he sat up and brewed black coffee. He'd had nothing to eat all day except the lumps of stale baguette, and his mouth felt sour from the wine he'd been drinking at lunchtime. And, as he drank the coffee, he took himself to task. He was close, he realized, to cracking up, though heaven knew what form it would take.

'Get a grip on yourself,' he said aloud. 'Routine.'

He remembered what they'd dinned into him as a trainee, that it was routine that solved crimes, not luck or intuition. And through quite a long career this had proved true. Well, approach the thing this way: a crime had been committed, now set up the routine for solving it. Just like any other crime. Except in any other crime, he hadn't been a prime suspect. Except in any other crime the other candidate for that place wasn't a gold-skinned, strong-willed woman who wandered round in the nude. Except that in any other crime the victim hadn't been the lover of . . . But that was just the line of thought he was supposed to be avoiding. If this were any other murder, if he'd been there simply as an observer, what would his next step be? And the answer was obvious: he'd be giving a very close questioning to Miss Nimue Hawthorne.

The oblique approach, he decided, had been a waste of time. Why go round asking all and sundry if they'd seen her the night before, without putting the question of where she'd been to Nimue herself? The answer, he knew, was that he was flinching away from the memory of how they'd lumped Shunner through the sand dunes, but routine could take no account of feelings like that. He looked at his recovered watch and found it was just after eight o'clock. If Nimue had been on duty at the pool she'd presumably be returning to reception about now with the key.

At least he'd got that much right. She was there behind the counter of the reception building along with the assistant, Marie. To his relief, both women were wearing tracksuits, although the woman holidaymaker Nimue was speaking to was in the camp's usual state of nudity. She was a small, grey-haired woman, with the sort of voice that suggested dog obedience classes, and she seemed to be quizzing Nimue about catering arrangements.

'A lot of us are vegetarians, and a barbecue is simply roasted flesh.'

Nimue said patiently, 'We realize that. We have some very good nut and soya steaks sent in especially every week.'

The woman was unimpressed. 'Do they contain animal fat?'

'Of course not.'

'Or dairy fat? Some of us are vegans.'

'We realize that too. They're made of nuts and soya and olive oil and herbs ...' The woman was looking almost approving. '... especially grown by a Buddhist commune in Provence.'

Birdie wondered if Nimue was sending the woman up, but the effect on her seemed to be entirely satisfying. She said in that case they'd all join in and left looking as happy as a well-walked terrier. This left Birdie, Nimue and Marie as the only people in the office, and Marie was dealing with what sounded like a bad-tempered telephone conversation in French.

Nimue gave Birdie a rather tired smile and said, 'The beach barbecue tomorrow night. It's a good job nobody's against cruelty to soya beans.'

Marie, hand over the mouthpiece, said something to Nimue who took the receiver from her and fired off a decisive burst of French too fast for Birdie to catch. She put down the phone and said to Marie, 'If they ring again, tell them it's their problem.'

She glanced at Birdie. 'You haven't been trying to hire a car, have you?'

'No. Why?'

'That was the local garage. Someone from here reserved a car last night and didn't turn up to claim it.'

'Not me.'

She shrugged and gave him the quick, efficient smile she'd given the doggy woman.

'Any problems?'

'I want a talk with you.'

He tried to make his tone hard and official, and was pleased to see a change in her expression.

'I'm just going for a work-out in the gym. You can come if you like.'

It wasn't quite what he'd had in mind, but it would have to do. Nimue lifted a flap in the counter and came round to his side.

'Will you be all right for an hour, Marie? I'll be back to close up.'

She and Birdie walked side by side, along the path bordered with rosemary bushes leading to her bungalow. Birdie was silent, sorting out in his mind how he was going to conduct the interview. She seemed quite composed, though some of the bounce seemed to have gone out of her. Instead of turning into her bungalow they walked on past it, to a large prefabricated building.

'The visitors don't seem to use it much, but I do.'

It was dusky inside, and Nimue turned on a neon strip light to reveal a quite well equipped gym with benches, wall bars and weight equipment.

'The job would drive me mad sometimes if I didn't have this place to come to. I never miss a day.'

Birdie had the feeling that she was on home ground and some of the initiative was slipping away from him. 'Let's sit down and have a talk first.'

'We can talk while I work out. I haven't got long.' And she was down on her back, cycling her legs in the air, in what was clearly part of a warm-up routine. Birdie, disconcerted, found himself talking to a slim bottom moving rhythmically under the nylon tracksuit.

'What were you doing last night?'

The legs cycled on for a bit, then changed their rhythm, as she touched the floor behind her head with each foot in turn, getting faster and faster. But her voice wasn't even slightly breathless as she replied, 'What I always do, I suppose.'

'You weren't. I know that much.'

No change in the rhythm. The legs went on threshing the floor. After a while she turned round and sat up, but not to answer him. She took the heel of her left foot in her hand and extended it so that the leg was pointing up in front of her face. From her expression, it seemed that her mind was entirely concentrated on the movement.

He said, more roughly, 'You couldn't have been doing what you always do. You asked me to take over at the pool, for a start. After that, nobody seems to have seen you until . . .' He paused.

'Until what?'

She was working on her right leg now, looking at him with a rather puzzled expression.

'You know very well until what.'

'Why does it matter to you what I was doing?' She stood up and he thought it might be a sign that she was beginning to take proper notice of him, until she pulled down the zip and threw off her tracksuit top.

'What are you doing?' She smiled at the alarm in his voice.

'I'm warmed up now. I don't need it.' And began taking off the tracksuit trousers. She smiled again when she saw his expression, and this time it had more than a touch of malice in it.

'I don't see why I should bundle myself up in a leotard just because you're here. You invited yourself.' And coolly she bent to pick up a dumbbell.

Birdie felt embarrassed and angry. He was getting used – almost – to the unthinking nudity around the camp, but this was something different. This time she meant it as a challenge. In other circumstances it would have been a clear sexual challenge, but not this time. It was more like a defiance of him, a statement that she'd do things on her own terms and his opinion had nothing to do with it. Or, it struck him, it might be a deliberate distraction from his line of questioning. One hell of a distraction. He tried to watch coolly as she swung the dumbbell between her straddled legs, then up at arm's length in a wide silver arc.

'So where were you, up to four o'clock this morning?'

Nineteen swings, twenty swings. She paused with the dumbbell above her head, ribcage stretched under the honey skin.

'I don't have to tell you that or anything else. I could ask what you were doing. If I didn't know.'

'You can't know.'

He heard panic in his voice. She turned away and picked up a second dumbbell from the rack, leant her body against a board hitched to the wall bars. Her small firm breasts stretched to flatness when she extended her arms, rose again as she brought the weights inwards. Birdie watched in silence for a while then, angry at his own embarrassment and lack of progress, tried another tack.

'Anyway, you don't have to worry for two days.'

This, for the first time, made her pause. She turned her head sideways on the board to look at him, dumbbells resting on her shoulders. Then went on with the exercise, but less forcefully.

'What do you mean?'

He said, slowly and deliberately, 'The woman Ralph Shunner was with thinks he's gone off to Paris. She's not likely to start getting worried for another couple of days.'

It was the first time he'd put a name to the body, and he watched her for any reaction. None that he could see, but then he'd never had to interview a suspect who was pumping dumbbells before. She didn't give any sign of having heard him until she was replacing the dumbbells on the rack, and even then her question sounded casual, uninterested.

'How do you know?'

'I've been talking to her.'

She stood turned away from him, her head bent. 'Why are you telling me?'

He said sarcastically, 'I thought you might just be interested to know you've got around forty-eight hours before they start tearing the place apart for him. I wondered what your plans were.'

'Why should *I* have any plans?'

She moved away to where a line of barbells stood propped against the wall and chose one of thirty kilos. He didn't take his eyes off her as she carried it over to a bench and settled it on the stand. She sat on the bench, a leg on either side.

'Is that meant to imply I should be making plans?' he asked.

She stared at him, seeming surprised. He pressed the question. 'You're pretending to think I killed him, aren't you?'

Now she was definitely registering surprise, or a convincing show of it. It angered him, put him off balance.

'I didn't kill him.'

His voice sounded alarmingly loud in the bare room. Without answering she lay back on the bench and began lifting the weight, slowly but steadily up and down, exhaling sharply as she raised it. From where he was standing he couldn't see her face, only the long thighs and taut stomach muscles, and the arms moving like pistons. He walked over so that he was looking down at her and found her face quite calm, intent on the weight.

'Stop that and listen to me.'

He felt like grabbing at the barbell but, angry as he was, didn't want to risk dropping it on her face. The steady pistons didn't falter. Five times more, with him looking down at her, she raised and lowered the weight before letting it settle back on the stand. Even then she stayed horizontal, letting her arms flop down by the sides of the bench to the floor. It was a defenceless, vulnerable position that seemed to emphasize her nakedness but, as before, he felt it as less a sexual challenge than a sign of her mental defiance: a complete refusal to do what he or anybody else expected.

'I didn't kill Shunner,' he said, still angry, but more quietly. No answer. She had closed her eyes and was breathing slowly and deeply.

'We had an argument. That evening. I hit him . . . hit him on the head and he sort of keeled over . . . but not where the body was.' It didn't sound convincing even to him. He rushed on. 'About half a mile away from where the body was, and a lot earlier. But the point is, I didn't shoot him. I haven't even got a gun. Somebody else shot him, after I hit him.'

She said, eyes still closed, 'You don't have to convince me.'

'But I do have to convince the police? Is that what you're saying?'

'I'm not going to the police,' she said.

'But you're pretending to think I did it. You must know I didn't.'

She sat up, unhurriedly, and looked at him, her eyes guarded rather than hostile. 'One thing I do know is that you have a motive.' And she smiled when he couldn't hide his alarm.

'He went off with your wife, didn't he? And he ran rings round the police in court. And he lost you your job.'

In spite of the smile the tone wasn't gloating. It came over as a cool recital of facts, all the worse because she wasn't mocking or threatening him. He felt dazed, remote from the rest of the world, the way he'd felt just before he hit Shunner. The sharp outlines of the gym had ceased to exist except as a blurred background to her face that was saying these things and he could feel blood pumping through his veins, fuelling up for action, while his mind waited, frozen, incapable of controlling whatever was going to happen. He might have taken a step towards her, because there was a sudden look of alarm on her face.

'How did you know?'

But she didn't move, and her voice was level, 'That doesn't matter.'

Then she tilted backwards and began moving the weight up and down again as if nothing had happened. He watched it, hypnotized, counting, trying to bring his mind under control . . . eight up down, nine up down, ten up down . . . at twelve the rhythm faltered and the piston arms were visibly trembling. She let the bar fall back with a clatter on its rest and lay there, panting.

'Tired?' he asked. To his relief it came out as he'd intended, calm and sarcastic. 'You can usually do better than that, can't you? It must be all that lost sleep.'

109

No answer.

'You didn't get any sleep last night, did you?'

Her rib cage rose and fell.

'What were you doing last night?'

No answer.

'What were you doing last night?'

She sat up, a few strands of hair that had escaped from her pigtail hanging lank and sweat-soaked down her neck.

'That's got nothing to do with you.'

'Hasn't it? When a man's been murdered? When you're pretending you think I killed him? When you come climbing over a back fence at four in the morning?'

She pushed the hair back, staring at him.

'Another thing. You knew his name, didn't you? When I said Ralph Shunner was supposed to be in Paris you didn't have to ask who I was talking about, did you?'

'People have to register here, remember. Names in a book.'

He hadn't thought of that. It shook his confidence for a second, but by now he had the feeling that the initiative was his. 'That doesn't explain where you were last night. Or why you had to come in over a back fence. Or why you hid the body.'

'I thought you were hiding the body.'

She stood up and grasped the barbell, apparently intending to return it to its place by the wall but she was either more tired or more shaken than she pretended. She stumbled off balance under the weight and let it drop back on the supports with a crash.

'Here.' Automatically Birdie moved forward, steadied her with a hand round her waist, his other hand on the bar of the weight.

'Let me help.'

'I can do it.' She twisted away from him and automatically his arm slid across her stomach, straining to pull her towards him.

'Are you going to answer me?'

'Let me go.'

She pulled sideways, throwing all her weight away from him. With sweat oiling her smooth skin she was as slippery as a fish. He held on to her but stumbled and they fell side by side on the bench, legs locked together.

Before she could get up he grabbed her by the shoulders, brought his face close to hers, 'Did you kill him?'

The only answer he got was the chop of her forearm across his throat.

'You little . . .'

On a swift reflex he grabbed her wrist, his fingers meeting round it easily, then let it go again as the nails of her other hand raked down his neck. His grasp became a yowl of pain as one of her hard, bare feet slammed against his knee. The knee with cartilage trouble, as it happened. She was on her feet and moving off but he stood up on his good leg and grabbed hold of her again, fingers digging into the hollow below her collar bone, his other hand bending her right arm across her back.

'Did you kill him?' he heard himself repeating, again and again. 'Did you kill him?'

And somehow the pair of them were on their knees, panting and exhausted. He wasn't sure how she'd managed that. His whole head was a fog of fury and confusion and he couldn't even trust his physical reflexes any more.

'Did you kill him?'

It had become a whisper, almost a plea.

Her eyes were a few inches away from his. Her expression told him nothing.

'Did you?' she asked.

The tone was one of polite enquiry, and she didn't wait for an answer. Without any more attempt from him to restrain her she was on her feet, zipping herself into her tracksuit. She paused at the door.

'Switch the light off when you leave, would you.'

That night, the little sleep he got was broken by nightmares in which the body in the seaweed had become Nimue Hawthorne.

CHAPTER EIGHT

The next morning Clancy Whigg, photographer, was at last getting down to some of the work for which his holiday supplement editor would be paying him: a typical day in the life of the Village Zoe. And, with the luck of the idle, he'd chosen a good day for doing it. One of the big events in the Village Zoe week was the barbecue and dance, held on a space of paving stones at a point where the sand dunes flattened into beach. The holiday makers themselves were encouraged to collect driftwood for the fires, and he spent several hours photographing family groups at the tide line who looked as if they were acting out summer versions of Good King Wenceslas. He noticed that the big Englishman who'd taken over as a temporary instructor was supposed to be organizing the wood gathering, but since he looked like a man fighting with a king-size hangover, Clancy was careful to leave him out of the healthy holiday shots. When he'd shot several rolls of film he managed to time his arrival back at the barbecue place to coincide with the noon arrival of drinks for the workers: orange juice for the kids and white wine for the adults. Practically everybody else seemed to have the same idea, and several dozen people were sprawled on the paving stones or sitting at the cut-down wine barrels that served as chairs and tables. As he got his drink Clancy cast an appreciative eye over Nimue Hawthorne, helping one of the French boys to string coloured light bulbs from poles around the dancing space.

'Hello, my lovely. Can we have a talk about some of these pictures?' She told him she'd be with him in a few minutes and turned her attention back to the coloured lights. It occurred to Clancy that she looked a bit tired too and he wondered if she and the English bloke might both have caught hangovers in the same place. He downed a quick glass of wine, poured another, then started wandering around the fringes of the barbecue space, with the idea of photographing some people relaxing sociably over drinks. His eyes immediately focused on a largish group clustered at a convenient distance from the drinks containers, providing a contrast in shapes and textures that no photographer could resist: a large white woman who could have modelled for Rubens, a woman in her thirties, so thin that her stomach was practically concave, and two men, one brown and scoutmasterly, the other pale and inclined to plumpness. They were all sitting together on the sand, the large white woman sprawled at ease in a diagonal that perfectly united the other parts of the picture. It might come out a mite satirical for the travel piece, Clancy thought, but there were always the trade competitions to consider. He strolled closer, unobtrusively, so as not to disturb them. They were all people he'd met over the past couple of days – the solicitor, Pollins, and his nervy wife, the poker player, Joan, and her eager little beaver of a husband. Two of the Pollins children were visible in the background, hauling a huge log up from the sea. He thought he'd try and get them in the picture. But, as he got closer, he found that it wasn't the relaxed holiday group he'd thought. In fact, a right royal row seemed to be brewing up between two of the characters. Clancy liked rows, as long as they were other people's. He squatted down in the sand a few yards off and, almost casually, took photographs as he listened. The thin woman was doing most of the talking.

'. . . plenty of time to get there and back this evening. We can't go home without seeing it.'

Peter Pollins shifted uneasily in the sand. 'The twins want to swim this afternoon, and Philip says he's seen plenty of châteaux anyway.'

Alexander, the plump woman's husband, added helpfully: 'But it's not just any chateau. Marie Antoinette stayed there.'

'I tried that on Philip. He said "And look what happened to her".'

Vinny made an impatient noise. 'Philip's just being silly. And the twins have got to do a history project on it, so we've got to go.'

'What about tomorrow?' Peter Pollins' face was pink with sunburn, but little white worry lines ran across the forehead.

'You know we can't go tomorrow, Peter. It's the volleyball finals.'

'All go, isn't it?' said Joan, lazily. The remark seemed to be directed at nobody in particular but Vinny gave her a glare and the next attack on her husband was clearly intended to ricochet off Joan as well.

'I really don't understand you, Peter. You seem to have the time to stay out all night playing cards with goodness knows who, but you can't summon up the energy to take your own children out for the day.'

Peter Pollins opened his mouth to reply, but Joan, for all her laziness, got in first.

'If you mean me, dear, when you say "goodness knows who", you can stop harping on about it. He wasn't there.'

Peter's mouth, which had been hanging open, closed with a snap. Joan went on, without changing her relaxed position by as much as a fraction.

'We waited for him in the car park, but he didn't turn up so we went without him. We thought he must have urgent business elsewhere.' A raking glance from her down Vinny's modest contours, then she moved in for the kill.

'So whatever he was doing the night before last, don't blame us for it.'

Clancy was just too slow with his camera to capture the look which Vinny gave her husband. It would have been an award winner for certain. Peter Pollins, it was clear, now had to struggle out from something worse than a château. But, for the present, he was saved by the arrival of the twins and their soaking wet log.

'Do you think it came from America, Mum?'

'Or from a wrecked ship?'

Painstakingly, after one more sideways glare at Joan, Vinny began to explain the operations of Atlantic currents and Clancy decided that most of the fun was over for the moment. But, being a man who liked gossip, when he met Birdie Linnet at the wine table he gave him a vivid run-down on what he'd just heard. And considering that Birdie looked as if the hangover were getting worse rather than better, he was surprised and gratified by his interest.

'You mean . . .' said Birdie slowly, 'he wasn't playing cards?'

'That's what Joan said, and she should know?'

'And he can't have been with his wife . . .'

'No.'

'So where was he?'

'That,' said Clancy, 'is what he's going to have to do some fast thinking about. Ciao.' He'd seen Nimue sorting out electric plugs on top of one of the wine barrels and strayed over to her, pulling a crumpled brochure from the back pocket of his denims.

'Hi, doll. How goes?'

'Hi.'

So far he'd found her cool but not downright discouraging. He perched himself on the barrel.

'Got some great pics this morning.'

'Good.' She went on sorting plugs, and added, 'Remember, you'll have to get people's permission before using them.'

'Sure.' He squinted through his viewfinder towards the sea. 'What I need now is some of the more out of the way stuff. You know, something to make this place look different. I've been looking at the brochure.'

'That one's last year's,' said Nimue.

'Shouldn't think it makes much difference. Just getting a few ideas. What's this hydrotherapy for instance?'

'We've got a special little warm pool with underwater jets. A therapist comes in three times a week and gives treatment in it, for arthritis and so on.'

'Oh.' Underwater jets might have possibilities for pictures, elderly arthritics less so. He glanced at the brochure. 'What's this alginotherapy thing?' He read from the brochure, ' "Wrapped from head to foot in warmed, mineral-rich seaweed, let all your tensions drift away." Sounds great.' He'd seen several girls around who'd look pretty photogenic in a few wisps of warmed, mineral-rich seaweed.

'It was a bit of a gimmick,' said Nimue. 'We're not doing it this year.'

'Pity.'

He read from the brochure again, his voice carrying over yards. ' ". . . a tonic for the skin and an aid to good circulation. The properties of seaweed were probably known to the ancient Romans as . . ." ' He broke off. 'Hi again.'

Birdie Linnet had suddenly added himself to the party.

'What's going on?'

There was such an edge to Birdie's voice that Clancy felt pretty well convinced he'd been off rioting somewhere with Nimue the night before. And Clancy had no intention of getting into a fight over any girl with a man of Birdie's size and muscle power, even if he did look several degrees under at the moment. He was conciliatory.

115

'Just discussing a few picture ideas with Nimue. There's this seaweed thing.'

'Last year's seaweed thing,' said Nimue.

Birdie was staring at her with an intensity that confirmed Clancy's guess about their relationship.

'Couldn't we revive it?' Clancy asked. 'Just for a pic or two?'

'There wouldn't be much point if people can't get it any more.'

'It might start a trend. People coming from all over the place to wrap themselves in your seaweed.'

'No,' said Nimue.

Clancy gave an exasperated sigh, but returned to the brochure. 'You still do yoga? People standing on their heads and things?'

A little more chat and he went away, leaving Birdie and Nimue alone together.

'He knows,' said Birdie.

'Don't be silly.'

'He must know. Coming up and talking about seaweed.' There were great drops of sweat on his face and chest.

'It came up quite naturally. He'd just got hold of last year's brochure.'

'He's a journalist. He'll be rooting around everywhere.'

'Well?'

'Now he's got seaweed in his head . . .'

'He's got practically nothing in his head for more than five minutes at a time.'

'You don't seem to realize, we've got to . . .'

'*We* haven't got to do anything.' She raised her voice. '*René, le tournevis, s'il vous plaît.*' And the boy was at her side in seconds. She started what sounded like a highly technical discussion with him in French about the electric wiring. Birdie stood and glared at them both for several minutes, then walked away, heavy footed, not looking where he was going, and almost trod on a plump, white calf.

'Mind me.' It was Joan. The rest of the party seemed to have deserted her, but she was still stretched out peacefully on the sand with a half full wine bottle propped in the shade of her beach bag.

'You *were* deep in thought. Sit down and have a drink.'

Dragging his mind back with difficulty from the problem of the seaweed he remembered that there were things he wanted to ask Joan – or should want to ask her if he were an efficient investigator and not just a man in a panic. He accepted her invitation and sat

116

down beside her as she poured wine into a glass.

'Somebody's already drunk from it, but we're all so bloody healthy round here I shouldn't think it matters. Cheers.'

'Cheers.'

They drank, and Birdie said, 'I gather there's been a bit of a row.'

She didn't seem in the least surprised by his interest. 'Yes, silly little bitch. She bloody near accused me of stealing her husband. I mean, married to that walking spare rib you wouldn't blame him if he fancied a cut off another joint. But it wasn't this joint.' She stretched her succulent body lazily, but Birdie was too worried to wonder if he were being shown the menu.

He asked, 'Was it true he wasn't playing poker with you?'

'Of course it was. There were supposed to be six of us going and we waited for him, but when he didn't turn up we just assumed she'd slapped the veto on it. So off we went.'

'You didn't stay in the camp, then?'

'No, of course not. That was the whole point – get out of this awful healthy atmosphere for a bit and go somewhere where you could let your hair down.'

'So where did you go?'

'Well, we had nowhere particular in mind. We just drove round the side roads for a bit, then we came to this little Routier place, you know, the sort of place long-distance lorry drivers use.'

'And you went in there?'

'Of course. Just what we wanted. Really friendly proprietor, lovely fug of cigarette smoke, couple of fruit machines. You'd have thought you were on a different planet from this place. And it stayed open all night.'

'Did you stay all night?'

She took another long sip of wine. 'Pretty nearly. It was after half past two when we threw ourselves out, and that was because a couple of them were falling asleep at the table.'

'And Peter Pollins didn't join you? Not at any time?'

For the first time she seemed surprised at his questioning. 'Of course not. He didn't even know where we were.' She pointed back towards the area of paving stones. 'Ask her, if you don't believe me.'

He followed the direction of her arm and saw Nimue, back on top of a stepladder, which the boy René was holding.

'Ask who?'

'Her nibs. Queen bee. Nimue whatsername.'

'How would she know?'

'She was there.'

He stared at her, wrinkling his forehead, trying to concentrate. 'Where?'

She sighed. 'You're not drunk already, are you?'

'No, it's just that I'm not clear what you're telling me. You're saying that Peter Pollins wasn't at this Routier place, but Nimue was?'

She nodded.

'She went with you? To play poker?'

Joan shook her head. 'Of course not. You can't imagine her in a poker school can you? She was nothing to do with our party. We found her there when we got there.'

'What time was this?'

'About nine o'clock. There she was, already sitting at a table in the corner with half a dozen lorry drivers. She must have got quite a shock when we all trooped in.'

'Lorry drivers?'

'They were all lorry drivers in there, except us.'

'Did she say anything to you?'

'She sort of waved. You know, the way you do when you want somebody to know you've seen them but don't want them to come over and talk. Like this.' Joan raised a hand from the wrist, and let it drop.

'And we just said hello and got on with the game. I mean, I suppose she's entitled to time off like everybody else, and it's her affair where she spends it.'

'Did she look embarrassed?'

'Well, it's hard to tell with her, but I suppose she must have been. I mean, it hardly fits in with the healthy image does it? All that bending and stretching and fresh air.'

'How long did she stay there?'

'I don't know. She was still there when we left.'

'After half past two?'

'That's right.' Joan looked at him closely over the rim of the glass. It had clearly occurred to her by now that his interest was more than casual, and she was storing up some questions of her own.

'With the same men?'

Joan paused and considered carefully. 'No, I don't think so. I

118

mean, we weren't watching them all the time, but I was naturally interested. And there was quite a lot of coming and going, especially up to midnight.'

'What were they talking about?'

She looked at him pityingly. 'They were rattling away in French. Her too.'

'Did they seem, well . . . tense?'

'Anything but. There was a lot of laughing, and as far as I could see she was telling jokes and so on with the best of them. And quite a bit of drinking. I'm surprised some of them could get back up into their cabs.'

'Did she . . . go out at any time? Go out and come back in again, I mean?'

Another pitying look, and a pause. Then Joan said, more quietly, 'Is what you're asking: could she have gone out and had it off with some of them in their cabs?'

He hesitated, then plunged in. 'Yes, I suppose it is.' Was that any better, he wondered, than asking if she could have gone out and shot a man dead?

Joan said carefully, 'I suppose the answer is, yes she could. I mean, we were looking at the cards most of the time. And, as I've said, there was quite a lot of coming and going.' Another pause, then, 'But I'm not saying she did, I mean, she could have just been practising her French, couldn't she?'

'Yes . . . Yes, I suppose she could.'

Birdie gazed into an empty wine glass and felt one of Joan's large soft hands descending on his shoulder. 'I'm not asking why you're interested.'

'Thanks.'

'But I'd be careful, if I were you. She looks to me like a girl that knows her way round, that one.'

He thought of Nimue with her hands tucked under the armpits of the corpse. 'You may be right.'

The hand removed itself as Joan rolled over to watch what was happening on the beach. From the sea edge there was laughter and screaming as a group of teenagers played in the surf, diving, ducking, standing on each other's shoulders. Clancy, camera at the ready, was the centre of attraction.

'He's enjoying himself, anyway,' said Joan. 'I wonder what's happened to the blue film girl.'

'The what?'

119

Birdie had been sunk in thought at what she'd told him so far, but he was beginning to realize that Joan, as a source of gossip, was more easily started than stopped. Her air of total laziness went with a very keen eye on what was going on round her.

'You know, little Melanie, the one from the telly series. She was all over that photographer the other day.'

'I know.'

Birdie decided not to tell Joan about the photographic session at the swimming pool, but he was still curious.

'Why do you call her the blue film girl?'

'Oh, you weren't there, were you? There was another right little dust up at the café two days ago. That man with the nice eyes . . . Ralph . . . Ralph Shunner – it turned out that he'd known her from years back and he as good as said she'd been making pornographic pictures. And she didn't deny it, just turned on her heel and walked away.'

Birdie swallowed hard. His heart hammered at his ribs from the moment Shunner's name was mentioned, and it was a struggle to make his voice sound casual.

'He really had known her? He wasn't just trying to be funny.'

'No, he was talking about when she worked in one of his wine bars, before she went into films.'

Birdie felt his head swimming from all the new possibilities that were being pumped into it. From having too little information he was now getting too much, and couldn't see how it all pieced together. If Joan was right – and he couldn't see what motive she might have for lying – the girl Melanie could have had a very substantial grudge against Shunner; could reasonably see him as a threat to a flourishing television career. And now Shunner was dead, and Melanie seemed to have gone off somewhere.

He said, 'Her manager was looking for her yesterday.'

She nodded. 'He was really getting his Y-fronts in a twist, wasn't he? I told him I hadn't seen Ralph Shunner all day either, and perhaps they'd gone off somewhere together to discuss the film industry. If looks could have killed . . .' She chuckled, and Birdie did his best to join in, although unconvincingly. He wondered if anyone else beside the sharp-eyed Joan had noticed Shunner's absence already.

'I think he's gone to Paris,' he said.

'So I hear.'

At that point there was an outcry of screaming and shouting

from the water's edge that made even Joan sit upright and had Birdie on his feet in a split second. The teenagers who'd been giggling and shouting were this time seriously alarmed by something, and there was no sign of Clancy.

'Bloody hell, there's somebody in trouble.'

Birdie could just make out, over a distance of thirty yards or so, that somebody was down and threshing in the surf. His lifesaver's instincts taking over, he sprinted down the beach and was just in time to see Clancy rising from the waves, spitting salt and fury, his denims dark with sea water and the camera still slung round his neck.

'You silly bitch. Look what you've done.' He was waving the camera in a threatening way at the woman who stood beside him, up to her knees in water: Nimue Hawthorne.

'You shouldn't have crept up on me like that. It's your own fault.'

'What's happening?' Old habits die hard, and Birdie's question came out in policeman-like tones. They both turned to him and Clancy spoke first.

'I was just trying to get some pictures and she comes rushing at me and cannons into me like some fucking demented hammerhead shark and before I know where I am I'm flat in the bloody water with my camera round my neck.'

Nimue said, 'I hadn't told him he could take pictures of me. I was just going in for a quick swim and I turned round, and there he was, practically treading on me.'

'Is there any damage done?'

'There is to my bloody camera. I'll have to get it stripped down before the salt starts eating away at it, if it hasn't started already. And the film's ruined, of course. God knows what she thought she was doing.'

'God knows what you thought you were doing. There are enough people to photograph round here without following me around.' She was angrier and more disturbed than Birdie had ever seen her.

'Anyway,' said Clancy. 'I've got her placed now.' He turned to Birdie. 'You know I said I'd seen her somewhere before? Well, I've just remembered where.' Then back to Nimue, 'And you didn't want to be photographed that time either, did you, sweetie? Was that the trouble? Brought back old memories?'

And she just looked at him and walked off without another word to either him or Birdie. The two men watched as she strode up the beach back to the barbecue place. The teenagers, sensing the drama was over, moved away.

Birdie asked, 'What was all that about?'

Clancy chuckled. The retreat of Nimue seemed to have brought back at least some of his good humour, although he was still clutching the camera to him protectively.

'You heard me. The reason why she didn't want to be photographed was because she remembered the last time. I didn't, till I saw her get mad like that. She got mad the last time too. She was about two stone heavier then as well.'

Birdie asked, 'Where was the last time?'

Clancy looked him up and down. 'Where d'you think? In prison.'

A silence. Clancy went on staring at him.

'Are you sure?'

'Of course I'm sure. It was spring last year. I was doing this piece for the *Observer* on a new women's open prison. The Home Office had said I could take pictures of the women in the workshops, back view or silhouette only, and only if they agreed to it. She didn't. Most of them were quite happy to see a new bloke, but she wasn't having anything to do with me.'

The tide was coming in, splashing up above their knees. Clancy stepped to dry land and Birdie followed him.

'So that's it,' said Clancy. 'But she needn't have pushed me in the water. I'd have kept quiet about her secret past otherwise. As it is . . .' He shrugged. 'Still, she's got herself together pretty quick. Better than most do.' He gave the camera a gentle shake, and drops of water fell from it.

'It's had worse than this, I suppose. Like the time I dropped it in the Ganges. But I'd better get it on the operating table. Ciao.'

Birdie deserted the beach. There were probably half a dozen things he should have been doing for the barbecue, but they'd have to wait. The urgency was to find somewhere quiet and sort out the mass of information that was dinning around in his head – dinning all the more loudly because of his feeling that time was running out. With the photographer showing an inconvenient interest in alginotherapy, Shunner's resting place seemed nowhere near as snug as it had been an hour or so ago, however calmly Nimue might treat it. It looked as if he'd have to deal with that problem on his own. And the hours were ticking away – perhaps less that forty of them to go now – to when Shunner's return from Paris would be so much overdue that Olivia would start pressing panic buttons. If the body were discovered, or Shunner missed with things still in their present state, he remained the prime suspect. He was becoming resigned, or numbed, to the idea of a grilling from the French police, but he couldn't face it without some ammunition to defend himself, and that meant producing some convincing theories of his own as to who had put a bullet through Shunner's head. The problem was that after what he'd learned that morning there were four possibilities, but all with some arguments against them. He found a large pine log in a clearing some way behind the sand dunes, sat down and considered.

The nervous solicitor, Peter Pollins. If Joan were to be believed, nobody knew where he was on the night Shunner was killed. And the photographer's account of the quarrel he'd overheard bore out everything Joan had said. Peter Pollins, unexpectedly, had not been with the poker school. Disastrously for domestic harmony, he had spent most of the night away from his wife, and the strangest thing was – from both Joan's and Clancy's accounts – Pollins seemed to have given no excuse for his absences. This was what puzzled Birdie most, because even on his slight acquaintance with the Pollins menage, he'd got Peter tagged as a man thoroughly cowed by domesticity. Yet in being out all night he'd committed an offence that would have had many tougher husbands frothing over with excuses and, apparently, he was staying obstinately silent. That, in Birdie's book must give Peter Pollins a place on the shortlist of suspects. The big disadvantage in drawing up a case of murder against him was the apparent lack of motive. As far as Birdie knew, there'd been no contact between him and Shunner before they came to the village Zoe, and only of the most fleeting social kind after that. But Pollins was a solicitor, and Shunner, at various points in his career, had spent quite a lot of time with lawyers.

Then there was the girl, Melanie McBride. Thanks to Jedd's rampagings, it was current knowledge around the camp that she'd disappeared without trace the night before last – the night of Shunner's death. Birdie had made nothing of it, mainly because it seemed unlikely that a girl so dim she couldn't walk off a springboard without help could procure a gun and shoot a man through the head. Also, there seemed to be no motive. But Joan's gossip had changed that. If Joan was to be believed – and it would be possible to check this from other people who'd been at the café – Shunner had teased the girl with hints about a past in pornographic films. One of the things Birdie knew about Melanie, since their conversation by the pool, was that her dim little mind was full of career ambitions. Was it possible that, if she'd seen these threatened, she'd have become efficient enough to commit murder? He doubted it – but where was Melanie?

But his mind refused to picture Melanie shooting Shunner and turned, almost against its will, to a very different woman. A woman efficient almost to a fault, physically strong, so lacking in squeamishness that she could lump a body through the sand dunes when his own nerve was almost failing him. A woman who, as he'd just learned, had spent a recent spell in prison. That, of all the things he'd learned on the beach, was the thing which rocked him most. He'd considered and rejected the possibility that Clancy might simply have been lying about it in revenge for the ducking Nimue gave him. He thought the photographer was a bit of a fool, but an easy-natured man. And not such a fool either that he'd spread a slanderous story which could easily be disproved if untrue. So Nimue, as recently as the spring of the previous year, had been serving a spell in prison. What for? Clancy wouldn't know that. An open prison suggested some non-violent offence, like fraud, for instance. But it could also be a preparation for life outside for a prisoner who'd already served a long term for a more serious crime. Like murder. Birdie did sums in his head. He didn't think Nimue could be much older than twenty-seven or twenty-eight, and surely if she'd been found guilty of murder she'd have done at least seven years inside. If she'd killed somebody at nineteen, say, and Shunner had known about it. . . ? It fitted, he thought, it fitted well. And yet, what didn't fit so well was a piece of Joan's gossip. By her account Nimue must have spent the hours between nine p.m. and after two thirty a.m. on the night of the murder chatting (and what else?) to lorry drivers in a beat-up little transport café. And Shunner's body was already cold when Birdie discovered it at four. But how far away was this transport café? Joan had agreed that she hadn't kept her eyes on Nimue all the time and suggested that she could have been popping out for quickies in lorry drivers' cabs. Would Joan and the others have noticed if Nimue had been gone long enough to kill Shunner? It depended partly on whether the café was within easy distance of the Village Zoe, and he was angry with himself for not getting more details from Joan. At least the checking of alibis should be work he understood.

And then, thinking of alibis, what was he to make of James Jedd? The man seemed to crop up somewhere whichever way he turned, and always with sinister implications. And, on the night Shunner died, Jedd and his gorilla-like minder, Don, seemed to have been ranging around everywhere looking for Melanie. It had been after one o'clock in the morning, for instance, by Jedd's own account, when he'd gone to Clancy Whigg's chalet – and found the photographer not at home. Supposing in the course of the search he'd found Shunner in the dunes, still groggy from the effects of Birdie's blow and, suspecting him of enticing Melanie, killed him? And if Melanie could be believed, Jedd was a violent man – had even broken an instructor's ankle in the short time he'd been at the Village Zoe. Having seen more of Jedd since the conversation at the pool, Birdie was a little less sceptical about the girl's story. But, if Jedd had shot Shunner, and on a very sketchy motive, why was he drawing attention to himself by making such a pother about looking for Melanie?

Birdie shifted his position on the log and scratched a calf, where a mosquito or some such had been feasting. At least some programme for action seemed to be developing: question Pollins, check the Melanie blue films angle, check the position of the transport café, question Jedd and have a long, serious talk with Nimue Hawthorne. After some thought, he decided to put the questioning of Jedd at the head of the list, on the grounds that he knew less about him than any of the others. He'd approach it by the Melanie angle. If he too were to pretend concern about the girl, perhaps even offer Jedd some manufactured clue to her where-abouts, it might be the quickest way to get the man to open up. Or, if Jedd really knew where she was all the time, make him snap shut like a menaced oyster. Either way, he'd learn something. Stopping occasionally to scratch various bites, Birdie made his way towards the centre of the camp and, after casting around for a while, located his man standing by the map near the main shopping centre.

Instead of walking up to Jedd immediately, Birdie waited in the shade of a clump of tamarisks a few dozen yards off. The man seemed intent, running his finger over the map. After a few minutes he apparently found what he was looking for somewhere on the outskirts of the plan and set off briskly. Birdie decided to follow him and observe for a while, without making himself known. Jedd's preoccupation with the map suggested that he was still on the Melanie hunt and it might be instructive to find out where that was leading him. For a few hundred yards, as Jedd marched along seawards, Birdie went hot and cold with the idea that he might be making for the alginotherapy building, but to his relief the man turned off to the right along one of the broad sandy drives between caravan pitches. There were fewer people in this part of the camp, and Birdie had to fall back quite a long way so as not to alert Jedd that he was being followed. Not that he'd given any sign of it so far, swinging along in the heat with the air of a man on the way to an urgent business appointment.

At the next bend Birdie lost him. The main drive swung inland and back towards the centre of the camp, with a slightly narrower branch, still just negotiable for cars, branching left towards the dunes. Reasoning that whatever Jedd had found on the plan was on the outskirts of the camp, Birdie took the left-hand branch and found himself in disturbingly familiar territory. It was the little area of sand and scrubland, with places for about half a dozen cars and tents, that he'd come to know so well during his first few hours in the camp, when he'd sat hunched on the dune above it, looking down at the tent which housed Olivia and Deborah and Shunner. The green Jaguar was still there by their tent, which gave him a shock. Surely its presence cried aloud to everybody that Shunner could not after all have gone to Paris? Then he thought that Olivia, who loved driving, might have insisted it should be left with her anyway. Which might mean Shunner was the customer who didn't turn up for his hired car. And where was Jedd? Assuming that he had come down the left-hand path, there weren't many places for him to be. The camping area was a cul de sac, ending in scrub, and there were only three tents standing on it, well spaced out. The one at the far end was full of laughing and shouting kids, the middle one a brown ridge tent, zipped up and silent, the third one – Olivia's. He stood indecisively for several minutes, watching it, but from that angle he couldn't see whether the front flap was open or closed. Then he caught a voice, Olivia's voice. He couldn't catch the words, but it sounded scared and angry. He covered the next few yards of sand at a bound and crouched beside a bush of giant heather at the end of one of the tent's guy ropes.

Olivia's voice again, '. . . got no right to come and talk to me like that. I've told you: get out.'

126

To his amazement it sounded tearful as well as angry. He had to fight an impulse to dash inside the tent at once, from an old habit of protectiveness.

Then Jedd's voice, lower, 'I don't know why you're getting so angry. It's a reasonable enough question in the circumstances.'

'It is *not* a reasonable question in any circumstances. Go away.'

And Jedd's voice again, level as ever, 'I don't understand your attitude. I've got a right to ask.'

Birdie, trying to catch up with what was happening, mentally cursed Joan's gossip. The woman should have realized she was playing with fire, putting ideas into Jedd's head. There was an angry, distressed noise from Olivia, sounding so close to Birdie that she must have been standing almost inches from the tent canvas.

'I don't have to stand here and take this.' And suddenly there she was, out in the sunlight and in Birdie's line of vision. She ran a few steps and there was Jedd too, with a hand on her elbow. Instantly Birdie was moving.

'Don't take it like this,' said Jedd. 'Can't we . . .'

'Leave me alone.'

His grip tightened on her elbow as she tried to pull herself free.

'Let her go,' yelled Birdie. He was on to Jedd in a bound, grabbed him by the shoulder, forcing him to release his hold on Olivia. She spun round and, for a second, looked into Birdie's face with an expression of horror and panic still frozen there from Jedd's attack. Then, before he could say anything, she swung away from both of them and threw herself into the driving seat of the Jaguar, slamming the door. Birdie let go of Jedd's shoulder and rushed round the front of the car.

'Olivia, it's all right. I won't let him touch you.'

Her face was pale and unresponsive. She fumbled in the pouch of her fisherman's smock for the ignition key, found it and switched on the engine.

'Olivia, for goodness' sake . . .'

He tried to open the driver's door but she locked it. The car began to move.

'Don't go dashing off.'

He leant on the bonnet, looking up at her set face. The car began to move forward and he had to throw himself sideways. It was slowed almost to a walking pace by the soft sand but she raced the engine recklessly. The wheels gripped and it began to move faster. Jedd was still standing where Birdie had left him, face blank, flanked by a line of open-mouthed children from the end tent.

Birdie yelled at him, 'You bloody fool. What are you trying to do to her?' then set off at a run in pursuit of the Jaguar.

Instead of taking the track to the main drive she was following a narrower path between scrub and sand dunes. It was a route nobody who wasn't severely panicked would ever have tried to negotiate in a large car, and even the Jaguar couldn't take it at much faster than ten miles an hour, with the engine labouring horribly. Birdie padded along behind, occasionally shouting to her to stop. He was desperately concerned about what she might do in this mood, and although the impulse to hold on to James Jedd and twist his neck round had been strong, the first necessity was to see that no harm came to Olivia. Even as he ran, he wondered how this protective instinct could still be so strong, after all that had happened.

'Olivia, stop.'

But luck didn't seem to be on his side. The path became wider and firmer and the car gathered speed. Ahead he could see a broad, sandy space where it joined one of the main drives. It must be this she was making for, and after that goodness knows where. In this uncharacteristic panic she shouldn't be on the public roads. He sprinted full out, but the gap between him and the back of the Jaguar widened. It had almost reached the sandy space.

'Stop. Stop, Olivia.'

And she did stop, but not because of him. The Jaguar's wheels hit a soft patch, a low cushion of wind-heaped sand that halted the big car as effectively as wet concrete. The engine protested and the car dragged forward an inch or two, then settled, its back wheels immobilized and half covered by sand. By the time Birdie got there she had switched off the engine and was out, trying to push, straining against the rear bumper.

'It's no good. You won't shift it like that.'

She looked up at him, face pale and sweating, wisps of hair flopping round her cheeks.

'I'll help you. But just cool it for now.'

She said, 'I had to get away from him.'

'It's all right. He's not here.'

'He's mad.'

'I know.'

128

She took a deep breath and he saw that she was shivering, either from fear of Jedd or the effort to shift the car.

'Just come and sit down for a bit.'

'But I've got to get it out.'

'Come and sit down first.'

He led her round to the driver's door, noticing that she made no attempt to remove his hand from her arm. When he'd got her settled in the driving seat he left the door open and crouched beside her on the sand. 'That's better. Just take a few deep breaths.'

Obediently she closed her eyes and breathed deeply for a minute or so, then, 'I'm sorry.'

'You don't need to be. The man's a bloody public menace.'

'He was asking me where Ralph had gone. He . . . he seemed to think I should be able to produce him, just like that.'

'What did you tell him?'

'That Ralph had gone to Paris, of course. That's all I could tell him. He just kept on at me.' She leaned back against the leather upholstery.

Birdie, still thinking hard thoughts about Joan, said, 'He's looking for his girl, that Melanie. I think some fool suggested to him that she might have gone off with Shunner.'

A sudden creak of leather as she sat bolt upright on the seat. Her eyes were wide and her face full of alarm. It was obviously a new idea to her, and one that she was taking more seriously than he expected.

He said, feeling guilty, 'It was somebody's idea of a joke. She should have realized it wasn't safe to make jokes to a man like that.'

But she was still full of tension, her eyes fixed on his face, not seeing him. He thought suddenly, 'It's not a joke to her. She's wondering now if he and the girl really have gone off together.' It should have been revenge for him – to know that this woman who'd hurt him so much was now facing some of the same bitterness herself, facing the thought that the man she'd gambled on was now galloping off on a different course. Instead, he felt wretchedly guilty, knowing that he could put her out of her misery. Quite a simple matter, it would be: no, your lover's not unfaithful, at least not as far as I know. You see, he's dead. And he thought, staring into her blank eyes, 'If I were to say that now, she'd be relieved first and only sorry afterwards.' Instead he said lamely, 'I'm sure he hasn't gone off with her. This man Jedd's just not sane where she's concerned.'

'Of course he hasn't.' She must have sensed the pity for her in his voice, because some of her pride was coming back, but there was still a haunted look in her eyes, a look he knew would stay there.

She said, 'The whole thing's so silly. I was just scared of him, alone there.'

'I'll warn him off.'

'No, I can manage.' She began tucking stray hairs into the knot at the back of her neck, looking away from him.

He said, trying to make his voice casual, 'Do you know when Shunner will be back?'

'He doesn't know himself.'

Pride again. She wasn't telling a downright lie, but was managing to imply that she'd spoken on the phone to Shunner recently, keeping up appearances. And he realized how completely a trap of misery was closing round her. From her point of view, her lover had left for Paris nearly two days before, and in that time she hadn't heard from him. And then comes Jedd looking for him, almost insane with anger, then her ex-husband with a piece of idle gossip coupling him with a particularly exotic blonde. If Birdie had actually planned to make Olivia miserable, he could hardly have done it more thoroughly. He felt as guilty as if he really had killed Shunner. After all, he'd wished the man dead, stunned him and buried him. And if he'd fired the shot that killed him it would have been to bring about a result much like this one: Shunner dead and rotting and Olivia with eyes that would stay haunted. Now he'd got it, and he didn't want it at all.

'Where's Debbie?'

'Tennis, of course. I'd promised to drive her into the village later.'

'He left the car with you, then?'

'Yes, he said he'd hire one. Jedd wanted to know that.'

'What else did he want to know?'

She shivered. 'All sorts of things. Mad, most of them.' Birdie said nothing, because his mind was escaping on a track away from Olivia's unhappiness. There was something which should follow logically from all this, and that was the relegation of Jedd to a low point on his list of suspects. If the bullying of Olivia proved anything, it was that James Jedd still believed Shunner to be alive – not only alive but lecherous. And unless the man were entirely insane, that was incompatible with the idea that he'd put a bullet through Shunner's head about thirty-six hours before.

'It's started raining,' Olivia said. 'I've got to get the car out.'

He realized that dark clouds, coming from the sea, had covered the sun and the first heavy drops were splodging the sand round him.

'Right. You switch on, I'll give her a push.'

Ten soaking minutes later he admitted, 'This isn't doing any good. We'll have to tow her out.'

'With your bike?'

Almost an affectionate tone from her. Their joint struggle with the recalcitrant car and sand had, just for the moment, submerged some of the bitterness between them.

'No. A tractor.'

'Where from?'

'There's a beat-up little machine they use for carting the camp dustbins around. I'll borrow it. Why don't you go and sit in the cafe and I'll let you know when I've got it out.'

'Thanks.' But she didn't move from the driver's seat.

'Why don't you get in here for a minute. I want to ask you something.' He was puzzled, then almost scared. Which way was her mind working?

'Come on,' she said. 'You'll get wet.'

He walked round and settled in the seat beside her. Rain fell steadily on the roof, isolating them in a sort of igloo of wetness.

She said, looking straight ahead, 'It's about you and Ralph.'

'What about us?'

Silence for a moment, then, 'When you followed us here, what were you doing?'

'I told you, I was worried about Debbie. I just couldn't stand the thought of her going abroad with him and me not being able to do anything.'

'And that was all?'

'All!'

'I'm sorry, I didn't mean it that way. I mean, there was no other reason? No professional reason?'

'Professional?'

No reaction from her.

'What do you mean, "professional"?'

She spoke slowly, almost apologetically, 'I mean, it wasn't police business? You weren't still . . . trailing him?'

He exploded, 'Fucking hell, we're not on that tack again, are we? You know I've stopped being a policeman, and you know damned

131

well why.'

'They say once a policeman . . .'

'Well, it's bloody well not true. As far as I'm concerned he could buy up all the poppies in Thailand and put them in kids' breakfast crunchies. As long as it's not my kid's. I've been there before, remember?'

Silence, then, 'I'm sorry. I had to ask.'

'Well, you got your answer.'

The intimacy of the igloo was broken. Her question had tapped such a well of anger that he'd even forgotten for a few seconds that Shunner was dead. It alarmed him and reminded him what a dangerous path he was walking.

'I'm going to get the tractor. You needn't wait.' He slammed the passenger door and began trudging through the rain, feeling her eyes on him through the car windscreen.

CHAPTER NINE

It was well into the afternoon before Birdie could begin looking for the café Routier. Dragging Olivia's car out of the sand had gone well enough, but after that he'd found another use for the battered little tractor and its trailer. It had meant a lurching journey to the seaweed building when most of the camp was enjoying its after-lunch siesta and a few minutes which he tried hard not to think about, though the seaweed smell clung to his hands and his clothes. Even then, it was only a temporary solution but enough, he hoped, to keep Clancy the photographer out of the picture. By the time that task was finished and he was free to hunt for the poker school's café the sun was blazing again, drawing up smells of pine resin and warm damp earth, bringing insects out to buzz and bite. After a few miles of it, he'd have welcomed the rain again. The bicycle he'd borrowed from the camp handyman was an ancient and sullen model apparently made from cast iron, with a repertoire of at least half a dozen different creaks, squeaks and rattles from pedals, chain and its remaining half mudguard, and a cracked leather saddle that had begun punishing his buttocks before he was even out of the camp drive. He ached, literally, for the comfort of his own bike, and supposed he was doing penance for his vandalism against it. What was worse, Joan had been pretty vague when he'd asked her for directions to the café. She hadn't really noticed, she told him. Somebody else was driving, and beyond a general idea that they'd started travelling south on the main road, then turned off somewhere and back on to another main road, she couldn't help him much. Except that there'd been a big motel by the first turning, and the café place was a white bungalow in a big parking space. She didn't ask him why he was so eager to find it, though he had an idea she'd be demanding an explanation sooner or later.

He found the motel easily enough, about seven or eight miles down the road from the camp, and turned left with a squealing of brake blocks into a narrow country road between two vineyards. The signposts from there on pointed not to any towns or villages but to wine-growing châteaux, mostly solid country houses of red brick rising like islands in a sea of vines that rippled gently towards the horizon. For half hour or so Birdie pedalled gently among the roads that parted this solid green sea, trying to visualize where Joan and her poker school might have turned. Then the sound of traffic and the sight of an occasional lorry above the vines told him that he was on the right track. He turned northwards at the main road, back in the direction of the Village Zoe, and hadn't gone more than a mile along it before he saw what he was looking for on the opposite side of the road: a low, white building, freshly painted, with a Routier sign at the door and a couple of trailers, almost as big as the café itself, parked alongside. He laid the bike flat in the shade of an outhouse, in case the sun should finally perish its ancient tyres, and walked in.

It was shady inside, and almost empty. The driver of one of the trailers was eating what looked like a very good omelette, and the other was zapping away at a Space Invaders machine. The proprietor, a small man with a face as leathery and creased as the old bike's saddle, was wiping down the counter. The smell and sight of the omelette had reminded Birdie that he hadn't eaten properly for days, and anyway, it seemed politic to order something before asking questions. In careful French he asked for an omelette and a demi-pichet of white, and sat down at a table close to the counter so that he could talk to the proprietor while eating and drinking. The omelette arrived, light and sizzling. Would the proprietor, Birdie asked carefully, care to take a drink with him? The man thanked him and poured himself a small glass from a bottle behind the counter.

'*A votre santé*,' said Birdie.

'Cheers,' said the proprietor.

'*Vous parlez anglais?*'

'I worked for three years in Australia. Showing them how to make wine.'

Birdie celebrated with another large gulp of his white wine. He hadn't been looking forward to conducting a delicate interview with the help of a French pocket dictionary. A little more chat about Australia, a compliment about the omelette, and he plunged in. 'Some friends of mine told me this was a good place. From the

Village Zoe.'

The proprietor nodded.

'They were in here two nights ago, playing cards till morning,' Birdie said.

A smile creased the proprietor's face even more thoroughly, suggesting that Joan and her poker school had been good customers.

'I think the fat woman won a lot of money off them,' he said.

'She would.'

They both smiled and drank.

'And the woman who runs the Village Zoe,' Birdie pressed on. 'She was here too.'

The proprietor looked thoughtful for a moment. 'The woman with her hair in a. . . ?' He lost the word and sketched out a plaiting motion with his hands.

'That's the one. Speaks good French.'

'And she is head at the Village Zoe?' There was doubt in his voice.

Birdie asked, 'You're surprised?'

'No, but . . .' The man spoke hesitantly. 'But if she is head at the Village Zoe I am surprised she is going away when the busy season here is just beginning.'

'Going away?' Birdie tried not to look too surprised. The proprietor shrugged.

'Perhaps it was a *blague* . . . a joke.'

'She talked to you about going away?'

The proprietor nodded. 'She came in here and asked me if I knew of any drivers who would be travelling to Marseilles that night. I told her that I didn't know of any, but if she wanted to wait, there might be somebody coming in. So she bought a drink and waited.'

'Why did she want to go?'

Another shrug.

'And she was unlucky?'

'It seems so. It happened that it was a night when most people were going north. Sometimes it's like that.'

'You often get that then? People who come in here hoping for a lift?'

'Not often. Some students sometimes, in the wine-picking season.'

'So you were surprised when she came in trying to get a lift?'

135

The proprietor was beginning to look a bit restive at the questioning, so Birdie ordered a coffee and Calvados. When he brought them to the table, he answered Birdie's question.

'Not quite surprised. But she didn't look like a student. She looked like somebody who could afford the fare to Marseilles if she wanted to go there.'

He looked sideways at Birdie. 'You are interested in this girl?'

He, like Joan, seemed to be classifying Birdie as Nimue's jealous lover. Resignedly, Birdie accepted that it was as good a cover as any.

'Yes, I'm interested in her.'

He invited the proprietor to get himself a Calvados and join him at the table. Two men of the world talking about the unpredictable behaviour of women.

'Perhaps she was trying to get away from you? A lover's quarrel?'

'Perhaps.'

They drank in silence for a while. Then Birdie asked, 'Was she here long, trying to get a lift?'

'Oh yes.' The proprietor spoke quite sadly, as if reluctant to let Birdie know that his girl had tried quite hard to get away.

'She was here before the card players came, perhaps eight o'clock. And it was very late before she left. I remember because my friend gave her a lift.'

'But I thought you said she didn't . . .'

'Not to Marseilles. But when she didn't get a lift she said she'd have to walk back to the Village Zoe. My friend said he was going that way on his motorbike and he'd take her as far as the other road.'

'What time was this?'

'After three o'clock.'

A thought struck Birdie. 'How did she get there in the first place? From the Village Zoe?'

The proprietor looked at him pityingly. 'She walked.' His look and tone seemed to imply that it must have been some lovers' quarrel.

'Walked! But it must be . . .'

'About twelve kilometres,' said the proprietor, gently.

That seemed to be it, but Birdie didn't intend to leave without every loophole closed.

'So she walked, got here about eight, stayed till after three and

136

then got a lift on a motorbike. And she was here all the time?'

The proprietor nodded. 'Except now and again she'd go outside and walk up and down the car park.' He added, almost apologetically, 'I was watching her. I felt sorry for her.'

Birdie finished the Calvados, paid and left. The sun was as hot as ever, the bike seemed to have acquired a new creak or two, and his head was muzzy from the drink. He decided to go home the way he'd come, rather than risk getting lost in the back roads among the vines. There should have been a lot for him to think about as he cranked along, but at first there was only room in his brain for one thing: unless both Joan and the café proprietor were part of some incomprehensible plot, Nimue could not have killed Ralph Shunner. She'd probably have been already in the café by the time Birdie had his meeting with Shunner back at the camp. The pillion lift after three in the morning would have just given her time to walk along the beach and climb over the back fence to find him standing by Shunner's cold body. And yet there were still so many questions to be answered: why had she been looking for a lift? Why, if she'd wanted a lift so much, had she simply given up and gone back to the Village Zoe? Surely she'd have had a better chance of hitching by daylight. And the old question: why, above all, had she, without hesitation or question, helped him dispose of Shunner's body? The only person who could give him the answers was Nimue herself, and although he shrank from another meeting with her after the way their last one had ended, he knew he had to see her before doing anything else.

When he reached the main road turning by the motel he waited for a while to let some traffic past, supporting himself with a hand on the low, white wall of the motel car park. As he was about to move off, he saw that a dark blue Renault was coming out of the car park on to the road, and decided to let that pass too. He swung into position behind it, noticing that it had British number plates and a Midlands garage sticker in the back window. It accelerated away before he could notice anything else, other than that there were no passengers and the driver was a dark-haired man. But professional training had given him a good memory for cars and number plates, and he was almost sure he'd seen the same vehicle parked beside a pavillion tent at the Village Zoe. The tent where the solicitor Peter Pollins lived, with his wife Vinny.

He got back to the Village Zoe at around six, returned the handyman's bicycle and went straight to the swimming pool,

137

thinking he might find Nimue on duty there. But the lifeguard was the French lad again, and he said he'd no idea where she was. At the reception building Marie told him Nimue had gone for a meal and would be back later.

'Where? In the café?'

But Marie just shook her head and turned away to an insistent group wanting to know about boat trips. He decided to look for Nimue in her bungalow, remembering where it was from the time he'd helped carry the injured instructor there. His feet crunched along the gravel path between hedges of rosemary. A window at the side of the bungalow was open and he could hear a tap running.

'Nimue,' he called, quite softly.

The water stopped running. 'Who's that?'

'Birdie, Birdie Linnet.'

'What do you want?'

'Can I come in?'

Silence, then round the corner of the building he heard a door opening. He found her standing on a low step, a green mass of endive in her hand.

'I was just getting something to eat.'

He followed her into the small, tidy kitchen. She dumped the endive in the sink and turned to face him. 'What now?'

She was wearing a T-shirt and a long skirt with a swirling batik print, the first time he'd seen her in more or less conventional clothes. Her feet were still bare.

'Can we sit down and talk?'

Without a word she led him through to the living room. A wooden slatted blind was pulled down and the white walls and big floor cushions were flecked with little dashes of light and shade. Again he noticed the one print on the wall: the silver birches with their shadows falling across the picture, like bars.

He said, 'Were you in an open prison all the time?'

She took her time, sat down on a big turquoise cushion and folded her legs to one side. 'No.'

'What were you in for?'

He stood on a fawn rug of nobbly weave, aware for the first time that he smelt of sweat from the cycle ride.

'Sit down,' she said.

'I'm all right. I . . .'

'Sit down. It was you who wanted to talk.'

He settled awkwardly on the cream-covered divan.

'Drugs,' she said, and waited for his reaction. He was careful not to show any.

'Who told you?' she asked. Her voice was quite level and she didn't take her eyes off his face.

'Clancy, the photographer. He'd seen you in there.'

She took a long breath, and he couldn't tell if it was relief or exasperation.

'What sort of drugs?'

But if he'd given her a shock it had only rattled her for a while, not floored her. He could see as he watched that the defences were coming back in place.

'I can't think of one good reason why I should be talking to you about it,' she said.

'I can think of several.' If she wanted a sparring match he wasn't going to let her have it all her own way.

'For one thing, I know now that you didn't kill Ralph Shunner.'

'And?' She waited.

'And I know that for some reason you wanted to get away from this place so much two nights ago that you spent seven hours in a transport café trying to hitch a lift on a lorry.'

'And that concerns you?'

'What does concern me is what you thought you were doing that morning. All right, you didn't kill Shunner. So why were you so eager to help bury him?'

She managed a smile. 'You didn't want my help, then?'

'It's a criminal offence, you know, helping to dispose of a body. It must be the same in France.'

'And you're going to tell the police, of course?' A more convincing smile this time, taunting him.

He said, 'I might just do that.'

Her eyes flashed, and her whole body was suddenly as tense as a cat's with anger. 'It's no good trying to bully me. I'm not taking that again from anyone. Tell the police what you like.'

He realized that he was in danger of mishandling the whole thing. If he continued on this tack he'd get nothing out of her, might even drive her to a hostility that would have dangerous repercussions for him. It hadn't occurred to him before that he could no longer rely on his old police assumptions, that he was out on his own now, and in deep trouble.

'I'm doing this all wrong, aren't I?'

It was what he'd been thinking, but he was surprised to hear his own voice saying it. The wine, the physical effort, the nervous battering of the past few days were ganging up on him at a time when he needed all his alertness. He sighed, and let his body sink back so that he was half lying across the divan, his shoulders against the wall.

'Are you?' she said.

He nodded, eyes closed. 'I've got problems. I need your help.'

She said, without aggression, 'That can be another kind of bullying.'

'I just want you to answer some questions, that's all. We've just got to make sense of this.'

'Not "we". You.'

It sounded discouraging, but the anger had gone from her voice. He opened his eyes and saw her sitting in exactly the same position on the turquoise cushion, seeming quite relaxed.

'All right, *I've* got to make sense of this. And I can't do it if you won't tell me what's going on.'

Silence while she considered, staring down at the patterns on her skirt. Then, 'It was heroin. Smuggling heroin.'

He'd expected her to start with the body, but it made sense to go along with her way of telling it.

'The summer before last I was in Morocco, staying with my mother's family. I'd been living with somebody and it had all broken up and I was . . . I was sort of at a loose end.'

'I know how it feels.'

'I met this Englishman out there. He ran this firm that did Moroccan tours – cut price, mostly people in their twenties, by coach. You know the sort of thing.'

Birdie nodded.

'He said he was out there for a few weeks looking for couriers. I knew Morocco, I've got bi-lingual French, I got the job.'

'And the job included smuggling heroin?'

She gave him a long look. 'You can believe what you like, but if I'd known that I wouldn't have sat at the same table with him. I was so bloody innocent it still makes me angry when I think about it.'

'When did you find out?'

She stretched her legs out in front of her, gently massaged a calf. 'He went back to England almost at once. I dealt with his manager out there, a Moroccan. I brought two parties out and back, no trouble. The third trip, the manager asked would I take this

140

package over to their office in London. Reels of photos for next season's brochure.'

'So you took it?'

'Why not. It seemed a reasonable thing to do. The fourth time he asked me would I take some more photos over. The first lot hadn't come out properly.'

'And that was the time when . . .'

She nodded. 'The police were waiting for me at Dover. Me and my reels of photos.'

'And the court didn't believe your story?'

Another long look at him. 'Do you blame them? If I'd been on the jury I wouldn't have believed it myself.'

'You take it very calmly.'

'I didn't then, I can tell you. At one time I could cheerfully have killed the whole lot of them – police, screws, the other women in there. Then after the first six months something happened and I got a grip on myself. I knew if I went under then, I'd never come up again.'

She stretched out an arm towards him, fist clenched. 'This all started then, you know.'

He thought it was some kind of solidarity sign, then realized he was simply being invited to observe the development of the muscles.

'You put on weight in prison, all pale and floppy. I promised myself the first thing I'd do when I came out was get my own body back. And I did. I'm not letting it go again.'

Her eyes challenged him, as if she expected him to deny her that right.

'I'd have felt the same way about it myself.'

She let the arm fall back to her side.

'And this Englishman. Did you give the police his name?'

'I told them the name he'd given me. It might as well have been Donald Duck.'

'A false name?'

'Of course.'

'What about the travel firm?'

'Two bent directors who'd never met him. Bank accounts in the false name and instructions by telephone.'

'So you couldn't give the police any lead on him?'

'I tried hard enough. I might have kept out of prison if I could have given them any more.'

He couldn't look at her. 'But what you did give them. . . ?'

'He never told me what part of the country he came from, but he couldn't resist boasting about restaurants or clubs he'd been to or this and that famous person he'd met. But you know all about that, don't you.'

Her voice was quiet. The room was becoming cool and dusky as the sun slipped round to the west. Scents of rosemary and damp earth came drifting through the slats of the blind. Birdie asked:

'How much do you know?'

'Not everything. I went abroad as soon as they let me out of prison. I only heard . . .' She hesitated.

Birdie finished the sentence for her. '. . . that the police had fucked it up.'

She nodded, eyes fixed on his face. The last thing he wanted was to tell the story again, but after her time in prison she'd surely earned that.

'You know I was a policeman, right? I was a detective sergeant. The word came to us from Scotland Yard that we might have a big wheel in the drugs trade on our patch. They couldn't put a name to him, only quite a good description, a list of the restaurants he'd used, the people he'd met and so on. I realize now that must have come from you.'

She nodded again, like an intent student at a seminar.

'We did a bit of casting around, and after a time we came up with a name that fitted. Big house, local benefactor, friendly with half the councillors, respectable as you like.'

He took a deep breath.

'Half the police forces in the country would have left it there and told Scotland Yard they'd got it wrong. I might have done it myself, but we had this Chief Inspector who wouldn't let a thing like that rest. And he decided to put me on the case because my wife and I did a lot of youth work in our spare time.'

'How did that help?'

'Our man was a great one for local youth charities. The idea was that I'd get friendly with him, let him take me out for dinner a bit and generally relax with him.'

'You mean,' she said, 'let him think you might be open to a bit of bribery?'

'If it came to that, yes. But generally to try and find out where all his money was coming from.'

'And it worked.'

'Oh yes, it worked.'

He was silent, seeing with particular vividness the golden regency striped wallpaper at one country club which was a particular favourite of Shunner's. Bronze light fittings with gold shades to match. The red hair of the woman Shunner had brought with him nodding towards Birdie, because Shunner himself was occupied with Olivia. Olivia's laugh at something he'd said to her. Evenings of large glasses and steaks wallowing in all manner of sauces and, by day, the dry and careful cross-checking of dates and places, of snatched interviews with scared little men in pubs and coffee bars. And Olivia growing more and more silent in the rare evenings at home with him, more and more animated when they were with Shunner. He said, 'She thought we were framing him.'

'Your wife?'

'She still does, come to that.' He stood up and walked over to the window, squinting out through the gaps in the blind.

Nimue said, 'What I can't understand is why they left you on the case when they knew he was having an affair with your wife.'

'They didn't know.' He turned blindly and began pacing across the floor. 'I couldn't tell the Chief. Just couldn't tell him.' He reached the far wall, turned and paced back again, struggling to explain to her and himself.

'It was like being in this nightmare. I kept telling myself that I'd got it wrong, that it couldn't be happening. And if I'd told somebody else, you see, especially the Chief, it would be admitting it was real. It was as if it wasn't happening as long as I didn't tell anybody.'

'I see.'

Her voice came from higher up. He was dimly conscious that she'd moved from the cushion to the divan, perhaps to avoid his pacing feet. He remembered too, though he didn't tell her, how he'd diverted his misery and anger into all the meticulous by-ways of checking the case against Shunner, working for the day when he could lay it down at Olivia's feet and convince her of its justice.

'And we got it to court – more or less in the teeth of the whole bloody county – and he'd told his fucking lawyers about him and Olivia and they . . . they . . .'

He stopped in the middle of the room, fists clenched, eyes tight closed, trying to shut out the memory of the coat of arms over the judge's bench, of the questions they shouldn't have been allowed to ask him.

'It's all right,' she said. 'That's the bit I know. You don't have to tell me.'

'And as far as the jury was concerned, it discredited our whole bloody case.'

He sat down heavily on the divan beside her, weakness flooding over him, sweating as heavily as he'd done that day in court.

'Are you all right?' she asked.

He nodded, eyes still closed.

'So if it hadn't been for me, we'd have got Shunner in prison for you.'

'His sort always get off one way or the other,' she said.

It was an odd remark, in view of what had happened to Shunner, but it seemed to him both wise and generous. He found his hand was touching hers and his fingers closed round it, mainly for its coolness.

'It's all right,' she said. She didn't take her hand away from him, and for a while there was silence apart from their breathing.

He said, 'It must have been a surprise for you when he turned up here.'

Her fingers tightened.

'Don't worry. I've said you can't have killed him. I just want to know.'

'It was. There he was, all of a sudden, just walking up to me on the tennis courts.'

'Didn't you recognize his name from the court case?'

'She signed them in under her name.'

So Shunner had lived and died at the Village Zoe under the name of Mr Linnet. 'He took the lot from me, didn't he?' He'd meant it as a flat statement rather than a cry for sympathy, and he was surprised, though not unpleasantly, to feel Nimue's arm round his waist.

'He took a lot from both of us,' she said.

'Quite a coincidence for you that he turned up here.'

She shook her head. 'That wouldn't have been coincidence. He was out to get me.'

'How do you know?'

'He wasn't an idiot. He must have guessed somebody shopped him to the police. And he must have guessed who.'

'You mean you thought he was coming here to kill you?'

In spite of that arm round his waist Birdie couldn't smother his professional instincts entirely. What a motive she had, if the alibi

144

hadn't been so strong.

'No. I don't think he'd have done that. Too risky for him. I think he was coming here to arrange a set-up. Get me in prison again.'

'Are you sure?'

'No. I'm just trying to follow the way his mind might work. Supposing the police were tipped off that somebody was running drugs from here, then they find out about my record. Back in prison and no chance of fighting my way up again. Wouldn't that be it?' She'd tried to keep her voice calm, but he could feel her body trembling.

'I tried to run off,' she said. 'That's what I was doing at the café. If there'd been anything going to Marseilles that night I'd be back in Morocco by now. But I had a whole night to think about it, and I thought, why should I let that bastard run me out? He was the guilty one, not me. So I came back.'

'Intending to kill him?'

She shook her head. 'No.'

'But not sorry to find him dead?'

'No.'

A silence. Then she said, speaking softly and quickly, 'Can you try to understand this? I hated them, even before this. Things that take your mind away. Even joints. They'd laugh at me sometimes in Morocco because I wouldn't. He knew that. And heroin . . . I had a row with my bloke once because I said the Ayatollah was right to shoot drug pushers. And that was before prison when I saw . . . saw what it did to people. And to know he'd got me into that . . .'

Her voice died away, but the eyes watching him were full of pain and effort. Her trembling seemed to have communicated itself to him. They sat staring at each other with a mutual horror at their physical weakness. When they fell back together on the divan it was not lust, but an animal desire to cling together against a threat from outside. She whispered to him like a confession of love, her mouth close to his ear, 'I didn't know what it was like to hate anybody so much.'

'Nor did I.'

He slid his arm round her shoulders and pulled her closer, her small breasts firm against his chest. After a while he must have slept because when he was next conscious of anything the sunlight on the wall was low and golden and the trembling had stopped. She was still lying beside him, awake, and he remembered something important he had to tell her.

'I've moved it. I was worried about that photographer poking round.'

'There was no need.'

'I thought if I put it . . .'

'I don't want to know at the moment.'

He knew he should tell her about the tractor trailer, but was glad to have an excuse not to do it then. There was comfort in lying close, so close he could feel her ribcage rising and falling in long breaths, the practised breaths of an athlete recovering from exertion.

He said, 'When all this is over, can I go on seeing you?'

'Perhaps.'

He began to stroke her hair, over the crown of her head and down to the smooth neck beneath the pigtail.

'And it will be over, you know. Quite soon.' He was talking to convince himself as much as her.

'That man Pollins knows something. And I think Melanie must too, or why did she go off like that?'

She turned her head sideways to look at him. A look more of sympathy than of interest, like somebody who'd heard it all before.

'I'm going to have a talk with Pollins. If I'm right, we may have this cleared up by tomorrow.' No change in her expression. 'Do you know anything about him? Had you seen him before?'

'No.'

'He's been behaving oddly. You can tell he's dead scared of his wife, yet he goes off . . .'

'Yes.'

'Then there's James Jedd. You know he's been going all over the place making threats? If I can get him to talk, and Pollins . . .'

She removed his hand gently from her hair and sat up. 'Look,' she said, 'it doesn't matter.'

He looked at her blankly, then realized what she was telling him: that she didn't believe any of this, that she was still sure he'd killed Shunner, but that he'd nothing to fear from her. And that scared him more than any hostility would have done.

CHAPTER TEN

Vinny and Peter Pollins had another argument that evening, round the table in front of their tent. Birdie heard them at it as he strolled past after leaving Nimue's bungalow, to check that he'd been right about the identity of the blue Renault. When they saw him, they froze immediately into happy family snapshot expressions, Peter with a wine glass, Vinny flourishing a chicken drumstick like a sceptre of domestic harmony.

'Nice evening,' said Birdie.

Lovely evening, they agreed. Only plump Philip's voice sabotaged the effect.

'I don't want to go to the rotten bonfire, Mum. Can't I go for a walk with Dad?'

Vinny and Peter told him simultaneously that he couldn't, then glared at each other over his head.

'Daddy's not feeling well. He's got a headache,' said Vinny, in a voice that made it clear she didn't believe it.

'Well, I have,' he protested.

'I wasn't denying it, was I?'

Birdie, watching in the dusk from a bench by the tennis courts half an hour later, was not surprised to see Vinny and the three children, minus their father, among the procession of people making for the bonfire place, she striding along at such a rate that Philip trailed yards behind. Nor was he surprised when he walked back past their tent to find that the Renault had gone. The question was, where. He was quite determined by now to find Peter Pollins on his own and scare him into answering some questions. Twice that day, to Birdie's own knowledge, he'd defied his wife's orders and gone off alone in a way that anybody could tell was uncharacteristic. He looked like a man with something heavy on his mind and, above all, he was taking some pains to hide where he'd been on the night Shunner died. The only thing in his favour

147

seemed to be a complete absence of motive. Ironic that Nimue should have limitless cause to kill Shunner, and an apparently unbreakable alibi, and Pollins no shade of an alibi, but no cause either. But that was something ten minutes alone with Pollins might well clear up.

Birdie loped off to the shed where the handyman's cycle was kept. The aches in his calves and buttocks made the idea of getting on the machine again a painful one, but short of borrowing the green Jaguar from Olivia, there was no alternative. And the idea of driving Shunner's car, even if it was to hunt for Shunner's killer, seemed worse than anything the handyman's cycle could do. He clanked out of the main gate and turned southwards, trying to plan his tactics. Judging by what the child Philip had said, Pollins had pleaded a headache and the need to go for a walk.

But Birdie, like Vinny, was sceptical about Pollins' headache, and far more interested in what Pollins had been doing at the motel that afternoon. It was possible, of course, that he'd simply slipped in there for a drink. He looked like a man who was drinking quite heavily. On the other hand, there were at least half a dozen bars or small hotels between the camp and the motel, all of them looking a lot more inviting. Had he gone there to meet somebody? Somebody, perhaps, who knew about Shunner and was trying to blackmail him? He remembered, suddenly, Pollins' anxious question at the café about changing travellers' cheques. But then, after all, why shouldn't a family man on holiday want to change travellers' cheques? He told himself that he'd got to be professional about this, got to stop making so much of any chance fact that came his way. But, after all, there were very few of them. And how could he be cool and professional when he himself would still be Number-One suspect the moment Shunner's body was discovered? He knew his latest emergency measures in that direction were no more than a stop-gap. Sooner or later—sooner probably—the body would come to light, and by that time, if he wanted to stay out of a prison cell, he must have a watertight case against somebody else.

And there was another reason now, had been since he woke up on a divan bed in a white room a few hours ago, with a woman's cool skin against his shoulder: Nimue. She'd given him something—a tenderness, an uncomplicated response—that he'd never expected to feel again after the hurt over Olivia. But she'd given it to him on false pretences, as the man who'd murdered

148

Shunner. He wanted more of it, but the thought of taking it on that basis made his blood run cold. To take it as an accomplice, to take it with the smell of decaying seaweed hanging over it, was impossible. He needed to be able to go to her, to say, 'This is the man who killed him. Now you know that, will you still let me sleep in your bed?' And if she said yes, then that was another kind of freedom, as important in its way as staying out of a French prison cell. Which was why he wanted Pollins as murderer far too much to be professional about it.

He hesitated for only a second or two at the main gate before pedalling straight down the main road. It was mercifully cooler now, almost dark, and not much traffic on the road. At every bar or hotel he passed he kept a look-out for the blue Renault, but without result. The journey to the motel seemed longer this time, reminding him that the days of tension and broken sleep were bound to have their effect. Another reason for wanting to end all this soon, before what was left of his mental and physical strength gave out entirely. The motel at last, even more ugly under floodlighting. Only a few cars in the car park, not as busy as it would get later in the season. And there, parked unobtrusively in the far corner, the blue Renault.

Birdie stood the bike against a wall and considered. Now he was proved right about where Pollins had gone, he wasn't clear on what the next step would be. If Pollins was drinking alone in the bar there'd be no problem. But suppose he had gone there to meet somebody? Was there any chance of hearing their conversation before they saw him? If the bar was as empty as the car park, probably not, and that was even supposing they'd let him into the bar in the first place. Birdie was suddenly aware that he was wearing the same sweaty tracksuit he'd been cycling around in all day, that his hair was unwashed and full of sandy dust, that his training shoes looked as if they'd done several marathons. Walking into a motel bar looking like that would make him as inconspicuous as a cart horse. There was nothing for it but to hope to make contact with Pollins before they bounced him.

It turned out that either the nerves of the management were stronger than he'd expected, or they were glad of any customers, however scruffy. Birdie walked unchallenged into the plush foyer, nodded to the young man at the reception desk and made for the open-plan bar, leading off it on the left-hand side. Several heads turned to stare at him – a couple who seemed bored to the point of stupefaction, a man who looked like a commercial traveller, the young barman. But just one glance around the pale wood tables and the parlour palms showed him that Pollins wasn't there. He walked back to the reception desk, thinking hard.

'*Pardonnez moi, je pense que mon ami est ici.*'

The young man turned out to have quite efficient English. Birdie described Pollins and his car to him, then brought out his excuse for wanting to find him, trying to sound as relaxed about it as possible.

'My friend has accidentally gone off with my car keys. I need them urgently, so I've come to ask him for them.' Neat, he thought. It would explain, if necessary, why he'd been sweating through the countryside on an old bike. And it worked. The young man was instantly solicitous, as if lost car keys were one of the great human tragedies.

'I think your friend must be the man in Room Twenty-Three.'

Birdie was surprised. 'He's staying here?'

A more guarded expression on the young man's face. 'He is visiting somebody.'

Better and better. Birdie was only afraid that the helpful young man would send somebody to Room Twenty-Three to ask for the non-existent car keys, but fortunately the motel seemed to be economizing on staff and there was nobody to send.

'What floor is it on?' Birdie asked, trying to guide him into a decision.

'The first floor.'

The young man looked slightly doubtful, so Birdie made for the beige-carpeted stairs before he could change his mind.

'I could telephone the room,' he suggested, as Birdie reached the bend in the stairs.

'Don't worry,' said Birdie, and went on climbing.

The stairs came out to a corridor with doors leading off it on the left-hand side. A trolley with plates and dish covers on it was parked outside the furthest door. Treading carefully, glad that the motel hadn't skimped at least on the thickness of its carpets, Birdie moved along, stopping outside each door to listen. Nothing from the first three. From the fourth, a man's voice speaking French, into the telephone by the sound of it. Nothing from the fifth or sixth. He moved very cautiously up to the seventh door. The plates on the trolley had the remains of a meal on them, and by the look of it had been a meal for only one. But there were two voices coming from the room, a man's and a woman's. And without being able to hear them at all distinctly, Birdie thought from the rhythm of the words that they were talking English. Praying that nobody would come along the corridor, he knelt down with his ear against the door. A phrase in the woman's voice came to him quite distinctly, '. . . no good expecting me to go back there. Not after all this.'

The last time he'd heard that voice, its owner had been sitting next to him by the swimming pool at the Village Zoe, hinting of vague dangers and asking him to look after her. It sounded now as if Melanie McBride had found somebody else to look after her, and was not pleased with his efforts so far. The man's voice was replying but more quietly, inaudible to Birdie except as a wordless monotone. They seemed to be speaking from somewhere over on his right, well away from the door. He stood up and shifted cautiously a few steps, then found there was an eighth door he hadn't noticed, of metal and reinforced glass, set a little back from the others. He pushed it open and found that beyond it the carpet gave way to plain concrete. There was an open broom cupboard with a large rubbish hatch in it on the right, and uncarpeted stairs descending to what were probably the service regions of the building. But for Birdie the important thing was that the left-hand wall was also the end wall of room Number Twenty-Three and very little money had been wasted on soundproofing it. There was not even any need to put his ear against the wall. The two people sounded no more than a yard or so away from him, and their voices came as clearly as if they were talking to him directly.

Peter Pollins first, reasonable but weary, '. . . don't have to come back with me. I've told you. I can see you again in the morning and . . .'

'I'm not going to spend another night here on my own. I don't like the way the manager keeps looking at me.'

'Oh, for heaven's sake.'

A silence in which he could even hear Pollins' heavy, exasperated breathing.

'And I get so bored here.'

The child's tone of voice that seemed so much more natural to her than the seductive one she used for the next few words, 'And so lonely.'

All the same, it seemed to work for a while.

'Poor darling,' Pollins said, and a few seconds later, 'I didn't mean to be cross. It's just so much to think about, that's all.'

And she, seizing the advantage, 'You wouldn't have so much to think about if you didn't go back to that fucking place tonight.'

'Look, I've explained, love. I've got to.'

'You shouldn't have anything to do with him. You don't know what he's like.'

'For goodness' sake, don't start that again. You keep telling me I don't know what he's like. But it wasn't his idea anyway.'

'So why's he bringing it?'

'I don't know why he's bringing it. Somebody's got to, I suppose.'

'But why him?'

'I've got to be there anyway. I promised Ralph Shunner.'

'Fuck Ralph Shunner.'

'You could wait in the car if you liked and . . .'

'Fuck the car.'

A silence in which Birdie could imagine them glaring at each other. It occurred to him that, in or out of matrimony, Peter Pollins didn't seem to have much luck with women. But he was feeling, if anything, more confused than ever. If the last bit of conversation meant anything, it surely meant they both believed Shunner to be alive. Otherwise would Pollins be bound by a promise to him or Melanie so casual with her obscenities? But assuming that one of them was the murderer and the other didn't know it, wouldn't they have spoken in exactly the same way? Still silence from the room. He decided that he wouldn't solve anything by haunting the service stairs, and that there was something to be said for making an attack on both of them at once. He stepped back into the main corridor and tried the door handle. The door was locked.

'Who's that?' came Melanie's alarmed voice from inside.

'The lifeguard from the Village Zoe.'

Pollins' voice, equally alarmed, 'What are you doing here?'

'Peter, you know me. It's Arthur Linnet. I just want to come in for a chat.'

'Well, you can't.'

Time for the below-the-belt stuff. 'I've got a message for you from Vinny,' said Birdie loudly. The door flew open and there was Pollins on the other side of it, at once anxious and furious. Anxiety won.

'The kids,' said Pollins, holding on to the edge of the door. 'Has something happened to the kids?'

Immediately guilty, Birdie shook his head. 'No, they're all

right.'

'Vinny?'

'She's all right too.'

Pollins, clearly trying to come to terms with what was happening, let go of the door and Birdie stepped into the room, closing it behind him. An untidy room, in which stale fumes seemed to have been substituted for air. One light on over the dressing table. Melanie, in white lacy bra and French knickers, was lying on her side on an unmade bed, her hair the brightest thing in the room. As Pollins followed the direction of Birdie's eyes towards the bed fury got the upper hand over anxiety.

'I didn't realize the Village Zoe ran to morality police as well.'

'Look,' said Birdie. 'Can we . . .'

'How does it work? Do the wives have to fill in a card or something? Do you send a report back to them in triplicate?'

'As far as . . .'

'Does anybody ever punch you on the nose?' asked Pollins. And tried it. Birdie blocked the blow and gripped hold of him by the elbow before he could try another. Melanie, from the bed, gave a little screech like a vole in pain.

'For heaven's sake,' said Birdie, 'shut up and do some listening. For a start, as far as I know your wife's got no idea where you are.'

'Then how did you. . . ?'

'And there's no message from her. I just wanted you to open the door.'

'You bastard,' said Pollins, sounding the word with great precision, as if he didn't often get a chance to use it.

Birdie let go of his elbow and moved to sit on a chair near the bed.

'I've a damned good mind to ring for the manager and have you thrown out,' said Pollins.

'I don't think any of us want that sort of fuss, do we?'

Melanie's eyes were following every move they made, her mouth slightly open.

'Oh. What do we want then?'

'What I want is some answers to a few questions.'

'Like what?'

'Like what you were both doing on Sunday night.'

'Two questions to that. Firstly, why? Secondly, what's your authority for asking?' Pollins, perhaps conscious of Melanie's concentration on them, was recovering fast.

153

'Two answers then. First, there was an incident at the Village Zoe and I'm trying to find out more about it. Second, I'm acting as an employee of the village.'

Melanie said suddenly, 'Don't answer him. He's from him.'

'Who?' asked Pollins.

'Him. Jedd of course. Jedd's sent him.' She was on her feet, whirling towards Birdie. 'He sent you, didn't he? He sent you.' And before either of them could stop her she was out of the door and into the corridor. Birdie, although further from the door, recovered more quickly than Pollins, and went after her just in time to find the food trolley flying at him, propelled by Melanie with more force than he'd have expected of her. It took him at mid thigh level, bowling him backwards on to Pollins, who was just coming through the door, and the two of them fell back into the room in a confusion of slithering plates. Unsure whether their curses were meant for each other or Melanie, they got to their feet and dashed to the service door, which was still swinging from the speed of her exit. From there they'd probably have gone rushing on down the concrete stairs if Birdie hadn't heard noises coming from the broom cupboard. He went close to the door.

'Melanie?'

No answer except for the sound of a mop or something falling over.

'Melanie, I promise you I've got nothing to do with Jedd. Just come out of there and let's talk sensibly.'

Always assuming the blighted woman was capable of talking sensibly. 'Come on, Melanie.'

He put his hand on the door handle and found she hadn't bolted it from the inside, began opening it slowly so as not to panic her. There was a scuffling in the room as something went from one side of it to the other.

'There's no need to be frightened.' Frightened? For all he knew she might try to brain him with a bucket. He pushed the door full open, standing well to the side, and was just in time to see her small, silk-covered behind sticking out of the opening to the rubbish chute.

'Melanie, don't be silly, that's . . .'

She twisted round somehow so that he could see her terrified face and her fingers clutching at the edge of the chute, gave another of her vole-in-pain screeches, and was gone, with no more noise than a cardboard box might make tumbling down. Birdie stood there aghast, staring at the gap where her face had been.

'It's all your fault,' said Pollins.

Birdie glanced at him, then rushed down the service stairs two or three at a time. He was telling himself on the way that they'd only been on the first floor, that the rubbish chute couldn't be so very long. But his mind was full of pictures of the girl tumbling and turning in the dark down an endless tunnel to God knew where. The thought that the chute might lead direct to the boilers had him jumping down the last ten or so stairs without touching them, landing with a jar fit to drive his backbone through the top of his skull. He found himself in what looked like an annex to the kitchens, full of sacks and several crates of vegetables. Nobody around. He'd been conscious of Pollins' footsteps behind him on the stairs, some way back, but the man hadn't caught up with him. Then he heard the sound of the footsteps clattering on, down a further flight, presumably to the basement boilers. But Birdie wouldn't face that possibility yet. What he hoped and expected to find was the dustbin bay, and that must surely be at ground level. The night air hit him, cool after the fustiness of the room, as he stepped out into the yard.

Again, nobody around. Just a parked van and some more crates. And, on his right, a single-storey building sticking out from the main body of the motel which looked very much like the place where they'd keep the rubbish. He raced round it to find the door, a wooden door with a bolt but no lock on it. Inside, four huge metal bins about seven foot high, with wheels for moving them around. He saw with relief that one of them was directly beneath the end of the rubbish chute and heard a scrabbling sound coming from it that was too loud for even the largest of rats. Moving more cautiously now, he manoeuvred one of the empty bins on its wheels so that it was blocking the door shut. Then he moved to the occupied one, knocked on it gently, and called, 'Melanie.'

Fiercer scrabblings from inside, and a muffled voice saying something he couldn't hear.

'What was that?'

'. . . can't get out.'

It was dark in the shed and he couldn't find a light switch. He felt around the walls but there was no step-ladder, not even a crate, to stand on. To have gone out poking around the yard would have been another risk of attracting attention.

'Can't breathe,' said the voice from the bin. It sounded terribly

155

distressed. 'Can't breathe.'

Then there were choking sobs, quiet at first, then more desperate.

'Hold on,' said Birdie. 'I'll come in and get you.'

He'd had some idea of keeping the girl in there until she told him what he wanted to know, but if she were hurt, or suffocating – or even simply hysterical – that course was ruled out. He gripped the edge of the bin and, without much difficulty, pulled himself up until he was looking over the top into a dark mass that smelt predominantly of tomato and overripe melon. He didn't see her until she moved and a pale face, streaked with something dark, was looking up at him. The bin was two-thirds full and she seemed to be crouching on the surface of the rubbish, in no immediate danger of slipping further in.

'Don't worry,' he said to her. 'Just keep still.'

The sobbing stopped for a second or two, then began again as he edged round the bin to try to find a foothold.

'It's all right, I'll get you out.' Something firm and horizontal under his track shoe, possibly a handle. 'If you could get yourself round this way and grab hold of my hand . . .'

But she couldn't. Shocked into near paralysis, she had no idea of leaving whatever firm island in the rubbish she'd managed to find.

'Right then, I'll come in with you.' He pulled himself over the edge, stepped cautiously down on the rubbish, and immediately sank up to his knees in something slimy and fish smelling.

'Damn.' He reached towards the sound of the sobbing and put a hand on what he hoped was her shoulder. She shrank away from him.

'I'm not going back to him,' she said.

Birdie breathed deeply. 'Will you please get it into your head that I'm nothing to do with James Jedd. Anyway, why are you so scared of him?' Silence. He pressed on. 'It's not just this business about your contract, is it? There must be something else.'

'I want to get out,' she said. 'I want to get out.'

The smell of overripe melon came from her direction, at least preferable to his reject fish stew.

'Of course we'll get you out. But since we're in here together, you might answer a question or two, don't you think?'

Now he knew she wasn't suffocating and was pretty sure that nothing was broken there seemed a chance for a variation of his original plan. He didn't enjoy the idea, but this mournful hump in the darkness was, after all, one of his two remaining suspects.

'Why did you run off like that, on the night . . . Sunday night?'

'I told you. I tried to tell you at the swimming pool. I was scared of him.'

'Yes, but why that night in particular?'

'I don't know why you keep asking me questions. I want to get out.' The child's wail again.

'I'll get you out, I promise. Just answer me: why that night?'

A silence. He fancied that she was trying to get control of her brain, such as it was. She said at last, in a normal voice, 'It was that fucking photographer.'

'Clancy? What did he do?'

Then resentment against Clancy came pouring out.

'I'd told him about Jedd, and he said not to worry about Jedd, we'd leave the fucking village what's-it-called together and go off to Cannes, and he knew a film producer who had a villa there, and by the time Jedd knew where we'd got to we'd be staying at the villa, and the film producer would have lawyers who knew about getting out of contracts, and there was this film he was casting and . . . fuck him.'

'So what went wrong?' Birdie asked, thinking he could guess.

'We were supposed to be going off to Cannes that night, and when I asked him wasn't it time we were going there were all these excuses. He still had work to do at the camp, he said, and he wasn't sure his friend would be at the villa after all, and anyway we couldn't go to Cannes because he had to take the hire car back to Boulogne.' She said 'hire car' and 'Boulogne' in a way that made them sound like obscenities.

'So he stood you up in a big way?' Birdie said.

She seemed to find his tone unsympathetic. 'What are we doing, sitting here and talking in this shit? I want to get out.'

'I've told you, I'll get you out but I want to know exactly what you did that night. I really need to know.'

'Do you swear you're not from him?'

'For the thousandth time, I've got absolutely nothing to do with James Jedd.' He'd spoken too loudly and he heard his voice echoing round the bin. He hoped there was nobody listening back up the chute.

'And you swear you'll get me out?'

'Yes. Now go on with what you did after you left Clancy Whigg. For a start, what time was that?'

157

'How would I know what time it was? I was too angry and upset and . . . and scared. I knew Jedd would kill me if I went back to him after going off with Clancy, and I'd got nowhere to go and no money and there was just . . . just nobody. And I was just sort of wandering around crying and not knowing what to do, and then Peter found me.'

'How long had you been wandering around?'

'I don't know. It felt like for ever.'

'So what did Peter do?'

'He asked me what was wrong and I told him, and he said he'd take me to a hotel. And he drove around for hours and couldn't find anywhere, then we found this place.'

Birdie was amazed how she took it for granted that Pollins should help her, even sounding annoyed at his failure to find a hotel straight away. She seemed simply to absorb masculine help as a right. Even, perhaps, to the extent of expecting somebody else to kill for her?

'Did he stay here all night?'

'I wanted him to, but he wouldn't.'

'What time did he go?'

'Don't keep asking me about time. I've told you, I don't know. Just get me out. Get me out. Get me out.' Her voice rose higher and higher and Birdie was horrified to hear a tapping on the door.

'Now you've done it.' He clamped a hand over her mouth and waited, listening. More tapping, then mercifully Peter Pollins' voice.

'Melanie. Melanie, are you in there?'

Birdie called out as quietly as possible, 'Yes, she's here. She's all right.'

'Open the door then.'

'Just wait a minute. And for goodness' sake, don't make such a noise.' Birdie said, with his mouth close to Melanie's ear, 'I'm going to bend down. I want you to stand on my back and get hold of the top of the bin. Understand?

The first step presented no great problems, but the second was more complicated. 'Now pull yourself up a bit.'

Her weight came off his back and he straightened up, but she was sobbing again. 'It hurts my hands. I can't hold on.'

'You don't have to hold on for long.'

Finding a moderately firm foothold on some cardboard cartons, he supported her round the waist and persuaded her to hook one

158

knee over the rim.

'Now put a hand on my shoulder and get the other knee over.'

Pollins' alarmed voice came from outside, 'What's going on in there?'

'We're all right,' said Birdie, gasping as Melanie's nails dug into his shoulder. 'Get the other knee over,' he repeated.

Pollins' voice again. 'Get your hands off that girl and let me in.'

Melanie, with both knees hooked over the rim, rocked backwards with a sharp little cry of pain. 'Not that way,' said Birdie desperately. 'For goodness' sake, keep the right way up.'

Pollins' voice was loud and scandalized. 'Stop it, stop it. Can you hear?'

'I can't stand it,' Melanie sobbed.

'I'm going to get the police,' shouted Pollins.

'What for?'

'You're raping a girl in there and you ask . . .'

Birdie howled, 'Raping! For heaven's sake, I'm not even touching her.' Which, for the moment, was literally true, Melanie having managed to manoeuvre herself into an upright perch on the rim of the bin. 'I'm just helping her out of the bloody dustbin. For heaven's sake, you tell him, Melanie.'

'I'm scared,' she said.

'And if you don't keep quiet she'll bloody well fall in again.'

Which quietened Pollins for a while but did nothing for Melanie's nerves. Sweating great fish-smelling drops at the possibility that Pollins might really call the police, Birdie had to stay patient and persuade her to reverse her hand grip and let herself down so that she was hanging at last on the outside of the bin.

'It's only about a foot to the ground. You can let go.'

But she wouldn't, not till her fingers gave way and she slithered down the outside of the bin with a little cry, by which time Pollins was becoming restive and wanting to know what was going on again. Birdie got himself out of the bin within seconds, checked that Melanie was more or less unhurt, and rolled back the barricade from the door.

Pollins pushed past him and seemed struck incoherent by the smell. When he recovered he said, 'I've had enough of this. We're all going back to the camp.'

Melanie was still sitting on the floor, sobbing gently.

'Is she all right?'

'I think so,' Birdie said. They managed to get her standing and, speaking in whispers, to reassure her.

'We can go straight out to my car,' Pollins said. 'I'll come and collect her things and settle up in the morning.'

Melanie said, 'I want a bath.'

'You can have one back at the camp – or a shower at any rate.'

'I don't want a shower back at the camp. I want a bath here.' She planted her bare feet firmly on the concrete and refused to move. 'And I want to wash my hair.'

Pollins sighed and the two men looked at each other over her head.

'She can't go back inside in this state,' Pollins said. But Birdie was determined to have a few more answers before either of them left the motel.

'I don't know. If nobody's noticed all this going on they're not going to start now. If we nipped up the back stairs . . .'

So, with Birdie going in front to make sure there were no staff around and Pollins murmuring encouragements to Melanie as if she were a nervy colt, they made it back to Room Twenty-Three. The minute they got inside Melanie gathered up an armful of tubes and bottles from her bag, rushed into the bathroom without looking at either of the men, and slammed the door.

'Well . . .' said Pollins. He collapsed onto a chair, looking drained. 'Well, of all the . . .'

'What were you doing on Sunday night?' asked Birdie ruthlessly.

Pollins stared at him for four or five seconds. 'This was where we came in. I asked you why you were asking and what your authority was. And it's no good just telling me there was an incident at the camp.' He sat back a little more easily in his chair and Birdie walked across to the window to gain time. He'd seen this coming. Pollins was, after all, a solicitor – but was still reluctant to take the next step.

He said at last, 'I'm a police officer. We've reason to think somebody at the Village Zoe may be involved in drugs trafficking.'

'A British police officer?'

'Yes.' So there was another crime for the charge sheet: impersonating a police officer and no defence to say that eighteen months ago he had been one.

'Where's your identification?' Pollins asked.

'I don't carry it in my tracksuit. It's back at the camp.'

'Force, rank and number?'

Birdie reeled them off glibly and was sure Pollins was stowing them away in his memory. Another vision of the coat-of-arms over the judge's bench flashed on his consciousness, but he pressed on: 'So I'm asking you again: what were you doing on Sunday night?'

'And you're not going to tell me what the incident was?'

'Not yet.'

Pollins said, 'I'd be quite within my rights to refuse to co-operate, but I'm willing to answer that.' He paused. 'As long as it doesn't get back to my wife.'

'We'd have no reason to communicate what you say to anybody else, unless it's relevant to our investigations.' Birdie was shocked to find how easily the official manner was coming back to him, as if nothing had happened. And it certainly seemed to be working with Pollins.

'From what time?'

'From about nine o'clock.' Birdie estimated it was about nine when he'd hit Shunner.

'I'd accepted an invitation to go out for the evening and play poker.'

'From Joan?'

'Yes. I'd agreed to meet the rest of the party at a quarter to nine in the car park outside the gates. I left our tent at exactly twenty-five minutes to nine.'

'Your wife could confirm that?'

Pollins winced. 'My wife could confirm that. I hope you won't find it necessary to ask her.'

'I hope not. But you didn't turn up at the car park. What happened?'

Pollins nodded his head towards the bathroom door, and the sound of angry splashings from the other side.

'She happened.' There was an odd mixture of embarrassment and pride in his voice.

'How did she happen exactly?'

'I was walking up the drive to the main gate, and there she was sobbing her heart out and practically staggering along. I had to ask her what was the matter.'

'And what did she say?'

'She . . . that she was desperately scared of a certain person at the camp. I gathered that they'd come on holiday together and the relationship had deteriorated.'

161

'Was that person James Jedd?'

'Yes.'

'Did she say exactly why she was scared of him?'

'No . . . not exactly. I understood he was what you might call a rather dominant personality.'

'What time was it when you met her?'

'It must have been about twenty minutes to nine.'

'And what time was it when she'd finished telling you this?'

'It took some time to get it out of her. About five minutes past nine.'

'You seem very precise about times.'

'I was looking at my watch quite often, wondering if Joan and the others were still waiting.'

That rang true to Birdie. He could imagine Pollins, already embarked on one piece of domestic defiance by accepting Joan's invitation, being totally flustered by Melanie.

'So she was with you from twenty to nine to five past nine. Were you standing on the drive all that time?'

'Some of the time. Then I found a bench.' He stared at Birdie, a growing doubt in his eyes. 'It's not her . . . I mean you don't think she. . . ?'

Being holed up in a motel with a beautiful blonde was bad enough. Add beautiful blonde drug smuggler and Vinny could do war dances on her husband from now till doomsday.

'We have to investigate everybody,' said Birdie.

'Yes, but . . .'

Birdie might have felt sorry for him if his own position hadn't been so desperate.

'And then what happened?

Pollins avoided his eyes. 'I . . . I suggested that it might be a good thing if she spent the night away from the camp to give both of them a chance to think things over.'

'And you volunteered to arrange it?'

'What else could I do?' He put the question at first as a challenge, and the second time as an appeal, 'What else could I do?'

'Did you leave straight away?'

'No. She wanted to collect some things from her chalet. I went with her. She made me go in first to check that he and the other man weren't there. She packed a bag, then we left.'

'What time was this?'

162

'About twenty-five minutes to ten.'

'Did anybody see you go?'

'There was a man on duty at the gate.'

And he'd surely have noticed somebody as spectacular as Melanie, Birdie thought. 'Then what?'

'I drove her to this restaurant place first. We had a couple of drinks and I tried to get her to eat something. They didn't do rooms there, so we had to leave at about half past eleven to find somewhere else.'

'Was that difficult?'

'Yes. The first two places we tried said they were full up and I turned inland looking for a farmhouse or something and got lost in all those vineyards. And Melanie by then was getting very tired and a bit bad tempered . . .'

'I'll bet,' thought Birdie, remembering his own journeyings through the sea of vines.

'And when we found this place at last it was already past one o'clock.'

Birdie was depressed at how well it all squared with Melanie's version so far. But Pollins could have left there after one o'clock and still had time to get back and kill Shunner.

'So you settled her in and left?'

'Yes.'

'What time did you leave?'

Pollins' face grew red. 'It . . . it was quite light. Soon after four.'

'She took a lot of settling in then?'

Pollins gave him an angry look. 'We . . . we talked. And made love.'

'Oh.' Melanie hadn't mentioned making love. He'd like to think that invalidated at least one of their stories, but he had the feeling it would have been a far less significant event in her life than in Pollins'. He persisted, 'Sure of the time?'

'I told you: soon after four. It might have been about a quarter past. You could ask the reception desk if it's so important.'

'So what time did you get back to the camp?'

'A quarter to five.'

'Your wife was awake?'

'Yes.'

Birdie tried to stop the sequence there for the moment. By that time Shunner's body was already on its way to the seaweed, and there was no need to pry into Pollins' husbandly sufferings. He tried another tack.

'Now what's all this about somebody delivering something to the camp tonight?'

Pollins' face and body became even more tense. 'That's nothing to do with anything you're investigating.'

'How do I know unless you tell me?'

'Wine. That's all. Just a case of wine.'

Birdie felt an old excitement stirring; the feeling that some things were adding up.

'Who's bringing it?'

'James Jedd.'

'The man Melanie's so scared of. So why's he bringing you a case of wine?'

Pollins bit his lower lip. 'It wasn't Jedd who arranged it.'

'Who then?'

Silence.

'Was it Ralph Shunner?'

Birdie found it hard to say the name, but Pollins was too wrapped up in his own worries to notice that. He nodded miserably.

'And why should Ralph Shunner arrange a case of wine for you?'

Pollins flared up, 'I've had about as much of this as I can stand. I don't see why you're making such a drama about a perfectly simple business of taking some claret home. I was even going to pay duty on it, if you must know.'

'So how come Ralph Shunner's involved in the perfectly simple business of taking some claret home?'

Pollins explained to him with sarcastic patience, 'He's an expert on wine. He used to run wine bars. He knows this château where he can get a 1975 St Emilion at about the same price as supermarket plonk. He very kindly offered to get me a case and asked me to take another case of it back for him.'

'So if Ralph Shunner was getting it for you, why's James Jedd delivering it?'

'I don't know. Jedd just came up to me yesterday and told me. Shunner's wife said he was in Paris, so I just assumed he'd got held up on business there.'

Birdie breathed hard at 'Shunner's wife' but let it pass. He asked: 'When's it arriving?'

'Half past one.'

'You mean to tell me that Jedd's going to drive up to your tent

164

with a case of wine at half past one in the morning?'

Pollins hesitated. 'Actually,' he said, 'it's coming by sea.'

'What?'

'To the beach. He's bringing it in a boat.'

'And did he say why he's bringing it in a boat?'

Birdie tried to stay calm but he wasn't succeeding and Pollins was looking jumpier by the minute. He said, 'They've got all sorts of marketing regulations, closed shop to keep the prices up. Shunner said this château would be put out of business if anyone found out they were selling it at such low prices.'

'So they usually smuggle it to campsites in motor boats, do they?'

Pollins said nothing.

'It actually pays them to hire a boat to take one case . . .'

'Two cases. There'll be Shunner's as well.'

'. . . to take two cases on to a beach at dead of night so that they can sell them to tourists at supermarket prices. Is that it?'

Pollins said miserably, 'It's a favour to Ralph Shunner.'

Birdie felt drunk with triumph at the picture which was suddenly coming to life. He wanted Pollins to see it too, to the extent that he threw away all caution.

'Would it surprise you to know . . .' He asked the question slowly, drawing it out. 'Would it surprise you to know that Mr Shunner stood in dock last year on a drugs charge?'

A gasp from Pollins, and the colour drained from his face.

'I didn't . . .'

'Would it surprise you to know that a former associate of Mr Shunner's has served a prison sentence for drugs smuggling?'

Pollins was squirming to and fro in his chair as if leeches were sucking at him. 'Are you saying . . . I didn't know. For heaven's sake, how was I supposed to know?'

'Aren't you wondering yet why he went to such trouble to deliver a couple of cases of wine?'

'Oh my God,' said Pollins. 'Oh my God.' He wiped his shirtsleeve across his forehead. Birdie, against his will, was convinced that this man was every bit as shocked as he looked, had genuinely no idea about Shunner's drug connections. With the excitement of the investigation still on him, Birdie crossed the room and tapped sharply on the bathroom door.

'Are you nearly finished in there? We're going.'

But when Melanie came out of the bathroom about five minutes later, in a skirt and sun top, her damp hair piled in a careful chignon, there were no signs of movement. Pollins was sitting on a chair with his head in his hands and Birdie had hooked a knee over the little table and was staring at her.

'Now, young lady, I think it's time you answered a few more questions.'

She moved closer to the door. 'If you're from . . .'

Pollins said, sounding bone weary, 'Do stop that. He's from the police, and it's serious.'

She was motionless, staring at Birdie, eyes wide.

He said, 'Your Jedd and Shunner were great buddies, right?' He regretted the slip in using the past tense, but she didn't react to that or anything else.

Pollins said to her sharply, 'For goodness' sake, sit down and answer his questions.'

She moved over to the bed and sat down, still without taking her eyes off Birdie. He repeated the question.

'They . . . they worked together sometimes.'

'From years back?'

'I suppose . . . yes.'

'And what was it they worked together on?'

'All sorts of things. Clubs and . . . things.' She shook her head, tendrils of damp hair flying, as if in despair at the complexities of business life.

'Go on. What sort of things?'

Her eyes flickered to Pollins but found no help there. 'Records and . . . and films . . .'

'Go on.'

'And a clothes shop and . . .'

'And drugs?'

Eyes on him again, blank with fear.

'That's why you were so scared of Jedd, wasn't it? Because you knew they were in the drugs trade and you knew what sort of thing happens to people who step out of line.'

She nodded, so slightly that if it hadn't been for the swinging tendrils of hair he wouldn't have been sure she'd moved at all. Then she murmured something, so faintly that Birdie couldn't catch it at first.

'What was that?'

'His ankle,' she said.

At first he didn't understand, then the memory came back to

him of his first morning at the Village Zoe, helping Nimue up the drive with the man whose ankle was broken. And of Melanie at the pool, and his feeling that she was only being self-dramatizing when she said it had been no accident.

'You're telling me that Jedd broke that instructor's ankle because he'd stepped out of line? Because he was one of them?'

She nodded again, more decisively.

'What had he done?'

'I don't know. I think . . . I think it was something to do with a boat.'

'He was supposed to be driving the boat for them, then backed out? Was that it?'

But she just repeated, 'I don't know . . . I don't know,' in a voice that became more and more like a child's.

'I think that was it,' said Birdie. He glanced across at Pollins. 'It all fits, you see.'

Pollins was slightly more balanced by now, but scared. 'You've got to believe I knew nothing about all this. Nothing. I'd no idea . . .' He banged his fist up and down on his thigh, helpless. 'Ye gods, and I thought people didn't get convicted for things they hadn't done.'

'You and me both, brother,' thought Birdie, but didn't say it. But it didn't matter any more because the rock at the mouth of his particular cave had rolled away. He was no longer the prime suspect for the killing of Ralph Shunner. He'd despaired almost when Pollins and Melanie had seemed to corroborate each other's alibis, but after all they'd given him what he needed. Only one doubt remained.

'James Jedd – would you say he's a good actor?'

Melanie looked surprised. 'He wasn't an actor. He was the producer.'

'I mean in real life. If he wanted to make people believe he was worried about something when he wasn't – that sort of thing?'

She nodded again, but this time quite emphatically.

'That's it then. Let's go.' He got to his feet and they both stared at him.

'Where are we going?' Pollins asked.

'Back to the camp. We want to collect that wine of yours, don't we?'

CHAPTER ELEVEN

The weather had been good for the bonfire, with the faintest of breezes blowing from the land, still carrying with it the day's scent of warmed earth and pine sap. At midnight it was still mild enough for some of the guests to be sitting around the fire naked, although Joan wore another of her gold-embroidered caftans that glinted from the reflection of the flames. There was a half moon and the sea was, for once, behaving more like the Mediterranean than the Atlantic, lipping almost apologetically at the flat sand. The party had been scheduled to end around eleven, after songs from a boy with a guitar. The songs had been sung and applauded, the coloured lights switched out, the boy was sprawled drinking red wine with the rest of them, but nobody showed any signs of leaving.

'Perfect,' said Alexander, Joan's husband. 'Just perfect.'

He was sitting with his arms clasped round his bony knees, naked except for his leather sandals, staring into the dying flames.

'Pity some of us are missing it,' said Joan. Her glance travelled round in a wide arc, from Olivia at one side of the fire to Vinny at the other.

'How's your husband, dear?'

'He's got a headache,' said Vinny shortly.

'Oh dear. Too much sun perhaps?' Joan's voice managed to imply that whatever Peter Pollins had been getting too much of, sun was the least likely. Vinny didn't bother to reply.

'What about your husband, dear? Still in Paris?'

Olivia replied, a little more politely than Vinny, that yes, Ralph was still in Paris. She hadn't been saying much at the party and more of her attention seemed to be on the children who, without any prompting, had formed a breakaway group about a hundred yards up the beach round their own smaller fire. She was watching them now, even while answering Joan.

'Don't worry about them,' Joan said. 'They're having the time of their lives.'

'The twins are very sensible,' Vinny added.

Olivia gave her a dirty look. 'Debbie's very sensible too. But it's past twelve and time she was in bed. She's got a tennis final in the morning.' (The twins had both been knocked out in the early rounds.)

'The child's on holiday,' Joan protested.

But Olivia got up and moved slowly out of the circle of their firelight, towards the smaller fire. Half way between the two of them she stood, a dark silhouette, still watching the children but apparently hesitating to be the first to call her daughter away. If she'd been hoping that other parents might follow her lead, she was unsuccessful.

'Is there any more wood?' asked one of the adults, poking at the fire with a half-burnt pine branch. The bonfire was well burnt down, more embers than flames.

'No,' said Nimue. 'The kids took some of the driftwood for their fire.'

Alexander was on his feet immediately, all helpfulness and resolution. 'What about the old brushwood fencing stuff? Up by the main gate.'

Nimue frowned, trying to place it. 'Oh, I know. Yes, we could burn that, but it's a long way to carry it.'

'It's already on the tractor trailer.'

'I'm not even sure where the trailer is at the moment.' Nimue, with work to do in the morning, was clearly less enthusiastic than the rest of them about prolonging the party, but Alexander was like a hound on the trail.

'It's back near the gate,' he said. 'I noticed when I was out jogging.'

Joan said, 'He's been wanting to drive that tractor all week.'

Nimue, bowing to popular demand, told him how to get the tractor moving and he left at a steady lope.

Joan giggled and leant back luxuriously on her Lilo pillow. 'Proper little pyromaniac, my husband. D'you know, he insisted on having our honeymoon on Stromboli?'

The three of them, Birdie, Peter Pollins and Melanie, heard a tractor in the distance as they walked down the main path to the beach. Pollins stopped, alarmed.

'What's that?'

169

Birdie stopped too and Melanie, who'd been clinging to his arm and staggering along in high-heeled mules, rested all her weight on him. He listened to the sound, coming from the direction of the main gate.

'Somebody having engine trouble by the . . .' Then, in a totally different tone of voice, 'Oh God, it's the tractor.'

Pollins stared at him, more alarmed than ever by Birdie's reaction.

'What's happening? What are they doing with a tractor at this time of night?' His voice trailed off but he remained tense, turning towards the sound. He was having to fight the impulse to run towards it. A few seconds later the engine was cut off. Pollins sighed with relief. 'That's it. They probably took it down there to collect the empties. They'll be all finished for the night now.'

Back at the motel it had taken Birdie some time to convince him that his best way out of the mess he'd got himself into was to co-operate, to let Jedd deliver the wine as arranged. But once the decision had been taken he'd become almost pathetically eager to get it over, hustling them through the dark camp and glancing every few minutes at the face of his luminous watch. Melanie, on the other hand, had lapsed into a misery so total she wasn't even talking any more, beyond the occasional squeak of pain and protest when she turned an ankle or got a heel stuck in the sand. She'd protested that she wasn't going anywhere near Jedd, that he'd take her away in the boat, that they didn't know what he was like. Only Pollins' unkind remark that in that case she could damned well wait on her own in the car park had persuaded her to change her mind and go with them, and after that she'd refused even to look at him.

Pollins began walking again and Birdie prised Melanie loose from the sand and followed, still trying not to think about the tractor. It was too late to do anything about that, and he needed all his attention for what was going to happen on the beach.

'What's the time now?'

'Twenty five to one.'

They toiled up the small slope towards the beachguard hut where Shunner had slumped. From there they could see the whole stretch of beach.

'Damn,' said Pollins. 'They're still there.' He pointed to the bonfire place about fifty yards up the beach and the dark figures silhouetted around it. They could even hear their laughter and talking above the sound of the sea.

'It was supposed to finish at eleven. What are they doing still there?'

Birdie asked, 'Didn't Jedd know they were having a bonfire tonight?'

'Yes, that was the point. He said the bonfire would be something to steer for when he was out at sea. Then he'd wait for it to die down and come in two hundred metres down the beach. He thought everybody would be gone by then.'

'He might not know they're still here. If he's been standing off out at sea all he'd see would be the fire.'

'You think he'll come in anyway?' Pollins was turning indecisive again, but for Birdie everything was now staked on the belief that Jedd must come in, that he must deliver the bottles and those bottles must hold something besides claret. It was unthinkable that things should work out any other way.

'Yes, I think he'll come.'

'If he . . .'

Then another exclamation from Pollins. 'Look, there's another fire. They've made two bonfires.' Taking a step forward he'd seen the other, smaller bonfire made by the children.

'There weren't meant to be two fires, were there?' he appealed to Birdie.

'Not that I know of.'

'How will he know which one to steer by?'

'It shouldn't make more than fifty yards difference either way.'

But Pollins stood staring at the fires, full of indecision. Birdie took charge again.

'He's more likely to risk it if he can see you where you're meant to be. Just you, not us. And we'd better cut behind the dunes. We don't want half the bonfire party tagging on.'

The dune path would lead them straight past the place where he'd found Shunner's body sprawled, but it was no time for bogies. He led the way back a few steps and on to the path between the two lines of dunes, but as soon as she felt the softer sand Melanie jibbed like a bolshie pony.

'I can't walk on this.' By the sound of her voice she was crying.

'Take your sandals off then.'

Pollins, standing a little way behind them, said, 'That tractor's started up again.' And it had, the sound coming towards them this time. Birdie, with all his attention on it, suddenly found a pair of

171

sandals in his hand.

'What am I supposed to do with these?'

'. . . pocket,' she sniffed.

And for Birdie, having no pockets, the tensions of the moment were not lessened by having a pair of high-heeled shoes stuffed down the front of his tracksuit, as well as Melanie attached to his arm. And all the time the sound of the tractor engine was getting louder.

Joan stood up, arm extended towards the tractor, wine glass in the other hand. The firelight glinted on her gold brocade, and she might have been Brünnhilde welcoming Siegfried.

'He's made it.'

Her husband, grinning like a sated leprechaun, drove the tractor and trailer once round them in a lap of honour before coming to rest alongside the flagstones. She, more animated than anybody had seen her, was there to meet and kiss him as he jumped down.

'Lots of good stuff there,' he said, his small, sinewy arm straining to encompass her waist. 'Should go beautifully.'

Some of the others fell on the mass of brushwood that was brimming out of the trailer, dragged it across the flags, upsetting wine glasses in the process. Sparks fizzed up as it hit the embers and the party that had been dying quietly along with the fire flared up again.

'Here, there's still some hooch.'

'. . . my glass. Well, we'll share then.'

'Here's to the healthy life, eh, Nimue?'

'. . . is some fire.'

The brushwood burnt enthusiastically but had no staying power. Before the rediscovered cache of wine had been finished the fire was dying down again.

'Any more of that stuff in the trailer?'

'Hang on.' Somebody wandered over to look. 'All gone. Wait a minute though, there's some thicker stuff done up in a tarpaulin. Don't know what it is though.'

'Bring it over. Let's have a look at it.'

Amid laughter the man manoeuvred the large tarpaulin-covered bundle from the trailer and waltzed it over to the firelight. But by the time he got there his face had changed.

'I don't think it's wood. And it smells awful.'

Another man caught at the edge of the tarpaulin and pulled. The bundle began to unroll itself, moving closer and closer to the fire. A curious circle formed round it, but at a respectful distance because of the smell.

'Perhaps it's fish.'

'Or somebody's washing.'

'Perhaps we shouldn't . . .'

A little scream from somebody as the bundle, in its last layer of tarpaulin, reached the edge of the flames. A last jerk from the man who was making it unroll. 'Does anybody bet me . . .'

Then suddenly a silence. The first voice from the man still holding the tarpaulin. 'Oh my God.'

Then a scream in earnest, instantly shushed by Joan. 'No, the children. And her.'

And they stood unmoving for seconds on end, staring down at a body that, either from the seaweed or the effects of the firelight, looked already antique, like something dug from a prehistoric bog and irreverently draped in the rags of elegant clothes.

'Get it off the fucking fire.'

It was the smell that roused somebody to action and the thing was dragged clear of the bonfire by a few yards.

Then Nimue, who'd been standing staring with the rest of them, said, 'Take it over in the corner there. And cover it up.'

She and several of the men managed it, watched by the others. The silence was still almost complete, except for a small engine in the distance. Somebody said, irrelevantly, 'There's a boat out there.' And was at once shushed by the others.

Nimue looked up. 'Somebody, make sure the children don't come here. Don't tell them anything, just get them away.'

'The police?' Alexander suggested.

'Yes. You speak French? Right, there's a phone box outside reception.'

He ran off again into the darkness, less jauntily than he'd gone for the tractor.

Nimue said, 'And the rest of you, if you'd just go to your tents and so on. The police will be wanting to speak to all of us, but there's no point in waiting here.'

There was no immediate movement. The man who'd unrolled the tarpaulin said, haltingly, 'I think we all want to know . . . I mean, he must have been . . . I mean, somebody must have killed him.'

Nimue turned on him. 'That's just what I mean. It doesn't help

173

anybody. If you all go away now, you'll be told as soon as there is anything to be told.'

They wouldn't go away completely, but there was a general withdrawal from the bonfire place and the tarpaulin covered bundle to the beach guard's hut. The only ones left in the immediate circle of the firelight were Nimue, two of the men who'd decided she needed somebody with her, and Joan.

'What about her?' Joan asked.

'Where is she?'

'I think she was going to the kids.'

A look of alarm on Nimue's face. 'For goodness' sake, somebody should . . .'

'Like me to?'

Nimue stared at Joan for a second, then nodded. 'Take her up to my bungalow. Make her some coffee or something. I'll be there as soon as the police get here.'

Joan, arms clutched across her chest for warmth, walked out into the darkness towards the smaller bonfire, watching for the tall silhouette of Olivia. In the background to her more immediate concerns she too was aware of the sound of a boat's engine not far out at sea.

Birdie, Pollins and Melanie, standing about two hundred yards away at the edge of the dunes, saw the sparks flying from the bonfire when the brushwood was dumped on it, heard faintly the shouts of excitement. But after that all their attention was concentrated on another noise, the sound of the boat's engine that had been nothing more than a distraction to the bonfire party. Birdie judged that it could be no more than a few hundred yards out, but he could see nothing except the occasional white line of foam as a wave gently overturned itself on to the beach. The sound became louder and Melanie shrank back against him as if she expected Jedd to drive straight up the beach and seize her. Almost against his will he slid his arm round her waist.

'It's all right.'

Then she was relaxing, not because of his arm but because the sound was receding again.

'You see,' Pollins whispered. 'It's those two fires. They're confusing him. He doesn't know where to come in.'

'It's not time yet, is it?'

Pollins glanced at his watch. 'Nine minutes to go.'

174

The boat sound was well to the north by now, probably past the bonfires. Pollins said, 'I think he's giving up.'

'No.' Birdie was concentrating his mind on the sound, as if he could drag Jedd to the beach by sheer force of will. Even Pollins, although necessary to what had to be done, was becoming a distraction.

'You'd better get down there, right by the water. So he'll see you when he comes back this way.'

Pollins looked at Birdie, then at the long empty expanse of sand between the dunes and the water's edge. Now that the time had almost come, Birdie could sense in him a great reluctance to go there on his own, to meet Jedd and speak to him. After all, the last time he'd talked to the man it was as a fellow holiday maker. Since then he'd had to adjust his mind to Jedd the drug smuggler. Birdie tried hard to put into his voice the authority of a police officer, having found already that Pollins would respond to it.

'Now, you're clear what you've got to do? Unload the wine, keep him talking and I'll be there before he has a chance to start the engine again. Then it's our job to make sure he doesn't get away.'

Pollins said yes, licking his lips nervously. Birdie was sure that if it came to a fight it would be him against Jedd, with Pollins dithering on the sidelines, but he was almost looking forward to that.

'You're sure you'll . . .'

'Don't worry. As soon as he's handed that wine out I'll be across the beach so fast he won't know what's hit him.'

Pollins looked miserable but nodded and glanced at his watch again. 'Six minutes. I'd better . . .'

'Yes, he's coming back.'

The boat still sounded distant, but now the sound was definitely coming towards them again. Birdie thought that the party round the bonfire seemed to have gone quiet and imagined them all trailing off to their beds at last. Their normality seemed like another country.

'Off you go.'

And Pollins went.

When he was out of earshot Birdie asked Melanie, 'Do you know if Jedd always carries a gun?'

Her head moved infinitesimally against his shoulder.

'No, he doesn't always, or no, you don't know?'

'Don't know.'

175

He sighed and, without taking his eyes off Pollins, disentangled her and persuaded her to sit down on the sand. She'd probably squawk like a moorhen when he sprinted off and left her, but that would be the least of his troubles.

Four minutes to go. Pollins was at the water's edge now, a dark shape against the pewter-coloured sea, and the boat was still coming. A small boat, judging by the engine noise, but then it wouldn't take a large one to carry Jedd and two cases of wine. Birdie thought he'd almost certainly have picked it up from a ship, but all that could wait till later. The only important thing now was to get his hands on Jedd and the evidence. Not conclusive evidence, perhaps, that Jedd had shot Shunner, but the clearest possible of motives – the falling out of two pushers. If Jedd had a gun with him, and if that gun proved to have fired the shot still resting in Shunner's brain, then the evidence might be conclusive after all, even more damning than whatever proved to be in those wine bottles. And, wrapped up in Jedd's guilt – Shunner's guilt as well – the chance he'd never had to prove to Olivia that what he'd said about Shunner had been true all along, that there'd been no frame-up. The chance to show her how she – and Debbie too – had been used as a front for Shunner's latest consignment. He daren't think too much about Debbie, about how she'd been dragged into this. The thought made him almost insane with anger, against Shunner, against Jedd, and now above all he had to be calm. Everything depended on the next few minutes.

Three minutes.

'I'm cold,' said Melanie, from the sand.

He ignored her, straining ears and eyes northward. There were, he could see now, still a few people round the bonfire. Well, they'd be witnesses, no more. As long as Jedd didn't see them too and take fright. They too must have heard the motorboat. He fixed his eyes on the motionless figure of Pollins and the sea beyond it. Two minutes.

But there was something wrong. From the sound, the boat should surely have been in sight by now, coming in to where Pollins was waiting. But there was no boat, just the insistent phut phut of an engine. And the sound, too, was in the wrong place: well to the north of where it should have been, as if it was making direct for the bonfire. Then, glancing in that direction, he saw the boat quite clearly, so close to the shore that it must have been almost scraping the sand. But it was more than a hundred yards away from where Pollins was waiting, and a mere fifty yards or so from the bonfire group, although nobody there seemed to have noticed it. Birdie cursed, realizing that Pollins was right after all to worry about the second, unexpected bonfire. Jedd must have taken the wrong one as his mark, ending a long way too far up the beach. Which wouldn't have mattered, but for the unexpected presence of the other people. Surely it was only a matter of time before one of them went to see what was going on, and Jedd took fright and made off like a scalded cat, cargo undelivered. And, at that point, the boat's engine cut.

'Move!' Birdie yelled to Pollins, but the man seemed frozen by this change of plan.

'Get to him, damn you!'

Pollins turned, shouted something that Birdie didn't hear, then set off towards the boat at a slow, lumbering run. Birdie cursed again and shot off in the same direction, but much faster. He was dimly conscious of things round him, of Melanie's shoes digging into his chest, of the change underfoot from dry sand to damp sand as he got nearer the sea, but over it all was a desperate determination to get to the boat before Jedd could take fright.

Twenty yards to go. Sand water-logged and obstructive now, feet having to be dragged from it, as from cement. Upper body lurching forward, trying to go faster than the feet would let it, one of Melanie's shoes falling. A shout, probably from somebody near the bonfire, but he wasn't sure. Cursing the sand, he plunged on. He could see a figure in the boat now, bending over the back of it, desperately trying to restart the engine.

'Jedd,' he yelled.

No time for caution now.

'Jedd!'

An ankle gave under him and, no more than ten yards from the boat, he fell to his knees. But even as he fell he was dragging out Melanie's remaining shoe, launching it with all his force towards the bent figure in the boat. A little exclamation of pain told him it had connected, and that gave him just the few seconds he needed to drag himself up and cover the remaining yards. There was sea water splashing round his thighs and the smooth fibreglass side of a boat under his hands. He threw his weight against it, almost overturning it, and found Jedd's surprisingly calm face looking down at him.

177

'Don't play silly buggers,' said Jedd. 'You've got all the rest of the sea if you want it.'

'The wine,' Birdie gasped.

With the same calm, Jedd turned away from him and started the engine. The sea around Birdie churned up and he had to throw himself backwards or be chopped up by the propeller. He surfaced, gasping, to see the boat already moving off.

'You're not bloody going, Jedd. Jedd!' The yell was loud enough to be heard by the bonfire group. The boat hadn't got up much speed. He went after it at a fast crawl, looping out to avoid the propeller, and got both hands hooked over the side again, spewing salt water from his mouth. Jedd, hands on the controls, glanced at him and threw his own weight to the other side. The boat began to go faster, so that Birdie's substantial body was dragged alongside like trailing weed. They were past the first bonfire now and coming level with the second, about thirty yards out. Birdie spat sea water and yelled the name again.

'Jedd!'

He thought he heard other shouts from the beach, but they were meaningless in a world that consisted only of engine roar, of a boat's smooth sides and water that was trying hard every second to pull him away. Jedd turned to look at him, said something inaudible, accelerated. One numb hand pulled away and Birdie could feel muscles ripping as all the strain came on his other shoulder. Knowing that he could hang on for only a few seconds more he fought for a firmer grip, trying to blank out the pain in his shoulder then, with the hardest effort of his life, managed to hook a knee over the boat side. His head trailed under the surface with water smashing in through the nose and mouth, but somehow the second knee was over and he was pulling himself up and falling forward into the boat. His knee struck something as he fell – a square wooden case. Kneeling, he hooked an arm round Jedd's legs, pulling him backwards and away from the controls. Jedd half fell but recovered and kicked Birdie hard in the throat, looked down at him and kicked him again, this time in the face. But the second kick kept him away from the controls too long. The boat began to arc shorewards, still at a fair speed. Jedd dived for the controls, stepping on Birdie's chest as he went. More in a reflex action against the pain than anything, Birdie curled his whole body round Jedd's feet, trying to throw him against the side of the boat. It tipped

178

sideways with the combined weight of them, propeller screaming in the air, and suddenly Jedd lost his balance and fell backwards into the water, arms flailing. Birdie, too dazed to roll away in time, followed him. The boat righted itself and ploughed on its unpiloted course towards the beach, knocking Birdie into unconsciousness as it went.

'Olivia.'

Joan had last seen her alone on the beach between the two bonfires. But Olivia was still yards away from her and didn't seem to hear. With a couple of half-wits larking around in a motorboat just offshore, it was hardly surprising. Joan plunged on, unaccustomedly hot with the urgency of reaching Olivia and telling her gently before she heard some other way, angry at the men in the motorboat for their noise. How could you tell a woman her man was dead with all that going on? And one of the half-wits kept yelling something.

'Jedd, Jedd,' it sounded like.

Well, if the man Jedd was one of the half-wits, he'd be hearing about it in the morning.

'Olivia. Olivia,' she called.

But the damned engine was making a whining noise now, like a circular saw, worse than ever.

Somebody else was coming along the beach behind her: Nimue, at a long, loping run from the direction of the larger bonfire. Joan assumed that she'd left somebody else to guard Ralph Shunner's body and had decided after all to share the burden of breaking the news to Olivia. She pointed to the motorboat, meaning to ask if the noise could be stopped, but Nimue was running straight past her, unseeing. Then suddenly Olivia was running too, both women converging from their different angles on the sea, on the motorboat. Joan stood there staring at them, appalled. With what Nimue knew, what Olivia was about to know, was it possible that they'd be playing games in the sea with those two fools? She shouted to them:

'Nimue. Olivia.'

She took a few wobbling steps of her own in the same direction, then stopped, understanding that it wasn't a game. The motorboat, engine still screaming, was at the beach and seemed to be trying to burrow into the sand. But beyond it, yards out past where the slow waves were breaking, a man was struggling and screaming and something else was bobbing up and down passively with the movement of the sea.

Nimue and Olivia seemed unaware of the existence of each other until they got to the water. Even then, swimming out in a powerful crawl side by side, they wasted no breath. The first words were Olivia's to Nimue, when they reached Birdie's floating, unconscious form.

'Can you take him? I'll get the other one.'

'Can you manage?'

'Yes.'

Nimue already had her hands hooked under Birdie's armpits. Twenty yards or so away Jedd was shouting for help but seemed to be treading water. Birdie looked so bad that there was no time to be lost. Nimue towed him backwards to the beach where Joan, salt water soaking into her caftan, helped to drag him up the sand.

'Is he. . . ?'

'Alive? Yes.'

Nimue knelt over him, bent down and clamped her mouth against his. There was a smear of green seaweed on his cheek. Joan watched, horrified, as Nimue drew her mouth away and spat explosively, and vomit and sea water poured out of Birdie.

'That's better.'

Nimue had her palms on Birdie's chest, pushing up and down.

'What's going on out there?'

Joan tore her eyes away and looked out to sea. 'I think she's got to him. Or near him.'

'Can you do this?'

'I . . . I think so.' Under Nimue's instructions Joan knelt beside Birdie, imitated the regular pressure.

'Whatever happens, keep at it until he starts breathing properly. Somebody should be here soon.'

Shouts from down the beach showed help wasn't far away and Nimue was on her feet and back in the water, going like a torpedo to where Jedd had been. But she found there only Olivia – Olivia scarcely able to keep afloat from exhaustion, with eyes staring and face dead white.

'I . . . I think he's gone.'

'I could have saved him,' Nimue said.

It was evening, with the sun just clear of the sea. They were sitting in a dip in the dunes, because that was one of the few places at the Village Zoe not currently occupied by French police, examining magistrate or consular officials – every one of which, it seemed to Birdie, had questioned them at some time during a long day.

'If I'd known she couldn't cope. But I could see she was a strong swimmer. She sounded so confident . . .'

From the glimpses he'd had of her through the day, in between the questions and the bandaging, he knew that Nimue had been in control: calming the camp as much as it could be calmed, interpreting, dealing with what were obviously anguished phone calls from her head office in Paris – and, of course, answering those endless questions. Now, alone with him, she was letting the strain show.

He said, easing his throbbing ankle into a more comfortable position, 'After all, you were busy saving my life at the time.'

She caught from his voice something he hadn't meant to put there.

'You're worrying about that, aren't you? That she left it to me to bring you in?'

'No.'

'You don't have to. Either she thought you were dead and couldn't face it, or she thought she could cope better with getting Jedd.'

'But she was wrong, wasn't she?'

'She told me he was panicking. It can be hard to deal with that if you're not a trained life-saver.'

Birdie said nothing. He stared out to sea where the boat with the frogmen was still operating, as it had been for much of the day.

'And his leg was really mashed up, you know. I saw it when the frogmen pulled him out. He must have got it caught in the propeller.'

Birdie watched as another frogman entered the water.

'What are they looking for?'

'What do you think? They want to know if there's any more heroin down there.'

Birdie sighed. 'There's not. I explained to them about six times over. So did Pollins. Two cases, one of them OK for Pollins to take back with him, the other one with the stuff to hand over when he met Shunner – or Jedd, as it would have been.'

'Sixty grammes,' said Nimue. 'Five to a bottle in little polythene capsules.'

181

He looked at her face. 'Was that the way they did it when you. . . ?'

'No.'

'And Jedd shot Shunner for sixty grammes?'

She shrugged. 'We don't know what happened before that.'

He'd like to have put his arm round her for warmth, except that it was bandaged from the elbow up, tight against his ribs, which was apparently meant to stop his shoulder hurting so much, but didn't.

'They . . . they don't think you had anything to do with it?'

Another shrug. 'Once a drug runner, always a drug runner as far as they're concerned. But I think they know they can't pin anything on me this time.'

He didn't need to remind her that they were still waiting to hear what the French police would do to them both for illegally disposing of a body, but her thoughts were obviously running in the same direction.

'Why the hell did you have to put the damn thing in with the brushwood?'

He said, 'I tried to tell you. We couldn't leave it where it was. Not with that photographer poking around.'

'Great. So out it pops like pass-the-parcel with practically everybody in the place standing there.'

'I was going to get one of the boats and hide it down the coast somewhere.'

She looked at him, shaking her head. 'If I ever do commit a murder, remind me not to take you along.' But the tone was almost affectionate. He edged awkwardly closer to her.

'What are you going to do now, when all this is over?'

'Assuming we're not in a French prison for interfering with the corpse?'

'Assuming that.'

She was silent, as if thinking about it for the first time. Then: 'I don't suppose they'll let me stay in France. Moving on time again.'

'If you wanted to come back to England . . .' He hesitated.

'Well?'

'Well, there's a spare bed in my living room. And I know this woman who runs a gym . . .'

'You and me. Ex-drugs runner, ex-fuzz?' She made them sound almost like qualifications.

'Ex-husband,' he said.

182

'Oh dear.' The smile she gave him was a tired one, but with a hint of devilment in it. 'Sounds like the great dating computer blew its circuits.'

'But will you . . . will you think about it, I mean?'

She nodded, eyes on his, biting her lower lip. 'Yes, I'll . . . think about it.'

There seemed to be a lot of activity all of a sudden around the frogmen's boat. One of them surfaced, followed soon afterwards by his colleague. A man standing up in the boat seemed to be talking into his radio.

'What have they found now?' But he asked the question idly, with quite another scene in his mind – a bonfire, a tarpaulin bundle and a figure stained by the seaweed to the colour of a pickled walnut.

'Something you can tell me. Was she . . . was Olivia there when Shunner's body rolled out?'

She stared at him, looking almost horrified.

'No, of course not. You don't think she'd have been dashing along the beach rescuing people if she'd just found out her lover was dead, do you?'

'How did she know, then?'

Nimue sighed. 'I thought somebody would have told you this by now. Joan ballsed it up, that's what happened.'

She told him how Joan had volunteered to break the news to Olivia, but had wandered around the beach for several minutes without finding her. 'By the time Joan saw her, you and Jedd were trying to drown each other, so that was it.'

'That wasn't Joan's fault, was it?'

'No, it was the next bit she ballsed up – telling Olivia her husband was dead. I mean, after she'd seen you dragged out of the sea unconscious. I mean, what was the poor woman to think?'

An idea was beginning to form in Birdie's mind. 'You mean Olivia thought *I* was dead?'

'Yes. You see, by the time I'd got her out on the beach, you'd been lugged off on a stretcher. So here she is, nearly dead with exhaustion and panic, and Joan chooses this moment to come up and announce her husband's dead. Olivia goes all steely and determined and insists on being taken to see him, so we practically carry her along the beach and when she sees the body . . .'

'Shunner's body?'

'What else? When she saw it she just went unconscious. Blanked

183

out. Then, of course, when she came round we had this confusion of explaining that you were still alive but the man she'd booked in with as her husband seemed to have got himself murdered. So now you can see why I said Joan ballsed it up.'

'Oh ye gods.'

Silence again. The frogmen's boat was making its way quite quickly to the beach.

Nimue said, 'You haven't seen Olivia today then?'

'No.'

'Debbie's OK anyhow. I got her organizing some of the younger kids.'

'Thanks.'

He'd seen the child, busy with a rounders game, on his way from first-aid post to police incident room, but hadn't spoken. He wondered what he would say the next time he saw her and – for the first time in his life – dreaded it.

The boat had reached land and the man who'd been driving it stepped out, holding something carefully, and began to walk up the beach. Two more police officers with radio sets passed in front of Nimue and Birdie, walking to meet him. They met, apparently oblivious of the two people watching from the sand dune, and their three heads bent over the object. Then they turned and began walking as quickly as the soft sand permitted back towards the camp.

Nimue said, 'You saw what that was?'

'A pistol.'

'That ties the case up for them nicely, doesn't it? The pistol that shot Shunner. Jedd must have had it in the boat with him last night.'

Birdie's eyes were following the three policemen. By now they'd almost reached the beach guard's hut.

'But . . . but the boat was a lot further up the beach when we started fighting. How could the gun have got down there?'

Nimue smiled. This last brick in the wall of evidence against Jedd seemed to have lifted a load from her mind. 'We get some odd currents round here. Come on. If you can stagger as far as the bungalow I'll make you some coffee.'

CHAPTER TWELVE

Nimue's couch was softer than a tent groundsheet, but still not soft enough to give sleep to a body as battered as Birdie's. And even if his body had been disposed to sleep his mind would have had nothing to do with it. At around four, just as it was growing light, he got up. Nimue, pressed against the wall to make room for him, was still sleeping the sleep of exhaustion. She'd hardly changed her position all night. On the picture over her head the silver birches threw their black bars across the light. With difficulty he put on his crumpled shorts and shirt, leaving the left armhole draped empty across his bandaged shoulder, and went out, closing the door quietly.

There was a freshness about the morning, scent of pine, scent of rosemary. A few people about in spite of the early hour – one family loading surf boards and sun shields on the top of their Porsche. Quite a lot of families. Birdie thought, would have decided to get the hell out of the Village Zoe. There was a uniformed policeman on duty by the shopping centre, who stared hard at Birdie as he went past. They might have their case tied up, but they weren't forgetting that Mr Linnet had done his best to impede a murder investigation. More birch shadows across the light. Still, they could hardly stop him going to the place he was heading for. Down the main drive towards the sound of the sea, off to the right along a wide, sandy track, to where three tents stood in a kind of cul de sac. Two pairs of tennis shoes by the entrance. He stood undecided for a second, then walked in.

As he'd expected, she was up and fully dressed, in pale slacks and turquoise shirt. Quite composed, but with great rings of sleeplessness round her eyes. A mug of coffee steamed on the table beside her.

'You.'

He had to stand with head bent and shoulders stooped to fit

under the tent roof. It hurt.

'Is Debbie here?'

'Asleep.' She nodded towards the nylon wall.

'How's she taking it?'

'It's . . . it's hard to know with Debbie. She hadn't . . .'

'Hadn't got attached to him?'

'. . . accepted him.'

He asked, 'What about a walk?'

Without saying anything, they scrambled up the sand dune and stood looking at the pale, empty sea. A few small clouds were gathering in the west.

He said, 'Jedd panicked then?'

She said nothing.

'Nimue told me that's what you said. She said it was hard to deal with somebody panicking if you weren't a trained life-saver.'

Still nothing.

'She doesn't know how we met, of course, does she.'

She made a slight sound in her throat, either 'oh' or 'no'.

'When you were running life-saving classes at the baths. She doesn't know you taught me to life-save. And you were bloody good on what to do about people who panicked.'

Silence. He moved round so that he was looking into her face, standing between her and the sea. 'I haven't told her. Or anybody.'

'I don't care who you tell.' A total weariness in her voice.

'And another thing. You said he was in Paris. You implied you'd had a phone call from him in Paris. I thought you were just putting up a front because you thought he'd gone off and left you. But you knew he wasn't in Paris, didn't you?'

She nodded, not trying to avoid his eyes.

'Because you knew he was dead, although you must have been wondering like hell why nobody had found the body. Until last night.'

Another nod.

'By the way,' he said. 'They've found the gun.'

'When?' That had jolted her at last.

'The frogmen did, yesterday evening. They'll think Jedd had it with him in the boat and it fell out. They'll be able to match it to the round that killed Shunner. Open and shut case against Jedd, with that and the drugs.'

'It *was* an open and shut case. Until . . .'

186

'Until I started asking questions. But I'm not the first one to come asking you questions about Shunner, am I? That was what Jedd was doing when you got in such a panic and got the car stuck in the sand. He knew damn well that Shunner wasn't in Paris and he'd a suspicion what had happened to him. You wouldn't have got that panicked otherwise. Not like you.'

She said, with sudden anger, 'How do you know what's like me?'

And the truth of it struck him, made him pause. 'No, I don't know any more, do I?'

It was simple admission, but the sound of it when he'd said it made him angry too and he was battering at her with words, trying to break through that terrible shell of calm.

'I never knew, did I? Never knew you could shoot one man and deliberately drown another and stand there looking like a bloody martyr as if I'd done something wrong.'

She said, 'I didn't mean to shoot him.' Then, all at once, she was talking, fast and keyed up, not looking at him now but staring out at the sea as if it were a jury she needed to convince.

'I didn't mean to shoot him. I'd had this suspicion, ever since we left England, that there was more to this than a holiday. He was so . . . so intense about it. But I tried to tell myself I was wrong. Then I kept remembering all you'd said about him, all they'd said in court about him – and I knew they'd been trying to frame him. I knew it.'

A plea, in spite of it all, not for her own innocence, but for Shunner's. A plea abandoned.

'But then when he was so insistent about going to Paris – and he really was going to Paris – I started worrying again. And that night I thought I must have a talk with him before he left. I went back to the tent. I started looking through his things to see if he'd gone already. And I found it hidden in his binocular case.'

'The pistol?'

She nodded. 'He'd told me he'd never carried a gun in his life. And I thought, "If he's lied to me about that, what else has he lied about?" And . . . and I was half mad and I went looking for him . . . and I took the gun and I found him . . . in the sand dunes.'

'What was he doing there?'

Birdie knew that, among other things, he must have been nursing a sore head.

'He . . . he was just sort of wandering.' A pause. 'He seemed . . . he seemed odd . . . not co-ordinating. I think now he must have taken something . . . some drug.'

No need to tell her that what Shunner had taken was Birdie's fist on his face. Perhaps it helped her to believe he was drugged.

'I was so angry. So angry at him for dragging me and Debbie into this. And he was . . . odd. He didn't deny it, just kept hinting things in that dreadful, drunk sort of way. Boasting about big deals, about money. About how he'd have . . . have enough money to . . . to . . .'

'To what?'

It came out in a rush. 'To buy men like you ten times over before breakfast.'

So at least Shunner had died with, near enough, Birdie's name in his mouth. There was a kind of satisfaction about that.

'And then you shot him.'

She turned away from the sea and back to him, eyes hot and dry. 'I didn't mean to. Not that it matters, but I didn't mean to. He . . . he tried to put his arm round me . . . and the way I was feeling I couldn't stand having him touch me . . . I must have jerked my hand up and . . . it went off.'

Silence.

'So that's it,' she said. 'I just went back to the tent and waited for somebody to come and arrest me. I thought when they came I'd send Debbie to you and . . .'

'But nobody came. Nobody except James Jedd.'

'I wouldn't tell him. I'd have told the police if they'd come. But this man, I guessed he must have been part of whatever Ralph had been doing. I thought, people like that . . . they'd kill me if they knew.'

'Yes, they probably would.'

'So on the beach last night when I heard you shouting "Jedd" I knew he was out there. I decided . . . decided he wouldn't come out of the sea.'

Birdie said, 'There was heroin in those bottles.'

'I know. I'm not sorry. About Jedd.' She was looking out to sea again.

'That morning, when I saw you and Debbie in the canoe. You'd gone out to dump the pistol?'

'Yes. I didn't want it to be around where Debbie was.'

'There'll be no prints on it. Not after three days grinding about on the sand.' He was talking almost to himself.

She asked, 'So what are you going to do?'

'About Debbie?' His thoughts were racing off on another track.
'About me.'

For a moment he thought she was suggesting they should live together again, then he realized that wasn't what she meant.

'What am I supposed to do, for heaven's sake? Go off to the nearest *gendarme*?'

'Well what?' She put the question to the sea.

He said, from over her shoulder, 'Why do anything? They've got their body. They've got the gun that killed him. They've got their murderer in the morgue beside him and the heroin as evidence. Why upset it?'

'Yes, why upset it.' There was resignation in her voice, rather than relief. She turned and glanced at his face, shivering in the breeze off the sea. Automatically he raised his good arm, intending to slip it around her shoulders, but it fell back against his side as she flinched away. He followed her down the dune.

That morning he spoke to Debbie. They'd managed, in spite of everything, to play the junior tennis finals a day late, and she'd won in straight sets. He met her walking off the courts, face intent just like her mother's. But then she always looked like that after a match.

'Hello, love.'

'Hello, Dad.'

'Good game?'

'Nimue says I should have used my backhand more.'

'Lemonade?'

'Yes, please.' They walked together towards the café.

'You'll be back home soon.'

She frowned slightly. 'Mum says we might have to stay till Saturday. Because of seeing about the body.' From her voice it might have been no more than a car repair. He waited until they were sitting together at a table, she with her lemonade, he with a much-needed Calvados.

'Nimue might be coming to stay with me when we get back. You could come for weekends and play tennis with her.' Perhaps more than weekends. Olivia was in no position to be difficult now.

Again the little frown. 'I wanted to talk to you about that. About what I'm going to do.'

His heart sank.

'Nimue knows this boarding school where they give scholarships to people who're really good at sports. She's got a friend who's a teacher there and she says she might help me get in.'

'You'd like that?'

'It would make sense, Dad.' She sipped her lemonade while he stared at her, trying for the second time that day to adjust to a changed world. Debbie withdrawing from the protection of either of them. Debbie with her own life and her own plans.

'But is it what you want, love?'

A level stare at him over the glass. Then, at last, a smile. 'It's what I want, Dad.'